THE MORRIS MEN

Stephen E Mitchell

a *'Bainbridge Diaries'* novel

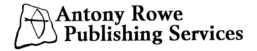

Antony Rowe
Publishing Services

THE MORRIS MEN

"For what shall it profit a man if he gain the whole world and lose the last hole?"   anon 1908

This book has been printed digitally and produced in a standard specification in order to ensure its continuing availability

Published by Antony Rowe Publishing Services in 2005
2 Whittle Drive
Highfield Industrial Estate
Eastbourne
East Sussex
BN23 6QT
England

ISBN 1-905200-36-6

Printed and bound by Antony Rowe Ltd, Eastbourne

ACKNOWLEDGEMENTS

My wife, Anne, for her unwavering support and belief; my children, Jennifer and Colin, for the motivation they provided; my parents, Irene & Roland, on celebrating their 60th wedding anniversary in 2005; Hotel Delfino in Italy, for its inspirational panorama; Manfred Schotten Antiques, in Burford, for their hospitality.

Stephen Mitchell is a freelance project manager living in the beautiful North Cotswolds village of Ilmington, just south of Stratford upon Avon. 'The Morris Men' is his first novel and is a reflection of his passion for collecting and restoring antique golf clubs.

The author is presently working on further novels, centralised on Bainbridge & Bainbridge, solicitors, under the collective banner of 'The Bainbridge Diaries'.

www.themorrismen.com

Prologue

Sometime around 1874

The sun was low in the sky and St. Andrews appeared crimson and magnificent. The ever weakening rays barely penetrated the grubby sash windows of the small workshop, yet were sufficient still to pick out sawdust hanging thick in the air. It was finally able to settle as the days turbulence subsided, adding a fresh layer to those undisturbed deposits which had gathered in all the tiny nooks and crannies across the years.

The cramped first floor workshop bristled with woodworking tools of all descriptions; workbenches, sanding gear, stools, shelves and wicker baskets full to the brim with roughly cut wooden golf club heads. Hickory shafts were scattered about in abundance, made ready for fitting to clubs that would cater for the massed ranks of players around the world. Several varieties of 'selected' shafts, those of ash and greenheart in particular, had been placed to one side in preparedness for a few bespoke orders. Hanging lines of thin leather strips were strung up everywhere, each waiting their turn to be formed into grips, all still reeking from the tanning process. There was practically little noise, just the faint hiss from a small jet of steam forcing its way through some faulty pipe joint.

It was the end of a fourteen hour working day, one which had seen the completion of a shipping order destined for a prestigious sports merchant in London, the largest order the proprietor had taken since trading began under his own name several years earlier. Humble beginnings and years of apprenticeship, alongside many of the great clubmakers of his time, were now paying dividends with merchants simply clambering to stock his goods. His three tradesmen and one apprentice had worked tirelessly that day, pulling as a team and taking turns in jointing heads, placing whipping, gripping clubs, waxing shafts, inspecting, rejecting, reworking, packing and loading.

Standing alone in his workshop, he was proud of their achievements that day. His men had headed home, but would be returning in less than ten hours to start all over again. Holding the one remaining club to be packed, he gave it his critical inspection. It was a perfect example he decided, solidly constructed and beautifully finished; a triumph of their collective skills. It had the familiar long slender head, made from dark stained beech, fixed tightly to the shaft in a spliced joint, and a fine grip made from sheepskin hide. It possessed a balance that set it apart from any his competitors could produce. All in all, he concluded, a putter worthy of any championship golfer.

Taking a small metal instrument from his top pocket, he held the putter upright on the nearest workbench. Placing the sharp end of the small tool on the nose of the club, he gave the broad end a sharp tap with a nearby wooden mallet. A small indentation, an exclusive mark sported by less than one in every hundred clubs, his seal of quality in fact, was now indelibly stamped on the club head. This privileged identification, small enough to be easily overlooked, was in the form of a tiny spider, a trade mark unique to the maker himself.

The putter was carefully wiped clean of any residual

dust, wrapped in cloth and finally placed into the one wooden packing case that remained unsealed. Laying there it appeared no different from the rest. But that particular club had just been given a separate identity; a unique impression that would make it forever distinctive.

Chapter 1

August 1931

Antique golf clubs adorned three sides of his drawing room at Kerrington Manor, all neatly regimented and all impressively displayed. Another group of clubs, this time loosely gathering in one corner, stood patiently waiting to be examined, cleaned and catalogued before adding to the ranks.

Sir Giles Pinkney sauntered slowly round the room, running a finger across his connoisseur clubs, a selection of particularly fine and expensive examples. There was a driver reputed to have belonged personally to James Braid the five times Open Champion, a putting cleek attributed to the great FG Tait and a driving iron abandoned by the infamous Harry Vardon following an exhibition match against his great rival JH Taylor. There were also scarce 'patented' clubs, mashies and niblicks of all descriptions, the best collection of smooth faced irons by Robert Forgan ever assembled, and several elegant 'long-nosed clubs' from the previous century. All these, and many others scattered around his imposing house, represented a lifetime's collection; an obsession that had cost him a small fortune.

Not that Sir Giles had any need to be concerned in that regard. He owned several successful trading companies and even though he had enjoyed a full and colourful retirement for the last eleven years, his personal income remained considerable, providing the means for his indulgences. Characteristically relentless in the pursuit of the unattainable, Sir Giles had employed an array of dubious techniques to amass a golf collection second to none in the country. Most were now irreplaceable, salvaged from pending destruction or obscurity in one form or another.

Yet despite all this, none could hold a candle to the one now displayed below a gilt framed golfing print hanging on the wall across the other side of the room. He moved over for a closer look, his favourite malt whisky filling the tumbler cupped in his hand. Standing in front of the print, he raised his glass, sipped his drink and savoured the moment. Closing his eyes briefly, he reflected on his hollow victory that day.

It had been nine years since he had last been able to savour a moment comparable to this; August 1922 to be precise. Since then, his arch rival had been the clubs' only custodian. But it was now on display in his home once more, back in its rightful place in Sir Giles's opinion. Quietly congratulating himself on his earlier achievement that day, he ignored the fact that it was purely academic. The club, or more precisely a putter, had no real value; it was merely symbolic. Placing his whisky carefully down, he leant forward and took the club down from the wall for a further examination. Sir Giles Pinkney adopted his somewhat unorthodox stance and proceeded to stroke an imaginary ball into an imaginary hole.

'*This feels good,*' he thought to himself, '*Yes, very good indeed*'.

But Sir Giles Pinkney was not thinking about the proficiency of his game on this occasion. In fact his thoughts were entirely unrelated to his golf swing. He was not an accomplished golfer by any stretch of the imagination and none of the clubs in his drawing room, despite their illustrious connections, could ever help him improve on his twenty two handicap. Instead, he was focused entirely on his achievement on the golf course, just a few hours earlier. He was experiencing overwhelming elation, coupled with absolute contentment in the knowledge that his golfing companion would be feeling catastrophically helpless and distraught at that precise moment. Yes, there was a cruel streak in Sir Giles Pinkney.

Still sporting his very best golfing garb, Sir Giles wandered slowly onto the elevated veranda overlooking his Gloucestershire estate, the putter still clutched firmly in his left hand. Surveying his surroundings, he thanked his blessings as rolling out before him were over forty five acres of the most beautiful pasture and wooded parkland which had been his family home for at least forty of his seventy three years. He felt emphatically safe and secure. His thoughts inevitably, however, drifted to the unusual contest he was still bitterly embroiled in.

'Surely the whole thing must end soon?' he asked himself, deep in thought *'How much life can there be left in that old dog?'*

Watching the sun starting to slip below the horizon, he was thinking of Sir Randolph Erskine, his close neighbour and firm adversary; the gentlemen with whom he had contested for so many years and the gentleman over whom he had emerged victorious that day on the golf course. He scolded his rival for not seizing the chance to leave this world whilst remaining ahead. After all, Sir Giles had given the fool nine years 'on account' in which to do the honourable thing.

'So, how much more time did that wretched man need?'

Sir Giles wondered, *'He should have died gracefully many years earlier ... ending all this nonsense once and for all,'* continued his thoughts.

But that would simply have been too convenient, Sir Giles then reflected. Despite his remorse that the contest seemed never ending, and virtually perpetual, a wicked smile had, nevertheless, gradually replaced his earlier frown.

'So be it, then. I'll just have to give him another chance to win this back ... if he's got it in him, that is,' he thought contentedly, looking down at the club. *'It should be much more fun ... now that I've got the upper hand.'* Sir Giles seemed to have suddenly altered his perspective on the challenge, preferring now to relish the prospect of a protracted contest.

Unlike other clubs in his collection, Sir Giles did not own the one he now held. It was merely in his care for as long as his proficiency enabled, and, for as long as his health allowed. He already had several similar on display; late nineteenth century 'long-nose' clubs with their elongated slender heads. Yet this one was much different. It could never be purchased for any sum, nor acquired through grace and favour. Instead, ownership was bestowed annually through contest, until either man, Sir Giles or Sir Randolph, ultimately conceded in the pre-determined way. In recent years, his opponent had retained the prize, but Sir Giles put this down merely to a lack of enthusiasm on his own part. For him, the whole challenge had now become ever so tiresome, with little satisfaction being gained from his obligatory annual round of golf, especially with a playing partner he detested so fervently.

Changed fortunes that day, however, might now inject

some fresh enthusiasm in him for its continuance. For the first time in ten years, or thereabouts, his opponent would be experiencing the ignominy of being regarded as '*The Challenger*', along with all the trepidation the title would bestow upon the holder. There may be some considerable amusement now, Sir Giles decided, in watching the aged fool suffer and squirm until the next match. After all, twelve months is a long time to wait for a further opportunity to play for the '*Trophy*'; long enough, indeed, for it to feel like purgatory for Sir Randolph Erskine.

Not so very far away, Sir Randolph Erskine, a rather frail man in his early eighties, shuffled into the library of his seventeenth century Cotswold mansion. Still wearing his tweed plus fours, his whole body was racked with pain from his exertions that day. His mind was bewildered and confused. As best he could, he headed straight for his faded brown leather winged-back chair in front of the fireplace, pausing every few steps to catch his breath. The ache in his chest was growing by the hour, but it would pass. It always had in the past.

Finally completing his advance, Sir Randolph slumped down into his chair, his complexion as white as a sheet. He stared at the wall in front of him for several minutes, without blinking once. His attention was not on the gilt framed print that hung there, but the space beneath that had, until that morning, been host to his most prized possession; a trophy that had no intrinsic value to speak of, but nevertheless one priceless in Sir Randolph's mind. But it was now gone. Perhaps forever, he concluded.

'What have I done?' he questioned himself.

Sir Randolph's extensive fortune was comparable to that of Sir Giles's, accumulated over many decades in a remarkably similar fashion. Trading was his business, but a business that would have flourished greater still had it not been for the frequent and unwelcome interventions of his competitor, Sir Giles. The constant bane in his life, he brooded.

Sir Randolph's dry mouth was gaping wide and his wheeze grew perceptively louder with each and every laboured breath. Anxiety began to consume his entire being as he dwelt on the consequences that were now facing him. He had gambled on the outcome of a game of golf for too many years, and was quickly losing the stamina to carry on. Sir Randolph was acutely aware he was now staring into an abyss, on the brink of an enormous black hole that he had fought so long and hard to avoid tumbling into. But his recklessness was now bearing down, and he was running out of time to make amends. He was not even sure his health could be sustained for yet another year. If that were the case, then he, and his family, were now facing unavoidable peril.

'Damn that man!' he yelled out loud, 'Damn that entire family!' he added venomously, his voice reverberating through the musty corridors of his palatial home.

Sir Randolph sat there dejected for at least thirty minutes before attempting to raise himself from his seat. His strength had deserted him entirely and he was unable to move, his brain too exhausted to transmit vital signals to his weakened legs. The print on the wall, the one that had provided him with such comfort and pride over the years, was now staring down at him in mock amusement. Suspecting Sir Giles Pinkney would, even then, be gloating over his own precious copy of that very same print, it upset him, greatly, to even to look at it.

Sir Randolph knew the print intimately, having spent many hours, over many years, studying it hard, imaging he was participating in the picture himself. The George Pipeshank engraving was an amusing caricature of Victorian golfing personalities locked in challenge and drawn many years earlier, to be sold in abundance to the golfing masses. It was entirely fitting that both men had chosen this image to represent the challenge they had laid down in a fit of peak during the summer of 1921. But there was no honour associated with their own particular contest, one which cast doubt on the old adage that golf was a game for gentlemen. Victory at any price was *their* own particular watchword, and the art of gamesmanship had taken on new and unpleasant dimensions throughout their contest.

Apart from the very first challenge ten years earlier, Sir Randolph had prevailed ever since. But his winning streak had ended that day. In defeat, complete ruin now confronted him, or at least those left to suffer the consequences of his foolhardiness.

'Why had I done it?' he muttered to himself dejectedly, bitterly disappointed with his conduct that day. 'I should have listened to the lad and not been so headstrong,' he added. 'That same shot ... that same blasted shot that had sparked the whole thing off in the first place!' He was punishing himself, which only served to compound his distress.

'My God! It's all been for nothing ...,' he desperately cried out in abject realisation, '... everything's been for nothing!'

A wave of exhaustion raced through his body as the chest pains tightened their grip. If he could grab some sleep he might feel less uncomfortable, he decided. Maybe he might even wake up the next morning, Sir Randolph contemplated, and miraculously discover a new lease of life.

Aching and tired Sir Randolph loosened his tie and closed his eyes as fatigue engulfed him. Twenty minutes later, his wheezing finally stopped, forever, as he passed peacefully from this world to the next.

It was unbefitting that Sir Giles Pinkney should consider attending the funeral of his adversary, but he needed to witness the ceremony, to satisfy himself that Sir Randolph Erskine was, indeed, dead and buried, and out of his life for good.

Positioning himself some distance away from the graveside, he ensured his presence remained unobserved by the congregation. After all, that would only be adding insult to injury. Sir Giles was not beyond acknowledging the sensitivity of the situation and the feelings of Sir Randolph's family. But keeping out of sight was more a case of self preservation than respect for their wishes as there was no certainty that Sir Randolph had not disclosed 'their secret' before drawing his last breath. Caution, therefore, was an absolute necessity.

Respectfully removing his hat, despite the teaming rain, Sir Giles watched on intently as the coffin was lowered slowly into the ground. A young man was seen placing his arm round an older woman for comfort sake, whilst the pair bent their heads in solemn reflection.

Sir Giles Pinkney also began to reflect on the moment and realised he felt no sympathy for the family standing just one hundred yards ahead of him. After all, it had not been he alone who had provoked the start of tensions between their families many years earlier. His thoughts began to recall recent events; those played out on the last tee at the Royal Stratford Golf Club where both Sir Giles and Sir Randolph had been members for more years than he cared to remember. With a wry smile as he cast his mind back to their final match on that fateful day, just a couple of weeks earlier. The images were still vivid in his mind and his recollection was complete in every detail.

The 18th hole at Royal Stratford GC is a challenge for even the most adept golfer. At that particular hole a player drives, or not as the case may be, across an old quarry enclosed by rock faces over twenty feet high. If he had ever attempted to drive over this quarry himself, he would have undoubtedly landed in its bowels with only the slightest chance of ever getting out again. He knew Sir Randolph Erskine was a steady, if not sensational player for the most part, but temptation had always gripped his opponent to have a go at clearing the obstacle. But whenever attempted, Sir Randolph had never been able to overcome the hazard and had invariably watched on helplessly as his ball descended from view into the chasm. It was for this reason Sir Randolph Erskine only ever 'had a crack at it' when nothing hinged on the outcome, a friendly match for example or when he already had a particular match securely under this belt.

Both he and Sir Randolph had been standing together on that very tee recently, the concluding hole in their annual challenge. As usual, they had been accompanied by their caddies and a nominated referee, the Club Captain.

This particular challenge had been a close encounter, most unlike any of their previous affairs over the last ten years. Sir Giles recalled that he had, to his complete surprise, come to the tee all square, with the match even and only the last hole to play. Having won the previous hole, it had been his honour to play first, and knowing he had no chance of clearing the quarry with his drive, had asked his caddie for his favourite club, the mashie; a mid iron club designed for loft rather than distance.

Each and every golf club that Sir Giles possessed, including his own playing set, had wooden shafts. The new trend towards steel shafts had brought a flurry and excitement to the game but he, along with many other elderly golfers, felt the soulnessness of metal was taking the finesse out of the game. After a few obligatory waggles, his over elaborate swing had somehow successfully connected club with ball, and yet, despite the usual lazy right-hand drift, his ball had landed a few yards short of the quarry, leaving a long and difficult shot to the green. But at least the quarry would have presented no obstacle for his second shot.

The red mist appeared to have descended upon Sir Randolph Erskine as, after witnessing Sir Giles's advantage, the man had then faced his usual dilemma, whether to play safe or go for broke. Normally, in competition, there would be no question at all, with common sense always prevailing. However, with so much at stake, the risk presumably had been worth taking. A drive over the quarry would have positioned Sir Randolph ideally to run a low ball onto the green, a much easier shot than Sir Giles himself then faced. The young caddie, reading the signs and sensing a mistake was about to be made, had pulled a mashie from the bag by that time and offered the club up to Sir Randolph for the taking.

'*Best take this sir,*' the boy had helpfully suggested.

Sensibly, Sir Randolph had taken his caddie's advice, teed up his ball, taken up his address and glanced down the fairway towards the quarry for a final time. But instead of playing his shot, Sir Randolph had looked across and seen his opponent's smug expression. Furious, he had then walked over to his bag, ramming the club back in, choosing instead to draw out 'the new driver'; a club bought just the week earlier and not yet used on any of the preceding holes. It had one of those new fancy steel shafts and presumably believing the salesman's pitch and the promise of, '*adding ten yards onto your drive, sir*', Sir Randolph appeared to have decided the time was ripe to try it out.

By now, Sir Giles recalled, he had turned away not wishing the amusement on his face to be observed. His opponent's determination had been so intense that, by then, the jacket had been removed and the sleeves rolled up for added agility. The club had appeared to suit Sir Randolph, he remembered noticing, as without hesitation the swing had been launched and the ball given an almighty strike hitting the sweet spot with a resounding crack. Everyone had followed the flight of the ball with envy as it first sailed towards, and then seemingly across the quarry, only to strike the opposing face but a few feet from the summit. The ball then disappeared inevitably into the void.

Sir Randolph Erskine had seemed dumbfounded at that moment, perhaps realising his recklessness had cost him the match. At that point, most golfers would have shook hands, congratulated each other on a fine contest and retired to the '19th hole' for a friendly beer or two. Instead, Sir Randolph had proceeded to embarrass himself unnecessarily further by firing three additional golf balls into the very same spot, each time becoming yet more hysterical over the outcome.

Having somehow been able to extract a concessionary handshake from his opponent, Sir Giles remembered how he had then left with his caddie and the Club Captain, and headed for the sanctuary of the locker room, leaving his opponent to continue thrashing away ball after ball. Some moments later, the Club Captain had dutifully presented the trophy to him beside the 18th green, the usual Tom Morris long-nose putter, and following the obligatory congratulations and reimbursement of his caddie, he had ventured on his way home, long before Sir Randolph Erskine had concluded his exploits at the base of the quarry.

Sir Giles Pinkney detached himself from his reminiscences for the moment, noticing the funeral was coming to an end. Having no wish to be seen, he promptly turned, to head discreetly back into town where he had earlier parked his car. He replaced his hat and, as he walked slowly away, he considered the situation Sir Randolph's death had now generated. With one or more of the 'interested parties' unable to fulfil the terms of the challenge, the torturous contest was deemed to have concluded. Sir Randolph Erskine, with his demise, had defaulted on the terms and would be unable now to present himself at the appointed place in a year's time.

He would make a call to Bainbridge & Bainbridge that afternoon and arrange the appointment that would officially settle matters once and for all. The solicitor had retained all the necessary documents, the very documents both men had lodged ten years earlier. All that remained, now, was for Sir Giles to present himself, in person, making sure he brought along the requisite golf club by way of certification. Very soon, he would be the most contented man in the world.

Sir Giles Pinkney weaved his way between the headstones and started down the grassy embankment. The rain was beginning to fall quite heavily by this time and having no umbrella, he decided on taking a more direct route back to his car, saving a good five minutes he estimated. Leaving the cemetery, he approached a little used footpath he knew ran alongside the old canal, noting somewhat anxiously he was very quickly alone and vulnerable in such an isolated location. A poor choice he now realised. But rather than going to the effort of retracing his steps, Sir Giles elected to push on with haste.

It was a grave mistake. Pre-occupied with his thoughts, he failed to notice a small group of ruffians gaining ground on him from behind. He was attacked without warning, his first realisation being a solid blow with something heavy, landing between his shoulder blades. Falling to his knees, he felt a follow up strike hit the very same spot, softer this time, yet still sufficient to knock him to the ground. Sir Giles struck his forehead painfully on a large stone and lay there, slumped face down.

Immobilised, but still aware of his predicament, he felt himself being rolled over roughly, his pockets rifled, his wallet seized, his hunter watch and chain yanked free from his jacket and his gold signet ring pulled painfully from his little finger. His attackers had meant him no serious harm with their blows, being too light for anything other he realised, just sufficient to confuse him momentarily as they removed his possessions.

With their spoils discretely hidden, his attackers quickly departed. Sir Giles lay there isolated, on his back, staring up at the grey sky trying to regain his composure and strength, whilst the rain washed his face. A severe ache erupted deep within his head and his vision very quickly became alarmingly blurred. The ache turned quickly into a piercing pain. A dark veil descended and his sight deserted him completely.

In next to no time, Sir Giles Pinkney had joined his counterpart, Sir Randolph Erskine, in the next life. Both men had died in quick succession and unbeknown to anyone other than their unsuspecting solicitors, Bainbridge & Bainbridge, their sombre secret had passed along with them into obscurity.

The Present

Several generations on, the belated appointment with Bainbridge & Bainbridge finally took place at their Stratford upon Avon offices. Yet it was one neither made, nor attended, by any member of the Pinkney family.

'But *what* are you saying?' the young women enquired desperately. 'I don't understand … this is all too much for me to take in.' She was extremely agitated and clearly bewildered.

'I apologise for the distress this is obviously causing,' said Maurice Bainbridge, senior partner, 'but you must understand that this, too, is the first time I have really had a chance to read the documents for myself. I will need time to examine them closely, especially the wording of the *'Agreement'*.'

He shuffled the faded papers in his hands.

'I'll also need to put them through the usual legal tests,' he added, '... and I will, of course, give you the benefit of my professional opinion after I have given the matter more careful consideration, ... but I have to say, based on first reading, the situation you now find yourself in is very unfortunate indeed ... to say the very least.'

The solicitor had been genuinely sympathetic as he had spoken.

Taking deep breaths to try and regain her composure, the young women tried to summarise, more for her own benefit than that of the solicitors.

'So, if I understand you correctly, Mr. Bainbridge,' she paused to get her thought process into gear, '... and if *these* turn out to be legally binding,' she added, pointing to the papers in the solicitors grasp, '... then my whole world is about to be turned upside down because of a couple of old fools ... whom I've obviously never met ... decided to write ... *these things*.' She pointed once more at the papers, this time much more emphatically, '... And, and...,' she faltered as her composure finally crumbled.

'Please, may I?' interrupted the solicitor. No response to his question came forth, so he carried on.

'As far as I can ascertain from just a casual read, Mrs. Erskine, the *'Agreement'*, thankfully, remains unenforceable without the presentation of the golf club to which it refers.'

He paused.

'Do you, by any chance, know if you possess such a thing?' he asked encouragingly.

'How would I know?' she replied abruptly. 'Maybe ... I just don't know, ... I'll need to have a good look around.' She gave herself time to think before adding, 'What sort of golf club am I supposed to be looking for anyway? I don't know a damn thing about *stupid* golf.'

Maurice Bainbridge unfolded a further piece of paper, one that had seemingly been referenced in the *'Agreement'* he had just read aloud to Elizabeth Erskine.

'I have something here that might help', he offered politely. 'It's a partial description of the club in question. I can read this out to you, but I'm not permitted, you will understand, to let you to take this away or have it reproduced. But you're welcome to make notes if you wish.'

He slipped a pen and paper in her direction and she scribbled away as the solicitor slowly read out the passage.

'I'll start looking straight away, Mr. Bainbridge,' Elizabeth Erskine politely and calmly declared, '... and when I find it, I'll come back immediately.'

Sensing the young women may be suffering from shock and not fully absorbing the potential gravity of her situation, the solicitor added a few further words of caution.

'It's entirely possible you don't possess the golf club, Mrs. Erskine. If that's the case, it may well be lost forever, making this ...,' he pointed to the thicker document on his desk, '...making this *'Agreement'* completely worthless.'

Before the young women interpreted his comment as

false hope, he promptly continued with his cautionary advice.

'But I have to advise you, that the family of the other named individuals in this *'Agreement'*, may well have it in their possession. And should they, like you, stumble across the second print ... with its handwritten inscription on the reverse ...,' he left that thought hanging for a few seconds, 'then they too could well be curious of its meaning and come here seeking similar advice, ... perhaps even to make a rightful claim!'

His words, although intended to help and guide, only served to create greater alarm. He saw, from her changing expression, that the true significance of the discovery was beginning to dawn on her.

Treading now very carefully, the solicitor continued on with his obligatory advice.

'Regrettably Mrs. Erskine, you and your husband will continue to be at risk until such time as you can satisfy yourself that you indeed have ownership of the prescribed golf club, or indeed that it no longer exists. Until that time, I strongly advise you to keep this matter as confidential as possible and avoid its announcement. You have my word, as executors to the *'Agreement'*, we shall maintain absolute silence on this.'

Elizabeth Erskine, realising the discussion could serve no more useful purpose, offered her thanks to Mr. Bainbridge for his time and assistance, placed her notes in her bag, and headed out of the solicitor's office, into a cold winters breeze.

Despite the passing of so many years, it was apparent that her family, the Erskines, could now be pitched unavoidably headlong into a ludicrous race against time. Thrown into competition with persons she had never even met, nor with whom they had any previous quarrel, people who may not even realise that *they too* were at great risk. And all because of a senseless and reckless agreement, created by a pair of *'idiots'* in her opinion; idiots who were even incapable of successfully settling matters between themselves during their own lifetime.

'*How could her husband's great grandfather have been so casual with their inheritance?*' she asked herself. '*And how could that man have gambled so carelessly with his decedent's livelihood?*' she pondered.

And against the Pinkney's of all people, she realised, the same Pinkney's that live not so very far away from herself; the same Pinkney's who are also highly prominent in the community.

Elizabeth Erskine cringed at the scandal all this might possibly cause. But surely it would not come to that, she reckoned. The Pinkney's, like they, would surely have no interest in entertaining the idea of an unseemly conflict over what, after all, could be no more than just an unpleasant state of unresolved affairs. Yes, she was convinced they too would wish to let bygones be bygones.

Nonetheless, with her pragmatic streak coming to the fore, Elizabeth and her husband really had no choice but to unearth that club. Claiming it for themselves might safeguard all that they rightfully called home. A shiver shot down her spine as she soberly realised it all could, quite easily and legitimately, be snatched away from them. And anytime soon perhaps, leaving them penniless and homeless into the bargain.

That prospect was too sickening to contemplate. The humiliation, alone, would kill them, if not literally, then certainly socially.

'*It's got to be in the house somewhere,*' she silently convinced herself, '*... It just has to be!*' she repeated thoughtfully, only this time with much less assurance.

That evening a meticulous search of the Erskine's palatial household was frantically conducted from top to bottom. Yet the search had revealed nothing to match the description she had noted that afternoon. They did find an old tattered cloth golf bag in the basement containing eight or nine old wooden shafted golf clubs, along with a further club having a severely bent steel shaft. But after some initial excitement, they soon realised nothing in the bag came remotely close to what they were actually seeking.

Elizabeth and her husband, Robert, great grandson to Sir Randolph Erskine, inheritor of the magnificent Grange Manor, both sat down exhausted in their drawing room. Neither could really comprehend the absurdity of the situation they now found themselves in.

'Tell me again,' Robert Erskine asked of his wife, 'What did the solicitor *actually* say?'

'I can't remember exactly. I was in absolute shock,' she replied impatiently, having already answered the question at least twice already, 'All I know is this. We have to find that blasted golf club,' she emphasised, '... and at all costs. If we don't have it, then the Pinkney's almost certainly must.'

She paused briefly, then added, 'And that's the risk Robert. If we can't place our hands on it … then there's every chance *they'll* be sitting here in this house for Christmas dinner … instead of *us*,' she added emotionally, '… and it seems there's nothing we can do about it … it all seems to be absurdly legal.'

Robert Erskine attempted to offer some words of encouragement. 'Well, all I can say is this,' he said emphatically, 'if they do have it, then surely they'd have staked their claim already … wouldn't they?'

His wife was not at all convinced, unable to regard their situation as anything other than dire. Hanging her head she said dejectedly, 'It's more likely they simply haven't found the clues yet. It's that blasted picture of yours … the golf one … they've got one exactly the same I bet. The solicitor confirmed as much. The only thing that's keeping us in our house is the possibility they haven't read what's on the back of it yet.'

Robert Erskine, not the most self-assured individual, was beginning to panic also, albeit rather belatedly. His wife was right. They needed to put a halt to this whole nonsense somehow.

'Perhaps the solicitor could just lose the document,' he offered rather naively.

Elizabeth Erskine, on the other hand, was more worldly than her husband and much more adept at problem solving. She dismissed his comment with some blatant eye rolling.

'Don't be ridiculous,' she said scornfully. 'Come on … another search of the house and if it doesn't turn up this time … well … then we'll just need to get our hands on it somehow,' she announced, '…won't we, Robert?'

Chapter 2

'Are you still on that computer?' Anne Hudson called up the stairs to her husband, 'Your breakfast is out and getting cold.' She waited impatiently for the reply that never came. 'Tom, are you listening to me?' she asked bluntly.

Tom was not deliberately ignoring his wife's enquiry, it being more a case of poor reception rather than outright ignorance. He had closed the world out temporally whilst he wrestled with an over sized dictionary, trying to translate *'I will send you'* into comprehendible French.

'With you in a minute, my love,' he finally replied following some subliminal recognition of his wife's voice, 'I'll be right down.'

Disregarding instantly the promise he had just made, he carried on with his search, found something that offered possibilities and then typed away once more.

'J'envoyer vous,' he confidently wrote, hesitated, erased, then re-typed, *'Je vous envoyez.'*

Hearing the continued clattering of the keyboard upstairs, Anne issued her final warning.

'Tom … I'm not going to tell you again.'

'Je vous envoyer les balles de golf en Lundi,' he typed assuredly, before doubting himself once again.

'Just coming!' he yelled out automatically, oblivious to what he was actually announcing. The concentration on his work was, however, abruptly disturbed with the front door slamming shut downstairs.

The mood at the dining table later that day was decidedly subdued.

'Look Tom, I don't mind you spending so much time on the computer,' Anne announced with a serious tone to her voice, 'but you're simply leaving everything up to me … expecting me to do all the running around,' she explained. 'We're going over there in a few days and you've not even looked out your passport yet.'

'Plenty of time for that,' Tom proclaimed dismissively, somewhat irritated and embarrassed by the reminder, 'I've got to get the arrangements sorted with those guys I'm meeting on the way down,' he added by way of an excuse. Realising he had just aggravated an old sore, he quickly added, 'But we'll still have some fun on the way down … believe me, we will.'

They were only a couple of days from starting their first real holiday in five years, spending two weeks in the south of France, close to the Italian border. And they were intending to drive. Not a unanimous decision it seemed, as Anne generally hated travelling long distances in the car. Yet it had been a compromise on her part to accommodate her husband's desire, *'to do some business en route,'* as he had enthusiastically described it.

'That's good to hear,' she said sarcastically. 'So how many people are you actually intending to see?' she asked with markedly less enthusiasm than her husband had earlier displayed. Completely oblivious to his wife's cynicism, he outlined his plan once again.

'Well there's a Jean-Pierre, just outside Dijon, and this guy called Philippe who lives somewhere near Monaco. He's asked if I can bring along some of my more interesting clubs,' he proudly announced.

She thought about that for a second or two, before asking the obvious follow up question. 'You're quite sure he knows we're on holiday, Tom .... he does, doesn't he? ... He doesn't think he's going to monopolise all your time down there?

'Of course he won't,' replied her husband brusquely, 'I just happened to mention we were coming down next week on holiday .... and he's asked if we can meet up for an hour or two, that's all. Thankfully, he speaks quite good English so I'm pretty sure he understood what I was trying to say.'

'*Good for him!*' Anne thought to herself, before dropping the subject and pouring out coffees.

Tom Hudson was a kind-hearted soul who loved his wife enormously. He had a fairly mundane occupation, one which provided a steady income, but one that would never make them rich. But that did not bother his wife particularly, as they were comfortably off and managed to get by without too much difficulty. She had a husband she loved and they both lived in a wonderful stone cottage in the heart of the Cotswolds, the most beautiful part of all England, she had long ago decided. Village life suited them and everything was on an even keel. Yet Tom, himself, remained somewhat unfulfilled despite all that. As a consummate dreamer, he had convinced himself that one day he could change their fortunes for the better. Never quite satisfied with the prospect of dull, yet steady employment until retirement, he was forever scheming to make a 'fast buck'. His most recent idea, and arguably the least hair-brained to date, involved the buying and selling of golfing memorabilia. Starting out as a pastime, it had inevitably developed quickly into one of his obsessions, along with a desire to trade full-time.

Anne Hudson never believed any of her husband's schemes would ever amount to much, but she was happy to go along with most whilst they remained relatively harmless. This latest was no exception. She only had one issue, however, and that was the inordinate amount of time he spent on the computer each week, trying to sell the golf clubs on the internet. Not that the money it generated did not come in handy; sometimes he made hundreds of pounds at a time. Her concerns centred more on all the fuss that seemed to accompany it, all the emails that were sent and received, all the difficulties over payments, all the packing, endless trips to the post office, the incessant photography, the countless hours writing descriptions in the first place and so on and so forth. She simply could not understand the need to spend so much time over the whole process, especially when domestic chores were being neglected as a consequence. And she would never comprehend why Tom had chosen to sell to the Europeans despite being linguistically inept in any language, even his first and only. A strange decision and one she had often questioned.

Despite his wife's scepticism Tom was nevertheless convinced he had finally found his niche, spurred on by a couple of early successes. Notwithstanding his inability to structure meaningful sentences, he had miraculously managed to cultivate two or three dealers in France, dealers who appeared to be fairly eager to trade despite some initial reticence on their part. For now, at least, there was no third party competition and practically everything Tom offered up for sale was seized with enthusiasm, providing him with profitable returns. In Tom's mind, this was the golden opportunity he had been engineering for so many years.

Their trip to France would be the acid test, so to speak, and he would take along some special examples, if he could; higher end value clubs that might realise better returns. He would explore the potential demand. And if there were none at present, then some careful seeding would do no harm.

As the trip had grown closer, Tom had allowed himself to get ever more excited at the prospect. But there remained a niggling problem; there was simply nothing in his stockpile that could be genuinely offered up as special. It was necessary, therefore, to speculate a little on the acquisitions front.

The upcoming auction was well timed and would provide the opportunity to buy more expensively than before, finances and spouses permitting of course. The mental shopping list was already in place, but he was at risk, once again, of getting carried away with his pipedream. Tom's optimism however, was indefatigably reinforced and unwavering.

'I've got a funny feeling I'm going to hit on something big here,' had been his recurring thought for some time now.

At the same time, elsewhere in the Gloucestershire countryside, an elegant young woman approached a rather impressive oak panelled door. The sheer dimension of the entrance left her wondering what splendours lay beyond.

Outside were parked at least four vehicles; two transit vans, a Mercedes and an old Ford Escort that barely hung together. Surely some provision ought to have been made for all of these unsightly vehicles to have been parked somewhere round the corner she thought. *'I suppose beggars can't be choosers'*, she concluded.

The Mercedes was hers, of course, and for a moment or two she was concerned it might get damaged in someway, dented by some careless individual who had no appreciation for the finer things in life. She hesitated for a few seconds, halting her approach to the house, not in contemplation of moving her car to a safer distance, but more in trepidation over what she was about to do.

Elizabeth Erskine composed herself, straightened her skirt, fiddled with her scarf and with an outstretched arm, pointed an index finger towards the doorbell. Without even touching the button, the door unlatched itself and swung wide open with startling velocity. She jumped back in surprise, briskly moving to one side, as if clearing the way for someone's hasty departure. She also became acutely aware, in the same instance, she ought not to be standing there in the first place.

Somewhat embarrassed, acting as if she had been caught in some unseemly act, she bowed her head, trying also to hide herself behind a stone pillar. A larger than life character emerged energetically out into the daylight from a poorly lit hallway. Paying no particular attention to where he was heading, the man stumbled over the threshold, loosing his balance as he tumbled forward. Grabbing the pillar, the very one now masking Elizabeth Erskine's presence, the man quickly regained his footing and turned around to address the tall willowy figure standing in the doorway.

'It's been a pleasure,' he bellowed jovially out loud, waving his departure at the same time, '… and thanks for putting them to one side for me. I'll be round tomorrow with the rest of the cash. … Don't you go selling them to anyone else,' he instructed. The boisterous man's attention then shifted to the young woman who was standing almost apologetically, and quite deliberately, well out of his way.

'Begging you pardon, my dear,' he offered gracefully, tipping his hat, '… didn't see you standing there. I'm ever so sorry.' He edged forward towards Elizabeth. 'Here get yourself inside.'

Taking her by the arm, he called out to the doorman.

'Leave it open mate … you've got a pretty young lady here who wants to come in,' he announced, taking unnecessary control of the situation. A little inappropriately, he continued holding her arm, ushering Elizabeth unceremoniously through the entrance, leaving her no time to think and no time to object.

Any reservations Elizabeth Erskine may have harboured about actually being in *that* house were no longer of any consequence. She was standing within a grand entrance lobby with all its imposing slender and grandeur, panic stricken at the thought of what she was actually doing. It had been forced upon her, having been given no real choice in the matter. And now she was there, no turning back now, her only option was to go along with it all and play-act the part. This may be her one and only opportunity to take a good look around Pinkney's house, her only chance, perhaps, to discover the golf club she was desperately seeking. If it *was* here, as she suspected, then she would need to start coming to terms with the situation. But that prospect was far too horrific to contemplate. Despite her fears, she needed to know for certain if the sought-after golf club was actually in residence.

She was a nervous wreck by now, but was managing to disguise it well. A gentleman dressed in black tails, the same willowy man she had seen a moment or two earlier, emerged from behind the open door and startled her.

'Good morning, madam,' the doorman courteously offered his greeting. 'Are you here for the sale?' he enquired.

Elizabeth Erskine had to appear confident and convincing, but lapsed into a moment's hesitation instead. Unsure whether or not her uncertainty had been detected, she nonetheless commenced her unrehearsed performance.

'Actually, yes I am ... but I don't have much time, so perhaps you could point me in the right direction?' she replied with conviction.

'Of course, madam,' the gentleman responded, 'We've produced a guide book which may help you.' There was some pride in his words and he continued. 'Well not so much a book, more of a pamphlet actually. Here let me get one for you. It'll describe which rooms are open and which remain private ... they're all clearly marked and there is a floor plan on the last page, ... I drew it myself, so I apologise for its crudeness, ... I'm no artist I'm afraid,' he continued whilst moving across the hallway, taking a copy from the small table beside the door and handing it to Elizabeth.

'All the items for sale are listed by room ... all you

need to do is have a good look around. Mind you ... you might find many have already been sold madam ... this is our second day, as I'm sure you're well aware.'

'I understand,' she said, with more confidence this time, 'You're very kind.'

'Is there anything in particular you are looking for madam?' he enquired helpfully.

Elizabeth Erskine was undecided whether or not she should come straight out with it. She bought herself some thinking time by flicking through the pamphlet before replying.

'I imagine the fun will be in the searching. Wouldn't you agree?' she asked, having chosen to leave few clues to her intentions, 'Although, I would be interested to learn if there were any sporting items being offered?' she added speculatively.

Before the doorman could respond, an anxious thought crossed her mind. Clues, she scolded herself. She had just left the biggest clue of all, sitting there outside the front door, a personalised number plate that could well attract some unwelcome attention. Elizabeth Erskine could ill afford to introduce herself like that, especially knowing the purpose for her visit. But, it was all too late to do anything about that now, she decided, so best try and make this as quick as possible. Without waiting for a reply to her question, she excused herself and turned away quickly, heading with edginess in the direction of the nearest doorway.

Something remarkable had happened whilst Robert

Erskine had scanned the local papers that very morning, a chance reading of a small announcement, hidden on page six of *'The Cotswold Recorder'*. In the midst of their plight and turmoil, a guiding light had shone down, one of those remarkable events that occasionally manifest themselves when most needed, reinforcing beliefs in divine intervention, perhaps. They were desperate, but that advertisement had offered a glimmer of hope, an opportunity to take charge of the situation. For days now they had racked their brains, trying to come up with some ingenious way of finding out if their neighbours possessed that all-important golf club the solicitor had described; the golf club that would secure their prospects. And there, in the black and white print of the local newspaper was their open invitation to inspect the Pinkney household from top to bottom, without even attracting suspicion.

Robert Erskine had almost injured himself rushing to the phone to call his wife that morning, to interrupt her obligatory visit to the garden centre.

'Darling, you're not going to believe this, ... but they're having a house clearance ... today ... right now in fact,' he had spurted the words out excitedly, 'You'll have to get yourself across there this very minute.'

Stopping her car on the verge to take the call and not really comprehending what on earth her husband was talking about, Elizabeth had enquired. 'Who, Robert ... *who's* having a house clearance?'

'The Pinkney's, of course,' he had explained, '... Who else would I be talking about?'

'You're pulling my leg,' she had responded disbelievingly, 'How cruel you are, Robert!'

'I kid you not … you'll have to go right now,' he had instructed, 'It's already into its second day. You'll need to hurry or we'll miss it.'

'What do you mean, get yourself over there? You'll be joining me, won't you?'

'How can I do that, Elizabeth?' he had asked, '… they know my face, I'll be recognised. Just get over there and take a good look around. It'll be alright,' he had added encouragingly. 'They're having some sort of sale … probably to do with all those death duties they've got to find. Anyway, just …'

'Don't you *anyway just*' me!' she had interrupted forcefully, 'For a start, I don't have a bloody clue what I'm supposed to be looking for. You might know one from another … but I don't!'

'Calm down, Elizabeth … please calm down,' he had pleaded over the phone, 'We'll never get a chance like this ever again. It might already be too late.' He had left his words hanging just long enough to take effect before adding, 'You have to do it, my dear. It's an old golf club. It'll have a long wooden head, remember … just like the picture I showed you. Just go and take a look … and pretend you come from London or somewhere …. they'll never guess who you are.' He had again paused, waiting for a response, but none had come forth.

Without properly thinking about his next choice of words, and believing he was offering some form of compliment by way of encouragement, he had finally said, 'You're quite good at feigning things my dear, so it shouldn't be a problem.'

The phone had suddenly gone dead on him. She had cut

him off. He had wondered if he should phone back.

'*Best not,*' he had thoughtfully concluded.

Only twenty five minutes after receiving the call on her mobile phone, Elizabeth Erskine was now standing in the drawing room of Kerrington Manor, the ancestral home of the Pinkney's, close neighbours and close adversaries, or so it would now seem. She cursed her husband for sending her on her own, alone on this clandestine operation. But he was right. There was every chance he may be recognised and that would lead to all sorts of awkward questions at the very least. But worst still, it might even have led to an embarrassing and public ejection from the premises, given the history between the two families. That would have been disastrous, particularly if it ever got into the papers, she decided.

But what was she thinking, she asked herself? Everything she held so dear was now at risk, and all she was contemplating was the ignominy of public humiliation at being asked to leave. It was time for her to regain her focus and see this particular unpleasantness through to the end. And as swiftly as possible.

Elizabeth Erskine was not alone in the big house and it was positively alive with what she presumed were dealers. Legions of unfamiliar faces were pouring over virtually everything, searching out the hidden treasures and making copious notes. She was uncertain how she ought to be acting at that precise moment and quickly became aware that standing in the middle of the room was perhaps not the most inconspicuous thing she could be doing. Feeling somewhat awkward and very self-conscious, she moved around avoiding any eye contact as best she could. Disappointingly, however, she was beginning to attract some unwanted attention from two smartly dressed gentlemen standing by the window. They were talking to each other and frequently looking over towards her. She turned away and moved in the opposite direction, towards the entrance door in fact. A subconscious act perhaps, as she was not deliberately intending to beat a hasty retreat. But she was, nonetheless, convinced she had been recognised.

As Elizabeth's pace quickened for the exit, a cold sweat was beginning to develop on her forehead. A small gathering, engaged in discussion, slowly emerged through the doorway, interrupting her departure. They stopped before entering the room fully. The middle-aged man in the centre of the grouping, appeared to be offering a guided tour and he caught Elizabeth's eye. He courteously presented a smile, paused in his dialogue for a second or two, then continued with his conversation. She had no choice but to turn around again and retrace her steps, back once more into the spotlight.

Detaching himself from the other, the taller of the two gentlemen headed smoothly in her direction from his window position. Plotting his trajectory, she silently cursed her husband, realising her desire for anonymity was now a forlorn hope. As he came closer, they simultaneously recognised each other.

'Mrs. Erskine, how are you?' the dapper gentleman enquired charmingly, 'And what brings you here? Decided to cut out the middle man, eh?'

'Mr. Grayson, how nice to see you here,' she replied insincerely. In an attempt to direct the conversation away from his question, she then asked, '… So how's business with you?'

For the next few minutes Elizabeth Erskine and the inquisitive Mr. Grayson engaged in duel, each asking questions, but each offering very few answers. Mr. Grayson, an established local fine arts dealer, embarked on polite, yet obvious probing, trying patiently to extract a plausible reason for her being there. At the same time, Elizabeth Erskine expertly parried with courteous enquiries about the health of Mrs. Grayson.

The exchanges had been unwelcomingly lengthy and had exhausted her, but thankfully had bought her some time, time enough for the middle-aged man from earlier to depart to another part of the building. Wishing Mr. Grayson a fruitful search, Elizabeth then excused herself and floated out the room through a different door. She found herself in what was obviously the library, a quite grand, yet intimate room.

Books had always held a fascination for Elizabeth Erskine and she stood amazed at the collection that surrounded her. It was not that she read a great deal, in fact she found that her hectic lifestyle left precious little time to read very much at all. She was, nonetheless, very keen on old books, first editions, out of print editions, signed books and the like. She appreciated the splendour, the craftsmanship, the smell, the foxing and fading that only time could confer. In this room there must have been at least five or six hundred examples, all beautifully bound, volumes galore, unique specimens for sure. She was momentarily captivated.

'Hello there.' An unfamiliar voice came from over her left shoulder.

She was surprised at the interruption and turning on her heels, she saw that the middle-aged man, spied a little earlier, was now standing right beside her. It was going decidedly contrary to plan, she thought. How difficult could it be, especially during an open day, to simply breeze in and out without being noticed, particularly when that was all you really wanted to do, she asked herself? Yet despite that, and within the space of ten minutes, she was about to engage in her third 'one to one' conversation. Fighting the irritation that was bristling inside and praying her flushed complexion would go unnoticed, she smiled modestly. He noticed her obvious embarrassment and withdrew slightly.

'Please excuse me, I thought I would introduce myself and offer my assistance … Charles Pinkney is my name,' he said presenting his hand and leaving his introduction hanging. She remained silent, unsure whether or not she had been recognised, her reluctance to respond and shake his hand creating an awkward moment for them both.

'Forgive me, I'll leave you to carry on,' he added apologetically, after what seemed to be an eternal delay.

'I'm so sorry,' responded Elizabeth Erskine, suddenly realising she was being rude, 'You must find me awfully impolite.'

'Not at all. It is I who should apologise,' he replied graciously, 'You've business to conduct and I'm interrupting you. Please carry on. I hope there's something here to your liking?'

Feeling fairly confident her identity had remained concealed, she belatedly offered a name. 'Elizabeth … forgive me, … my name is Elizabeth.'

'Pleased to meet you ... *Elizabeth* ....?' He was clearly fishing. Realising this, she took charge of the conversation and altered the direction in which it was heading.

'Yes, I'm here simply browsing, Mr. Pinkney. It's a pleasure to meet you and thank you for allowing us this opportunity.' She waved an arm round the room. 'So rarely do we in the trade get a chance to acquire such fine objects at source. The more roguish elements of my trade often get their hands on the nicer, more important pieces and turn them over a few times, changing the character of the item completely in the chase for commercial advantage, ... completely destroying it's identity and soul.'

She surprised herself at the ease with which she had also changed her own character within the last minute. Noticing his eyebrows lifting and realising she was venturing unnecessarily far into the unknown, she promptly posed a question of her own.

'Are you expecting to do well over these two days, Mr. Pinkney?'

Charles Pinkney, feeling somewhat obligated to offer an explanation for the sale, carried on to explain how circumstances were forcing his disposals. No detail was omitted, which included an expression of sadness and an insight into the distress it was causing his family. He questioned the ethics of the taxation system, he thanked the good folk of the community for rallying round in times of need, he praised the generosity of the local tradesmen and dealers, rambling on for several minutes.

He was over doing it, she thought, suspecting he too was playing out some form of charade here, presenting himself in a fashion which perhaps belied the true character of the man.

She was becoming impatient and was not at all sympathetic over the plight of the Pinkney household. After all, and for all she knew, this man could be contemplating the destruction of the Erskine family, *her family*, at that very moment. She was just at the point of losing her self control when, over his shoulder, she spotted something familiar. Recognising it straight away for what it was, she became increasing oblivious to what was being said. Charles Pinkney continued his monologue, not actually noticing her distraction at first.

'Elizabeth, Elizabeth … I'm sorry. I'm being a dreadful bore,' he said after finally noticing her attention had wandered. Following her sight line, he turned round to see what was causing so much interest.

'Ah, I see you're interested in the *Pipeshank* print.'

Her heart sank. How could she have been so stupid and indiscrete? Blind panic took hold right there and then as a hundred frantic thoughts flashed through her mind and the ramifications of her discovery began to unfold. Not only had she practically announced the arrival of *'Elizabeth Erskine, arch rival'*, she had now pinpointing the very object that could reveal *'the secret'* , the one which could lead to her complete ruin.

She desperately needed to clear her thoughts and analyse the possibilities.

Was this bad news? Did this mean he was aware of the contest and the Agreement? She was uncertain what to think, but she did soberly realise that the next few minutes were going to be crucial. She turned to look directly at the print.

Time to start bluffing.

'Ah, yes … a *Pipeshank*,' she acknowledged, pretending to infer some kind of knowledge on the subject. She silently cautioned herself before saying anymore. 'Is it for sale?' she asked innocently.

'I'm afraid not,' replied Charles Pinkney firmly, 'It's got a special attachment within the family.'

A disturbing response she decided. *What does he mean exactly by that? What does he mean by 'special attachment'?* She was quite ready to convince herself he knew the true significance of the print.

'Not for sale … that's a pity,' Elizabeth said thoughtfully. She had to gamble by pushing this a little further, she decided.

'Look, I'm not having much luck today, and this is the one thing I'd be quite keen to get my hands on. I'm sure we can come to some arrangement,' she suggested.

Charles Pinkney was able to read the signs, suspecting this dealer may have sniffed a bargain. She was also beginning to turn a little patronising, he thought.

'I hate to disappoint you, but I'm sorry … just can't do, I'm afraid. It's been hanging there for as long as anyone can remember. My great grandfather had been particularly fond of it and apparently quite insistent that it should never leave the family. It's probably one of the few things in the house which we *won't* sell. Bad luck I'm afraid, but we've lots of other prints. Perhaps I could show you those instead?' he countered firmly, whilst at the same time encouraging a move towards the hallway.

Elizabeth was uncertain whether to press for a sale one

more time and was now having to think on her feet. He seemed quite determined to snub out her interest and that was a very bad sign in her opinion. If he knew about the words on the reverse, then he would probably know of the existence of the '*Agreement*'. If that were the case, then all was lost anyway, as he probably had the club in his possession as well. But if he didn't, then he would never be able to make the connection. She had to succeed, somehow, in getting the print out of this house, meaning her family would be safeguarded forever, with no absolute necessity to trace the club after all. On balance, it was definitely worth taking a chance, she finally decided.

'Two hundred pounds,' she offered to his turned back. Charles Pinkney halted his departure, then turned around. He looked at Elizabeth quizzically.

'I don't wish to be impolite Elizabeth, but I've already told you the print is not for sale.' His tone was now much less civil.

'Four hundred pounds then,' she heard herself saying. Looking into his steely eyes, she instinctively knew she had just made a wrong call.

Charles Pinkney, unblinking and uncompromising, simply said, 'I would be obliged if you would leave my house now.'

Those disturbing few words were delivered in a way that left Elizabeth Erskine feeling stone cold. She had scuttled any chance she may have had of learning the truth. No way now of ever knowing if Pinkney possessed what she sought. Those few words would now compound the uncertainty of whatever future lay ahead for Robert and herself. Life would now be intolerable, forever threatening that dreadful day when a letter might fall through the letter box demanding the submission of all they owned. And to make matters worse, she was utterly convinced she had just inadvertently lit the proverbial blue touch paper that would now lead to that eventual outcome.

With tears welling in her eyes and a feeling of absolute loss starting to envelope her, she headed straight for the front door as fast as her dignity would allow. The tall man in tails was standing expectantly and seemed pleased to see her approach, despite her valiant efforts to ignore him completely. Making a dive for the opening and keeping her head lowered, she failed to notice him stepping into her path in an attempt to intercept her departure. The sound of his voice was all that prevented the collision. Coming to a standstill and confronting the doorman, she was fearful of the reason.

'You asked earlier about sporting items, madam,' he said, speaking very gently.

'Sorry?' she said not fully registering his intervention.

'You asked earlier about sporting items, madam. We have quite a few equestrian pieces which are on display in the study. Perhaps you saw them?'

'Really!' she said dismissively, by now trying desperately to step around him.

'But I'm afraid all the golf clubs were cleared out about three weeks ago,' he added helpfully. Elizabeth Erskine halted abruptly and switched her full attention now to the man speaking to her.

'I'm sorry, what did you say?' she asked, suddenly much more attentive to the words being spoken, 'All the golf clubs went *where* exactly?'

'Sold the entire collection to someone locally. Not sure who, but his van was local. I helped him load them all in. It took about half an hour I remember.' The willowy man said in recollection. 'Mr. Pinkney's great grandfather had quite a collection, you know, but Mr Pinkney himself has no interest in golf you see.'

By now she was fully tuned in.

'Do you know who that gentleman was, by any chance?' she asked wishfully.

'I'm sorry madam, I never thought to enquire as to the gentleman's name … but I could ask Mr. Pinkney if you're at all interested.' Elizabeth Erskine's reply was hastily delivered.

'Please no … there's absolutely no need to disturb Mr. Pinkney with this.' Her curiosity had reached bursting point by this time and she needed more information immediately. 'Did he say what he was going to do with them by any chance?'

The doorman was only too eager to help.

'To auction I believe madam. He said he would be putting them into auction. I have to say, Mr. Pinkney might well have been advised to do that himself and make a better price. But it's not for me to comment you'll understand.'

'*Which* auction?' she asked impatiently, wishing the man would simply take the lead and just tell her all he knew, and all she wanted to know, without any need for prompting.

'I honestly have no idea madam, but he usually sells close by. I remember him saying just that.'

A few further questions confirmed no more useful information was embedded in the doorman's memory, so she thanked the man and completed her departure. Her face was beaming as she jumped into her Mercedes and sped off down the drive at top speed, the wheels casting large quantities of gravel into the flowerbeds. A few miles down the road Elizabeth Erskine pulled into a local petrol station and gathered up all the different newspapers from the stand.

Later that evening, she and her husband trawled through every page of every newspaper, searching without success for any auction notices remotely associated with sporting items. The only advertised event was an upcoming agricultural sale. Which, of course, was of no use to them, whatsoever. Their efforts had proved fruitless.

Charles Pinkney breezed back into his library having spent several hours reviewing the transactions from the last two days. The sales had been much more plentiful than he had either hoped or expected, with Mr. Grayson, especially, being particularly carefree with his cheque book. That one dealer alone would require an entire fleet of removal vans to collect his goods. Within a few days the whole consignment would undoubtedly be packed into containers and heading off in the direction of some unscrupulous overseas associates.

He was heartened by the day's takings, but equally saddened and resentful over the need to dispose of his chattels in the first place. Death duties and taxation had been crippling his finances as he struggled to meet his legal obligations. His errant sister was also demanding her share. And despite the successes of recent days, there would still be precious little left 'in the kitty' to permit a few indulgences.

But that was a concern best left for another day. He looked again at the *Pipeshank* print on the wall. He was a little ashamed of his attitude that afternoon, but she had been disrespectful. The money had been immaterial on that particular occasion; the issue being more at matter of principle. Yet he may never receive an offer like that again. A good offer, indeed, for what, after all, was just an ordinary print in a rather ordinary frame. No other dealer in their right mind would have waved four hundred pounds under his nose.

'*Four hundred pounds*,' he reflected, '*Why so much?*' He elected to take a closer look, speculating that he may be missing something important. If a dealer offers four hundred pounds, then it's got to be worth a thousand, he reminded himself.

Taking the print down from the wall he studied it carefully for the very first time, perplexed and unable to fathom why it held so much interest for the woman. He prided himself on being quite a knowledgeable amateur enthusiast and was convinced it was worth, at most, a quarter of what had been offered. Deciding she must have been either mistaken or incredibly affluent, and dismissing the possibility it was anything other than just an ordinary example, he went to hang the print back on the wall. But the hanging cord snapped in the attempt; hardly surprising given its age. Flipping the print over to examine the fault, he noticed some faded words written on the brown paper backing. In fact there were quite a few words, words

46

written by hand and words he had been unaware existed until that moment. As he began read the inscription, his curiosity began to grow.

'*Executors Bainbridge & Bainbridge, Stratford upon Avon,*' read the last line.

'Interesting,' he said to himself. He knew of the firm but none of the partners personally. Bainbridge & Bainbridge were long established solicitors in the town, a little old fashioned perhaps in his view and unlikely to be his first choice if he had reason to seek legal assistance. Wondering what connection there could possibly be between his family, these solicitors and, more curiously perhaps, the woman who was so keen to acquire the print, he undertook to call them first thing in the morning, to see if they had managed to retain any references on file.

Around the time Charles Pinkney had been examining his *Pipeshank* print, Stuart MacIntyre was adding the finishing touches to his arrangements.

There were going to be nearly 600 lots in his auction the following day and each had been carefully arranged in an adjacent room, with his rostrum strategically positioned in front of the stage facing about two hundred seats organised into neat rows. He wondered if that were going to be enough.

Viewing that afternoon had been brisk, busier than usual in fact and many dozen commission bids had been left with his receptionists and porters. Telephone enquiries from overseas had reached record proportions and Stuart MacIntyre was expecting a considerable volume of business to be conducted over the phone during the auction. It was going be a demanding exercise for his staff, keeping control, especially the proxy bidding. Those responsible for processing the paperwork would need to be diligent to ensure none were misplaced or overlooked. As principal auctioneer, he would have responsibility for conducting a smooth run auction, with everyone's interests catered for; bidders and sellers alike. Despite his intention to delegate some of his duties, it was nevertheless going to be a busy day tomorrow. Treddington Town Hall had been their preferred venue for several years and its familiarity was now his only reassuring thought as the sale approached.

The pre-auction viewing was planned to start at 9am prompt in the morning, so his final chase round the 'Lots' was vital that evening. There would simply be insufficient time to do it properly if left to the following day. He would be getting home late that evening but it was important he made sure all the items in his sale were correctly displayed and organised. The neat arrangements would quickly be disturbed nevertheless, just as soon as the first customer burst through the entrance doors. For now, at least, he could have them all looking good. It always amused him, that period five minutes before any viewing commenced, when a small group of over eager 'punters' would impatiently huddle together pressing their noses against the glazed doors, each trying to sneak a quick look ahead of the rest. He often wondered what advantage they thought they were gaining.

The next day's auction was entirely assigned to the sale of golfing memorabilia and was going to be the second of three sporting auctions the company MacIntyre McBride had scheduled for that year. An ever increasing interest in all things sporting had led to specialist sporting auctions becoming much more commonplace, with golf enthusiasts in particular demanding more and more frequent sales. So as the interest had risen and their popularity increased, a sound business opportunity had emerged, one that MacIntyre McBride had responded to quickly. They now possessed a reputation that many latecomers undoubtedly envied.

But an auction dedicated entirely to golf was still an unusual concept and remained un-chartered territory to some degree, Stuart MacIntyre was a little apprehensive. It was a departure from the more traditional format of bringing several sports together for a single auction such as football, cricket, tennis, in addition to golf. This combination was commonly borne out of necessity, with insufficient items, from any one individual sport, warranting a dedicated sale of their own. In fact tomorrow's sale had originally been promoted as a combined auction. But an eleventh hour proposal had promptly altered all that. Some hasty re-scheduling and the announcement of an alternative collective sale within the month had served to pacify most objections.

The opportunity had been presented to them as one of those *take it or leave it* propositions, only very recently. With Stuart MacIntyre barricaded, as usual, in his office behind a mountain of paperwork, he had been unexpectedly and hurriedly summoned to the front desk. One of his junior associates, Peter Harrison had been engaging in conversation with an unkempt gentleman, but had sought the assistance of the senior partner when placed on the spot and pressed to make a quick decision. It turned out the gentleman had purchased a significant and desirable collection of antique golf clubs recently, nearly four hundred in fact from a deceased estate, all needing to be sold quickly to release the equity they represented. Peter Harrison, quite rightly, had been willing to oblige on behalf of MacIntyre McBride, but his comment about *'having to wait several months before a suitable sale presented itself'* had gone down badly with the eager gentleman. Not wishing to squander a perfect opportunity to generate some serious revenue for the company, plus a chance to enhance their reputation into the bargain, the young man had thought on his feet. The gentleman's attempt to depart had been impeded with a well timed offer of a small whisky, which had given Peter Harrison the chance to call for Stuart MacIntyre's attendance who, in turn, had the gentleman's signature securely placed on the company's sales contract in no time at all. But it had been bought with the assurance that his goods would be sold at the hastily arranged auction and his funds would be released within seven days thereafter.

But with that assurance had come some difficulties, of course. Catalogues being withdrawn for a later date and new ones generated in double quick time were not the least of the troubles. Clients were informed, buyers and sellers alike, most of whom had no difficulty with the enforced change. The few who challenged the decision were politely reminded of the company's terms and conditions which granted the right to substitute the content of sales without notice. Stuart MacIntyre suspected he may have lost one or two customers in the process, but the longer term benefits from staging the country's most significant golfing auction to date, clearly had an overriding attraction for him. And the auction was happening tomorrow, having required a concerted effort of quite impressive proportions.

He paused in the doorway for one final look before handing over responsibility to the security guard for the evening. From the feedback he was receiving, the sale had generated some genuine excitement within the collecting and dealership fraternity. The catalogues had been issued and the website updated, yet despite the late notice, the pedigree of the 'Lots' had stimulated some serious international interest. A specialist himself in golfing memorabilia, he had been particularly impressed with the quality of the private collection he was about to sell. It was a unique collection which would inevitably attract some heavyweight bidding. He was content his decision to switch had been a shrewd one, having received many calls of support from an eclectic mix of professional dealers, most of whom he knew personally. This group alone were going to snap up the lion's share, he predicted. Serious dealers not shy at spending thousands of pounds at a time. He occasionally felt sympathetic for the small time collector who invariably went home with slim pickings, having to settle for run of the mill auction fillers that had little or no interest to the full-time dealers. This time however, he was sure there would plenty to go round, with something perhaps for everyone.

Stuart MacIntyre issued the security guard his final instructions before heading home for a few hours of much needed rest ahead of the main event. The guard dimmed the lights and settled down to listen to the radio. In the adjacent darkened room, some faint moonlight diffused through a window, illuminating one table in particular. And there in the centre, surrounded by other clubs much less prestigious, lay a lone Tom Morris putter, waiting unobtrusively to be auctioned and sold to the highest bidder the following day.

Chapter 3

Robert Erskine, somewhat careless at times, had actually remembered to buy the local daily newspaper as instructed, but had then gone on to blot his copy book by leaving it behind at the bank. It had been an easy mistake, he had explained, having been distracted by a familiar face whilst finalising a transaction. He had nevertheless vowed to make amends, reassuring his wife he would pop out especially that afternoon, and pick up a further copy. But first, the horses needed feeding and the stables cleaned out.

On the outside of the entrance door at Treddington Town Hall, a fine array of noses were pressed firmly against the glass, each eager to sniff out the bargains. Amongst them was one belonging to someone calling himself *'diggidys'*, a name chosen for his internet trading in golf memorabilia and one that had become familiar to many aspiring collectors across Europe. To everyone else, he was known as Tom Hudson, small time dreamer. Why *'diggidys'* he had been frequently asked, a question which invariably generated a boring tale of failed business ventures, each bearing the same name. Even so, he was convinced the trade name would someday be associated with success. Hitting on the right idea, so far, was all that had held him back. Five unsuccessful attempts had, nevertheless, failed to dampen his belief in the title.

The doors swung open, with those first through offered a warm welcome by a smiling Stuart MacIntyre.

The surge forward was disorderly and a few broke off to start a small queue in front of the receptionist. Catalogues were on sale, neatly arranged ready for purchase. But most that entered in those first few seconds were pushing and shoving their way forward to gain some sort of advantage, or so they perceived. Tom had bought his copy the day before, so opening his catalogue and retrieving a pencil from behind his ear, he cast an expectant glance around the saleroom. Quite a large room with so much on offer this time he thought to himself as he began to wonder if he had given himself enough time to view them all properly before the auction commenced. Nonetheless, he was impressed with the sheer scale of the event and grew excited at the prospect of spending a frantic hour or two browsing through the exhibits. He was once again on the brink of losing himself momentarily in that abstract world where he was no longer office worker but the entrepreneur he aspired to be.

A small group had already assembled in the far corner, presumably a select few whom had been granted special privileges to view ahead of the general throng. They appeared to be gathering with a purpose which did not go unnoticed by Tom. He foresaw an inevitable rendezvous with these gentlemen, very shortly.

With limited time though, he would need to be ultra selective and avoid spending too long looking at the 'grouped lots'. After all, they were not what he sought this time, a preference now for the higher end value rather than the bulk purchases. Having circled about twenty or so items in his catalogue, he stepped forward for a closer look, deciding to elaborately circumvent the clubs he was most interested in, just to see if there were others close by showing a similar interest. There was a game of cat and mouse to be played out here, he decided, with larger wallets than his to contend with. So a bit of deception might pay dividends, he thought, although not entirely convinced it was likely to make any difference whatsoever. But he might strike lucky, he naively believed, his ploy achieving that elusive 'maiden bid' success everyone so eagerly sought. Little chance of that he quickly realised, witnessing the never-ending procession of hopefuls pouring through the entrance doors.

Anne Hudson had issued her instructions that morning, in ever-so simple and understandable terms, she had believed. Knowing her husband had some self-control difficulty when it came to auctions, and troubled at the thought of him going there alone, she had felt the need to be explicit. His previous antics had resulted in a sizeable overdraft, made even worse by an attempt to disguise his misdemeanour. Granted he had gone on to realise a profit when his alleged extravagancies were eventually sold, but it did mean they were forced to borrow from her mother for a couple of weeks to pay for the essentials. She had been decidedly unimpressed with her husband on that occasion, so Tom now found himself issued with his final warning.

Heading out that morning, he had reassured her that his earlier profits would easily cover his planned spend and any need to dip into their savings would be completely unnecessary. She had no problem with that, providing he kept to his word. But there was a reckless streak in her husband which sometimes went unchecked. She was not going to be there to check his enthusiasm and that bothered her, especially knowing their holiday savings would be offering an irresistible temptation.

But that had been earlier and was now essentially forgotten. Squeezing now past a rather portly gentleman who was meticulously examining an aluminium headed putter, Tom made a mental note to come back and take a closer look later. But for now he was making a hasty beeline towards a far table where most of the clubs that interested him might be waiting. Already a threesome had gathered ahead, familiar faces he recognised, often seen at auctions like these. Despite their familiarity he was definitely not yet on speaking terms with these fellows and they made that perfectly obvious as he approached. Their noses were already starting to lift. He knew he was about to muscle in on the 'old boy's club' he had spied as he had entered, with membership reserved exclusively for those dealers who felt it essential to publicly display their importance. They were part of a select group who regarded themselves as the main players, with only they seemingly entitled to lick the cream. The rest could make do with the less flavoursome offerings. Being on first name terms with each and every auctioneer throughout the land was a prerequisite for joining their club, along with a little black book of international clients at the ready, to be waved aloft at every opportunity. With only the occasional sale on the internet to boast, Tom understood it left him lacking in all the necessary credentials.

Tracking his approach, each peering over the top of their reading glasses, all three checked him out to establish whether he was membership material. In less than two seconds, he had been unanimously dismissed as an irrelevance and all eyes had returned to their catalogues. Their collective response had been deliberate and well practiced, expertly executed to leave him feeling both uncomfortable and intimidated at the same time. It was a clear message that his positioning alongside was both unwelcome and inappropriate. Tom's sense of exclusion was heightened further when one of the three, the shortest, moved over to his other side affording the grouping an opportunity to talk straight through him.

'Where are you stopping tonight, Frazer?' the tallest enquired over the top of Tom's head.

'You know me, The Belfry of course, where else?' the man called Frazer cockily replied, 'What about you, Gordon?'

'Not stopping over. We need to be in Scotland tomorrow,' the man called Gordon announced loudly. Then placing an arm round the third member of the group added, 'Richard and I are meeting up with a couple of clients from abroad. We're playing golf at Gleneagles. Our treat naturally.'

Taking his cue to demonstrate collective solidarity and emphasise their disapproval at the newcomer's intrusion, the man called Frazer asked a question, 'Got your eye on anything in particular, Richard?'

Unable to stomach any more of their diatribe, Tom exerted himself.

'Excuse me,' he interrupted, and after pushing his arms out to avoid being totally hemmed in, Tom leant forward and picked up a wooden headed driver. All three checked out his selection, unaware it had been chosen because of its proximity rather than its interest. Tom created even more space for himself by twirling it aloft causing both 'Frazer' and 'Richard' to shy away from its flight path.

'So sorry,' Tom insincerely apologised, before replacing the club on the table and referring back to his catalogue. He read the description corresponding to the number on the club.

'Lot 192. A Robert Forgan transitional scare neck beech wood driver with sole insert, rear lead weight and hide grip with maker stamp to shaft. Illustrated £250-300.'

He pretended to mark his catalogue, making sure also his apparent interest had been duly noted by his three bystanders. He had no intention of buying this particular club of course, even though he felt a modest profit could be squeezed from it. It was more important he allocated his precious time to sourcing the exclusive items, those which would assist him best with his ambitions to trade in premiere stock.

To his amazement he watched as the man called Richard brazenly picked up the same club and began giving it a critical examination of his own over the top of his glasses. It was quickly rejected as inconsequential and tossed back onto the table. An obvious shake of his head and a patronising comment created some amusement amongst the three men as they closed ranks once more. Tom Hudson had just been taught his first lesson in auction gamesmanship. Yet despite this, Tom placed a small wager with himself that the man called Richard would, nonetheless, be bidding for that particular club later on that day despite the obvious distain that had been so blatantly displayed.

MacIntyre McBride were particularly good at

cataloguing their sporting sales Tom had decided and having attended several in the recent past, the format was now reassuringly consistent and familiar. The first sale items generally comprised many run of the mill items such as, mass produced hickory golf irons from the 1920's and 1930's grouped together in bundles to appeal to the casual collector or small time trader. Most were in average condition offering the enthusiasts small restoration projects to get excited over. Following on would be the individual clubs, those interesting enough to be offered separately. These were mainly the late 19th and early 20th century examples, those which were much scarcer to find. The third category would undoubtedly be the connoisseur clubs; the £1000 plus clubs that the man called Gordon and his fellow colleagues would be contesting later that day. These, in particular, were also the clubs Tom was most interested in tracking down at that precise moment.

He detached himself from the pack and set about flushing out the dozen or so 'lots' he had earlier earmarked. As insurance against later disappointment and the prospect of leaving empty handed, he would also bid on some of the earlier lots; the 'common' clubs for the masses, providing, of course, the prices were right. Having allowed, though, insufficient time to examine their condition thoroughly, he quickly picked out several that showed a profit potential, and wrote down his nominal top limits in the left hand margin of his catalogue. If any were struggling below the lower estimate, he would move in and snap them up at the time. However, with the clock ticking relentlessly towards kick-off time, he forced himself now to focus on his primary objectives.

Tom had a shopping list in mind and at the top were clubs by the established and recognisable club-makers. His new found customers across Europe were not altogether sophisticated and knowledgeable buyers in the main, not yet at least. No doubt that would change in time, but for now they demonstrated a preference for familiar names with familiar credentials. In a way, this made it much simpler for Tom, with no need to seek out the more obscure. A good mark up could be assured if he struck lucky. It was all beginning to sound too straight forward and he wondered why he had not recognised this much sooner. Perhaps the man called Gordon and his associates had good reason, therefore, to be overly protective of their well established and blatantly exclusive cartel.

Tom's attention, along with all others in the saleroom, was momentarily captivated. A voice was booming out across the room, but the words were indistinct. The exact pronunciation was masked by a pronounced Scottish accent an one, no doubt, few in the room had ever encountered before. Precisely what was actually being shouted was unclear but the message delivered was something along the lines of; *'Here I am ... Look at me ... Everyone look at me ... I'm here ...Look at me now ...'*

And by design, of course, everyone's attention switched immediately to the new entrant. He was a mature man with white hair, who strode arrogantly across the hall, soaking up the attention he was now purposefully creating for himself. In unison, the men called Richard, Gordon and Frazer flocked immediately forward to greet him, throwing themselves deliberately into the limelight, seeking status and glorification through association. Stuart MacIntyre, who had been otherwise engaged in conversation, recognised the voice immediately and was spotted looking up and waving across his greeting.

The elderly white haired gentleman, unabashed, continued with his excessive proclamation, loud enough to ensure each and every person in the room heard his voice.

'Where's *Lot 195?*' he was believed to say, 'I'm looking for *Lot 195.*'

His words caused a flurry of page turning as dozens of catalogues, around the room, were simultaneously consulted to find out exactly what *'Lot 195'* might actually be.

Tom Hudson, taking an instant dislike to the egotistical gentleman, refused to take the bait. Instead, he glanced around the saleroom and realised he was practically the only person who had not complied with the man's indirect instructions. He had to admit though, to being slightly impressed by the audacity of the man. Either this gentleman was a complete fool to bring his particular interest to everyone's attention, or he was the consummate professional, scaring off the opposition at this early stage. A touch of reverse psychology perhaps? Tom wondered if that was the case. Maybe he had just witnessed his second lesson in auction gamesmanship.

A small group now gathered around the white haired gentleman, listening intently to some tale he was telling. The man had successfully placed himself centre stage, a tactic designed, no doubt, to ward off any frivolous competition. An act of intimidation it would seem. He was also conducting a chorus of laughter that had heartedly broken out, much to the irritation of the many non-participants. They were joined, soon afterwards, by Stuart MacIntyre himself who wasted no time in starting a round of mutual back slapping before adding his own particular quota of laughter to the ever growing volume. The 'old boy's' network was, seemingly, fully assembled and already starting to dictate proceedings, even at this early stage. Tom, somewhat resentful perhaps, deliberately ignored the ensemble and switched his attention back to the job in hand.

'*Lot 195?*' he pondered, 'Sounds very familiar.'

After a quick check to make sure no one would catch him, he sneaked a quick look at his catalogue.

'Damn it,' he muttered to himself, realising it was one of his preferred items;

> *Lot 195. A fine Tom Morris long-nosed stained beech headed wooden putter, overall length 37.5", fitted with original hickory shaft and full length hide grip with original under-listing. Makers stamp to the head and shaft. A single worm hole to the head. c.1875. Illustrated. £1500-1750.*

Several of his European customers had requested a '*Tom Morris*' club. A club-maker of international renown and a vital addition to any self respecting collection, Tom was therefore keen to bag this particular club, despite the high estimate placed upon it. The price might be a problem and he was reluctant in many ways to commit such an amount for a single club. It would be the biggest gamble he had even taken thus far, but a calculated one he reminded himself. The feedback from his customers suggested high selling prices were not, generally, a discouragement, particularly as so few clubs of this stature ever became available on the Continent. And this was the only genuine

Tom Morris club in the auction, so he had no choice but to enter into its inevitable chase.

The white haired gentleman's obvious interest however, made him nervous. Just his luck, he thought, to be pitched up against someone who appeared to be king-pin, judging by the man's obvious popularity. Nevertheless, this was his opportunity to gain promotion into a higher league, so he was determined to come away with the club regardless. If his wife, Anne, had been present at that moment, she would have immediately spotted the tell tale warning signs.

The white haired gentleman, name still unknown, appeared to have quickly grown tiresome of his fair weather companions. After detaching himself from the ensemble, leaving them standing awkwardly in the centre of the room, he now came face to face with Tom as the pair arrived simultaneously at the table where *'Lot 195'* had been laid down for viewing. A confrontation, of some sort, looked inevitable as the older man moved swiftly to pick the *Morris* up first. The man appeared surprised to see someone in its vicinity, showing an apparent interest in 'his club'. His announcement, after all, had been quite explicit, he presumably had thought.

His hand hovered over the club, more in defiance than hesitation, and making no obvious attempt to lift the club, appeared to be challenging the younger man to make the first move. Tom, well known for being a little belligerent at times, was sorely tempted to shoot his hand underneath the older gentleman's and snatch the club out of pure impudence, but decided, finally, to give the older man his place.

'Please … after you,' Tom offered politely.

'That's very kind of you, sonny,' came back the patronising reply, as the older man slowly lifted the *Morris*.

Tom Hudson was enraged by the remark but elected to display no emotion. Instead, he simply stretched across the older man, without first excusing himself, and seized the next available club. The older and younger men stood shoulder to shoulder, quietly inspecting their respective clubs, whilst at the same time, sneaking quick glances at each others. Tom was holding 'Lot 194'. Consulting his catalogue once more, he read;

> *Lot 194. A reproduction Tom Morris long-nosed stained beech headed wooden putter fitted with a green heart shaft bearing oval makers stamp with full length hide grip and under-listing, overall length 35.5". £150-250*

Being no particular expert himself, Tom wondered how MacIntyre McBride had come to the conclusion it was a replica club, and not the real thing. As far as he could make out, there seemed practically little difference between the club he was now holding and the one clutched by the man to his left.

'Wouldn't fool anyone that!' said white haired man derisively, pointing at the same time to the club in Tom's hand, a comment which Tom took to be both unwelcome and unnecessarily antagonistic.

'You're right, most people aren't fools,' he replied without looking at the man, '… but there's always a few exceptions around,' he quickly added, this time turning to look squarely into the older man's eyes.

The white haired man pondered over this remark for a moment or two, not quite sure if he had just been insulted. Letting it pass, he chose instead to monopolise the auctioneer's time by way of public demonstration.

'Stuart!' he shouted loudly over the top of everyone's head.

'Just coming, *Gus* … With you in a second,' Stuart MacIntyre responded instantly, and equally loudly, from across the room.

Tom replaced the reproduction club on the table and eased himself from the vicinity, granting the auctioneer space to manoeuvre alongside someone clearly regarded as a preferential. The pair engaged themselves in some light hearted banter before the man called Gus hoisted the club aloft and pretended to seek some advice. It was all a bit of charade, of course, as 'Gus' clearly knew all that he needed without asking.

A few minutes later, the putter was lying back down on the table with the man called Gus having departed. Tom was now free to inspect the Morris club uninterrupted and he marvelled at its workmanship and the provenance it possessed. How many players had used it over the years, he wondered? Had any of them been famous perhaps? Tom was determined to buy this club simply because he viewed it now as a calling card, enabling him to demonstrate he could both acquire and supply scarce clubs on demand.

Quite excited, he could no longer wait for the auction to begin and with just half an hour to go, he set about making sure he was prepared to start bidding. Heading off towards the reception desk to register his details, he noticed the man called Gus was casting him a sideways and challenging look from across the room.

In a stable less than twenty miles away, Robert Erskine had completed the mucking out. Their two horses had been fed and watered, the old straw swept outside, the new straw laid down and the stable doors securely bolted. His tasks for the afternoon were all now complete, which warranted a small gin and tonic by way of reward, to be taken in the summerhouse immediately, of course.

After a quick change of attire from his working clothes into something more casual, he wandered into the study to pour his drink. Elizabeth Erskine was reading a glossy magazine and seeing her husband approach, casually asked if he was *now* ready to go back into town and collect the newspaper, as earlier promised. Playing down his earlier forgetfulness, he playfully suggested the newspaper could be delivered instead, and he offered to call the shop, there and then, to arrange it. His wife was less than impressed with Robert's attempted avoidance, instead presenting him with a short list of things to buy whilst he was out. Electing, quite sensibly, to postpone his liquid gratification, he set about making amends straight away, kissing his wife on the cheek and departing for town for the second time that day.

'I'll be back for five,' he called out informatively before closing the front door behind him.

'Good afternoon, ladies and gentlemen. May I welcome you all to MacIntyre McBride for our Golfing Memorabilia auction,' Stuart MacIntyre announced from high up on his rostrum.

The room was already full, but others were still filing patiently through the door. The chattering continued despite the auctioneers opening remark, so he adjusted his microphone to make sure it was positioned properly, increasing the volume in the process. He continued with the preliminaries.

'We have a full catalogue to get through today, ladies and gentlemen, so I'll keep the introductions brief. I expect we'll finish the bidding around 4pm this afternoon. Our porters will be on hand to assist you to collect your purchases. Please take them away with you by 6pm at the latest, thank you ...'

The auctioneer was still being ignored in the main as people jockeyed for position, concentrating more, it seemed, on introducing one another and squeezing into available gaps around the perimeter. Unperturbed, he pressed on.

'... And I shall be in the front office until seven this evening ... so that I can take your money from you all!' That bit at least was heard and a ripple of laughter shot round the auction room. 'And that includes you as well, Gilbert!' he added, pointing to someone over to his left. More laughter followed. The room had settled down by now, so he set the wheels into motion.

'Here we go then, the first lot ... lot number *one* ... a set of six Maxwell irons to include an Anderson of Anstruther. Nice lot this one. Who'll start me?' he enquired. 'Forty? ... thirty? ... twenty pounds surely,' he pleaded seeing no hands rise, 'I see you're all going to make me work hard today.' Finally a hand was raised.

'Twenty I have … thank you,' he announced as other bids started to follow on.

'Twenty five …was that a bid, sir? … Thank you thirty … and five … and forty thank you.' The auctioneer continued taking bids, his hand moving from side to side. The bidding, on this first item, picked up pace before ending abruptly.

'… All out then at sixty five pounds?' he asked the room, 'I'm selling,' he warned before dropping the hammer. '… Sold for sixty five pounds to one, one, six, five,' he declared out loud noting the buyer's bidding number being held up high.

Bidding was brisk and the auctioneer was flying through his lots. No delays were expected during in this auction, MacIntyre McBride being far too professional to allow that to happen. Unlike other auctions, the porters were not expected to track down items, to hold them aloft prior to bidding. All the items, in the sale, were securely assembled in the viewing part of the room, cordoned off with no access during the auction. Bidders were expected to take advantage of the viewing opportunities afforded ahead of commencement. And once the auction had started, the catalogue became the only source of reference from that point. Inexperienced bidders often found the auction pace a difficulty, with there being practically little or no thinking time between 'lots'. Bidders had to be on their toes, otherwise items might pass them by. The regulars were good at this, of course, and rarely lifted their heads, simply raising a hand or bidders card at the right moment, making brief notes and ticking through their shopping lists. Stuart MacIntyre knew there was no benefit in trying to tempt the experienced dealers to extend beyond their pre-determined limits, so little time was generally wasted in doing so. If the bidder was recognised, and the bidding had paused, the hammer was usually dropped without further delay, allowing the auctioneer to move swiftly onto the next item. It was quite a performance to witness, the regulars clearly holding the advantage over the casual or less experienced bidders.

Tom Hudson remained fascinated by the whole process. He could not be sure, but he often suspected that regular auction-goers benefited from being recognised. There had been a couple of occasions, in the past and at other auction houses, when he thought the hammer may have been brought down a little too sharply. But it was usually too quick to really notice what had often happened or to spot who had actually benefited, if indeed anyone at all.

There must have been a couple of hundred people in the room that day, he estimated, mostly buyers but no doubt a few sellers, there to watch their money roll in. He recognised one gentleman in particular, one with whom he had traded several months earlier. It was unusual for internet buyers and sellers to actually meet up and exchange cash and goods, but this old gentleman lived close to where Tom worked and seemed 'safe enough' to meet. It also saved the old gentleman a few pounds in postage. George, as he was known, became a regular customer afterwards and the arrangement suited them both. They had seen each other from opposite sides of the hall and made their respective journeys to a couple of unusually vacant seats in the middle.

Whispering polite *hellos*, he discovered George was selling and not buying; a couple of boxes of golf balls in fact, dating from the 1940's. Tom wished him success and tried to return his concentration to the auction as some of his lots were soon coming up. But George had carried on talking regardless.

Tom missed completely the sale of 'Lot 56', a JH Taylor autograph cleek estimated at fifty to eighty pounds, only managing to turn his head as the hammer came down on a price of forty, well under the estimate. He had let slip an opportunity to buy cheaply and silently cursed his friend George who, oblivious to the auction itself, had now moved on to enquire if Tom had been 'busy' recently.

'George, please?' Tom pleaded politely, lifting his head at the same time to catch the action, 'I've a couple of lots coming up in a minute or two ...'

'Sorry Tom, I'm only here to watch,' George apologised, 'You carry on and we'll chat later,' he generously offered. A follow-up question quickly came, however, 'Which ones?'

Pretending not to have heard, Tom concentrated on the action taking place in the room. He had bought nothing so far and noticing many items were selling below estimate, he decided it was time perhaps to start picking up some deals. Over the next sixty or seventy 'lots', he managed to secure five items sold well below estimate, all mixed groups of clubs which would keep him stockpiled for a while. Most would be in poor condition he suspected, but he enjoyed restoration just as much as the selling. Occasionally, these restorations revealed some surprises, pedigree clubs hidden beneath layers of rust which, when removed and the club polished for sale, often brought an exceptionally high price. The chance of a special discovery was the one thing that intrigued him and fuelled his prospecting.

His haul so far included twenty four irons, eight woods and a group of six brass headed putters; all completely oxidised and lacking grips of any description. He was feeling pleased with himself, each and every one likely to realise a profit after a bit of cleaning. It was a good omen for things to come Tom decided, and after adding a couple of old canvas bags to the list, he was now set up to see himself profitably through a few more weeks of casual trading.

The auction was temporarily interrupted whilst some confusion required clearing up. Someone had lost track of the lot numbers, placed bids and secured an item they were not intending. Realising a mistake had been made, they had then called out, declaring an error which, in turn, had sparked a short debate between auctioneer and assistant. A decision was taken to carry on, unfortunate for the gentleman concerned perhaps, but nevertheless a lesson for others. A bidder must take responsibility for his or her actions, a responsibility that was re-iterated by the auctioneer for the benefit of all. George seized his chance to strike up the conversation once again and chipped in with some words of encouragement.

'You're doing all right, Tom,' he said, 'And did you see that silly bugger?' he asked flicking his head in the direction of the troubled bidder. 'Are you here for the collection?' he added without pausing for either breath or reply to his first question.

'Collection?'

'Aye, someone's selling their entire collection. You must have heard about it. It was in the papers. Best collection of clubs you'll ever see. Why do you think there's so many people here today?' George asked, 'Bet you there'll be loads of phone bids as well. Think they started around lot one hundred and fifty.'

Stuart MacIntyre brought proceedings back to order, quelling the discussions that had broken out all around.

'Thank you please, I'd like to get on if you don't mind?' he asked. 'Lot 173 is an Auchterlonie scare neck driver in original condition ... quite unusual this ... looks as if it's never been used ... I have a bit of interest in this one ... and conflicting bids so must start at ...ninety pounds.' A hand rose immediately.

'Ninety five, ... thank you Peter.'

The bidding continued at some pace with the sale gaining momentum. *Lot 195*, the Tom Morris putter was coming up in a few minutes Tom had noted, so time to straighten his posture and present himself so as to be easily seen. He felt his heart racing and the tension building up inside. The man called Gus was no where to be seen. Looking all around he finally spied the man commencing a measured approach from the rear, slowly and deliberately passing lines of onlookers to position himself front left.

The positioning had been well chosen it seemed, not only affording sight of the auctioneer but in full view, also, of everyone else in the hall. The man was an egotist for sure, Tom thought. He heard the hammer come down on Lot 192; the Forgan transitional driver examined and flagrantly dismissed earlier by the 'old boys'. And sure enough, the man called Richard was raising his bidder's number aloft, ensuring it was clearly seen by all.

'*I just knew it,*' Tom thought to himself.

'Lot 193,' the auctioneer called out and Tom Hudson's concentration was absolute by this time. Stuart MacIntyre was seen to consult his notes.

'I have three hundred … and I see three twenty standing at the back … and fifty.' There came then a short pause. 'Another bid, sir … No? … A new bidder then at three eighty.' The auctioneers hand was sweeping from side to side.

'Four hundred anyone?' he asked, 'Disappointing this, I would have expected it to fetch more.' The auctioneer was attempting to tease out further bids. George lent over and cut in.

'Been on holiday yet, Tom?' he asked with inappropriate timing. Torn momentarily between his natural politeness and telling George to simply shut up, Tom eventually did neither, choosing instead to keep it brief.

'No,' he offered minimally, hoping that would settle it. The auctioneer had been successful in the meantime.

'Four hundred we have, thank you Sir!'

'We went to Margate again,' George carried on regardless. Tom's concentration was now irrevocably broken despite trying to block George's conversation. The hammer fell on an item and he started to become distracted and disorientated. 'Stayed where we went last year,' George added.

'Good!' came forth Tom's curt reply with little or no conviction to the conversation. He was trying desperately to regain his bearings, but Stuart MacIntyre was accelerating away from him.

'Two fifty I have.'

'Lovely place Margate but the weather was pretty poor though,' continued George unabashed.

'Three twenty,' the auctioneer was heard to declare.

'Really?' Tom responded unconsciously. Had the hammer just dropped, he asked himself? He simply could not be sure at all.

George continued relentlessly, '... Wanted to go and see my sister in Bournemouth ... but she was going into hospital.'

'Who's going to start me?' asked the auctioneer. Tom had completely lost his place by this time, unsure what was now being offered up for sale. He looked around for clues and saw the man called Gus raise an arm.

'She's not been feeling too good ... it's her legs you see.'

Tom missed a bid and watched on as the man called Gus raised his arm for a second time, uncertain what was being sold or what price had been reached. Could it be his 'lot' he wondered. Panic set in quickly.

'So we decided we'd go to Margate once again.' George was nothing if not persistent.

The hammer was hovering over the rostrum, being readied to fall. Stuart MacIntyre called out for the last time.

'Any more bids? ... I'm selling!'

Without hesitation, and without knowing what price he was bidding, Tom shot a straight arm high into the air. If the man called Gus was bidding, then it just had to be the *Morris putter.* The risk was certainly worth taking.

'New bidder in the centre … and two twenty I have …
any more bids?' The room fell silent, the man called Gus
shook his head and the hammer dropped. Tom was utterly
confused.

'One, zero, eight, three isn't it sir?' the auctioneer was
heard to call out. Tom realised he was being addressed.

'Sir … one, zero, eight, three isn't it?' the auctioneer
asked for a second time. 'Your bidders number sir!'

Ignorantly nodding his agreement, Tom began to
wonder exactly what he had just bought. It was obviously
not the Morris, he decided … not at that price anyway.

'Now we come to *Lot 195*,' Stuart MacIntyre
broadcasted, 'the Tom Morris putter … an excellent club
this … a lot of interest in this I have to say … and I have
bids on the books so can start at nine fifty,' the auctioneer
called out from his rostrum, 'Who's got the thousand?'

Tom was now certain he had just bought something
other than the Morris putter, but exactly what, he was still
unsure. He kicked himself for not having given the auction
more attention.

'Thank you, Gus … a thousand I have,' Stuart
MacIntyre was heard to announce.

Suddenly regaining his bearings, Tom knew he was
now onto the main event. After a swift glance at his
catalogue he realised he must have just bought that replica
putter he had been holding a little earlier. But there was no
time to dwell on that as the bidding moved swiftly on. The
auctioneer was inviting further offers.

'Twelve fifty?' the auctioneer was heard to enquire.
The white haired man called Gus was in the thick of the

action and nodded casually at Stuart MacIntyre.

'Thank you again, Gus. It's with the floor at twelve fifty. Telephone bids are out. Do I see thirteen hundred?'

Tom Hudson placed his first bid at one thousand three hundred pounds. The white haired man caught sight of this and nodded instinctively in the auctioneer's direction.

'And fifty we have … fourteen sir?' he beckoned from Tom, who responded with a nod of his own.

'Fourteen I have …and fifty perhaps?'

The bidding soon became a contest of wills, with Tom Hudson in the centre of the room and the man called Gus standing closer to the rostrum. It was a senseless duel with all reasoning flying straight out of the window. The bidding rose to eighteen hundred pounds, way above estimate.

'I'm looking for eighteen fifty … are you bidding Gus?' the auctioneer enquired casually before adding, 'Come on Gus … you know we've put it aside for you.'

Sniggering broke out all around and the man called Gus nodded once more, much to the delight of Stuart MacIntyre and the other 'old boys', now positioned alongside for a fresh dose of limelight.

'Eighteen fifty I have,' the auctioneer proudly announced as he eagerly accepted the latest bid with a smile and a wink. Worst of all, he was no longer looking across in Tom's direction. Instead was raising his hammer aloft.

It may have been a frivolous remark, and one meant not to be taken too seriously, but nevertheless it had stunned Tom. He knew he should simply let it go; after all, the price had now gone far too high. But in some unaccountable way it had just turned personal for Tom and no amount of rational thinking would prevent his recklessness from now taking charge. Recalling the patronising remarks of earlier, and forgetting completely his wife's explicit instructions, he fumed at the notion of a deal already struck. He was being dismissed and he was taking it badly.

'Two thousand pounds!' he heard himself shouting out, just in time to halt the hammer's descent. A few comments flew round the room as George patted Tom energetically on the back.

The auctioneer's mouth dropped open slightly and he looked over in the white haired man's direction. The man called Gus hesitated and looked across at Tom before despondently shaking his head. The auctioneer enquired optimistically.

'Any more bids, ladies and gentlemen?'

After what seemed an extraordinarily long pause, presumably designed to provide ample time for minds to change, the hammer finally came down, albeit rather limply.

Tom Hudson had just acquired himself an original Tom Morris long nosed putter and unbeknown to him, a club which, until very recently, had been very much an important part of the revered '*Pinkney Collection*'.

Chapter 4

Charles Pinkney was in his late thirties and lived alone at Kerrington Manor, a grandiose Georgian property with acre upon acre of beautiful parkland just outside Chipping Campden in north Gloucestershire, right in the heart of the Cotswolds. The death of his father a year earlier had meant that he, as eldest surviving sibling, had taken ownership of the manor. His younger sister had lived in Spain for many years running a successful estate agency and had, on the death of her father, made it plain she had no interest in returning to England to help run the estate. She was, however, very interested in receiving her share of the inheritance as soon as possible being very keen to progress with a certain property development project in Andalusia. Charles Pinkney, faced with crippling debt in the form of inheritance taxation and a need to find sufficient funds to 'buy out' his sister's interests, soon concluded he was broke as things stood at present. To maintain the status quo, however, and especially to pay the estate staff, he had needed to liquidise some capital urgently. He had become a desperate man and with only a modest income from his occupation in the City, his decision to sell the family chattels had been a regrettable yet necessary one, leaving him broken hearted and dispirited. The house would be an empty shell within a few weeks, but on the positive note, the recent sale appeared to have raised sufficient money to satisfy his immediate commitments. For now, at least, he would remain the 'lord of the manor'.

Despite his pre-occupation with managing his debts,

there was something else on Charles Pinkney's mind that afternoon, something which was beginning to cause him added alarm and uncertainty. Instead of visiting an old friend in nearby Stow in the Wold, to regrettably sell his beloved Land Rover, he was heading north towards Stratford upon Avon to attend a hastily arranged appointment with Maurice Bainbridge of Bainbridge & Bainbridge, solicitors. He had been surprised at the reaction to his call that morning; an innocent enquiry he felt, but one that resulted in an immediate alteration of both men's schedules that day. Maurice Bainbridge had been anticipating his call for some peculiar reason it seemed, or at least a call from someone with similar business in mind. It had been a further surprise for him to discover the solicitor had stressed an importance for a meeting to happen very soon, without undue delay. Despite it being Charles Pinkney who had called initially, strangely it had been Maurice Bainbridge who had some information to urgently impart.

Charles Pinkney had been perplexed after calling the solicitor. Why had his call been anticipated, he wondered? And why had the solicitor asked him to bring along the Pipeshank print and an odd sounding golf club? What, indeed, was this mysterious golf club which seemingly held some significance and connection with the discussions they were about to have? All very intriguing he had thought.

But he knew he would only be able to satisfy the solicitor's requests in part. The print would be an easy one to present; it just needed lifting from the wall in his library. But the golf club was a different proposition entirely. He was almost certain every golf club cluttering his house until recently, had been disposed of several weeks earlier.

Despite this, he would arrive without the club, interested primarily in what this curious solicitor had to announce.

He was en-route for his meeting now, intrigued yet anxious, having been left in no doubt about its importance. The solicitor had implied his property and belongings may be in jeopardy for some obscure reason and that concerned him greatly. Not that his possessions amounted to much at present, but the house was worth a few million. His mind was speculating. Surely not the house, he thought. How could that be? Surely the house has no connection to the Agreement referenced on the back of that print?

Whilst driving to his appointment, Charles Pinkney had made a few calls on his mobile phone, desperately trying to contact the dealer who had recently purchased his great grandfathers entire golf club collection. After a series of redirections, he obtained a number and an assurance it would connect him directly to the man he sought. But his attempts were frustrated with the number having been switched to divert. He left his voice message along with a request for an urgent call back, hoping it was not too late to recover one club, in particular, from the bunch; the one that apparently now held some special significance. Knowing dealers the way he did, its retrieval would cost him dearly. But if the solicitor was to be believed, then a modest uplift in price might be well worth contemplating.

Whilst waiting for yet another set of traffic signals to change to green, he wondered if Maurice Bainbridge was being a touch theatrical. What could the man possibly have to say to him that warranted such a drama?

For Maurice Bainbridge, this was becoming a most

peculiar state of affairs. A remarkable coincidence in fact. For the second time in just a couple of weeks, he was intending to sit with a very interested party in what was turning out to be a most extraordinary contractual agreement; an agreement formalised in the very same office over eighty years earlier. Since that date, there had been no mention of it, no reference at all, no enquiry made, nothing whatsoever in fact. No one at Bainbridge & Bainbridge had any recollection of it and had found the archive search both exhausting and laborious. Finally an entry had been discovered in a moth eaten register in the basement along with a recognisable reference number. Further searches, more focussed this time, unearthed some documents that were perhaps associated with the contract, a legal document with signatures entitled *'The Morris Men Agreement'*, a sealed envelope marked with the inscription, *'For Authentication'* displaying the same signatures, and a further piece of paper providing a description of some sort. The file was re-opened and the documents lodged within, the whole ensemble becoming live once again following an eight decade sabbatical.

Maurice Bainbridge had found time before the meeting to undertake a casual read of the documents. The larger, the one forming the body of the *'Agreement'* was a series of terms and conditions and referenced the other two documents that were found along with. He had managed to test its validity against contract law and was in little doubt the *'Agreement'* was both sound and enforceable, although he did wonder what madness had possessed both parties to create it in the first place. The second document appeared to be a description of a golf club and had no legal status it seemed, serving only to inform. The third document was sealed and unopened which, according to the *'Agreement'* must remain that way until specific terms had been satisfied.

Charles Pinkney was punctual and arrived at the Stratford office at precisely 3pm, despite the difficulties encountered in trying to get parked. He had brought with him the *Pipeshank* print and now waited in the reception for the solicitor's door to open. His heart was racing and his palms were damp with perspiration as a door swung ajar and the tall slim figure of Maurice Bainbridge emerged, arm outstretched and his hand offered in welcome. The two men shook hands and entered the office, the solicitor discretely wiping his palm on the side of his trousers. For Maurice Bainbridge this was his first opportunity to establish, with any certainty, that Charles Pinkney was indeed entitled to an explanation. After both men were comfortably seated, the solicitor asked his first question.

'Mr. Pinkney, have you brought with you the print to which you referred during your telephone call this morning?'

Charles Pinkney nodded and lifted the print onto the table and the solicitor gave it a quick examination, especially the reverse.

'Very good' said the solicitor, 'And you brought with you the golf club to which I referred?' he asked optimistically. Charles Pinkney looked a little sheepish and apologetic.

'I'm afraid I may no longer have such a thing, Mr. Bainbridge. It was probably in my possession up until just a few weeks ago but it seems I may have disposed of it rather too hastily. That being the case, then I'll try to repossess it as soon as possible.'

'Indeed unfortunate, Mr. Pinkney,' the solicitor said solemnly, 'and I would suggest you make every endeavour in that regard as its significance will become ever so apparent as I explain the situation in which you now find yourself embroiled.'

Charles Pinkney began to feel very uncomfortable on hearing those foreboding words.

'Would you mind if I took a closer look at the print?' the solicitor went on to ask.

Charles Pinkney, a little bemused and still thinking about the golf club, acknowledged the solicitor's request with a nod of his head. Maurice Bainbridge held it up in the light for a better view. It had a gilt frame, was quite large and reasonably heavy the solicitor noted, and showed several caricature golfers in various poses on the golf course, each attired in late 19th century clothing. There were three main scenes. An elegant gentleman was engaged in an over elaborate swing, watched by a group of onlookers. Another showed a couple of dogs diving towards a rabbit hole in chase of a lost ball and the third being an old man sat alone with buildings on the skyline, recognisable as St. Andrews, and a reference stating '*The GOM of Golf*', the meaning of which neither men seemingly understood. It was a nice print, but by no means anything of particular value. On that they were agreed. The solicitor, having examined the front, then reversed the print to look for something in particular on the back. And it was there, plain to see, a hand written inscription, faded yet still distinct.

'Where you aware of the words on the reverse of this print, Mr. Pinkney?' he casually enquired.

'I confess, not until yesterday,' he replied, 'It attracted unusual interest from a dealer which raised my suspicions, although I have to admit I discovered the text by accident.' He went on to explain. 'I called you immediately, as soon as I realised your firm had some association.'

'I'm pleased you didn't hesitate, Mr. Pinkney, because this is very significant indeed.' The solicitor pointed to the wording. 'I shall read it out if I may?'

'Please go ahead. Perhaps you can tell me what it means?'

'Very well, let me see.' Maurice Bainbridge fiddled with his reading glasses before reading out loud the inscription.

First day of August in the year of our King, Nineteen Hundred and Twenty One.

1 of 2 Retained by Randolph Erskine of Grange Manor, Gloucestershire.

2 of 2 Retained by Giles Pinkney of Kerrington Manor, Gloucestershire.

This being 2 of 2.

The Retainers to be known as 'The Morris Men'.

The 'Morris Men' will compete on the first Sunday of August, annually over the Royal Stratford Golf Course.

18 holes matchplay, threequarters handicap to be known as 'The Morris Challenge', playing for 'The Trophy' being a Tom Morris putter duly

'Authenticated'.

Referee being the incumbent Club Captain.

The winner of 'The Morris Challenge' to be known as 'The Victor'.

The loser of 'The Morris Challenge' to be known as 'The Challenger'.

Rematch to be called by 'The Challenger'.

'The Morris Challenge' to continue annually until such time as 'The Challenger' fails to call for the rematch or 'The Victor' is incapable of defence, hence passing over his title. 'The Victor' becomes thus 'The Claimant'.

'The Claimant' to present himself and 'The Trophy' to the Executors, Bainbridge & Bainbridge, Stratford upon Avon, for the liberation of the 'Morris Men Agreement'.

For the next fifteen minutes Charles Pinkney sat transfixed, listening with increasing horror as the precise nature of the *'Morris Men Agreement'* was read out and the implications explained. The solicitor was deliberate in his presentation and paused occasionally to invite questions. Charles Pinkney was practically stunned into silence throughout, but when the solicitor finally placed the document back down on his desk, Charles Pinkney gathered his thoughts and spoke.

'Thank you, Mr. Bainbridge, you've explained things very well and I think I understand the significance of what you have just told me. If you don't mind, can I try and summarise what you've just said to me?' He was trying to remain dignified and calm.

'By all means. Take all the time you need,' offered the solicitor.

Charles Pinkney altered his posture to one more upright, correcting his earlier slump into the chair. He took a sip from the glass of water in front of him and cleared his throat, trying to be quite composed about it all, but clearly having some difficulty in the process. After a short pause he spoke.

'If I've understood you correctly, Mr. Bainbridge, you are telling me that I may be contractually obliged to honour the terms of this *'Agreement'*,' he pointed to the document on the desk, 'even though I wasn't party to any of it in the first place.'

'Not *maybe,* Mr. Pinkney. I'm afraid you emphatically *are.*'

'*My God!*' he exclaimed before regaining his composure. 'Anyway … you're saying that the agreement you have just read out was made back in nineteen twenty *something* by a couple of old fools who had a score to settle … so they decided they would gamble everything they each owned in the form of a wager!' Charles Pinkney was beginning to lose his temper somewhat.

'Again correct.'

'And that it seems to be legally binding on their families even though these,' his voice began to rise, 'even though these *buffoons* are now dead and buried!' His anger could no longer be contained and he struck the desk with his fist.

'It is not a case of *seeming* to be legally binding, Mr.

Pinkney. In fact my examination would suggest it undoubtedly *is* legally binding. A most unfortunate state of affairs, I would agree, but nevertheless one which cannot be ignored now that it has unfortunately come to light.'

'So there is *nothing* I can do … is that what you are telling me? … I have to accept that this ridiculous agreement exists and I have to live with that fact for the rest of my life? … Is that what you're telling me, Mr. Bainbridge?' he demanded.

The solicitor collected his thoughts then spoke.

'I'm afraid not just the rest of your life. The terms are binding in perpetuity, it would seem, until such time as the …,' he referred once more to the larger document, 'Until … and I quote … *until 'The Agreement' is redeemed by 'The Claimant'* … Mr. Pinkney.'

'But surely this *'Claimant'* is now dead!' he suggested somewhat optimistically.

'Technically you are correct,' said the solicitor, 'but the *Agreement* has been drawn up in such a way as to permit a representative of *'The Claimant'* to act on his behalf. I presume this was included to make provision for infirmity or something of the kind.'

'A representative?' he asked, 'What does that mean?'

The solicitor straightened himself, adopted a sombre expression, the proceeded to offer his best advice.

'A representative, in the context of this contract, has not been specifically defined. Commonly a representative is simply someone who has been nominated to act on behalf of an individual who is party to a particular contract. There is often a provision in contract to allow for such a nomination, usually through endorsement of some sort. Whilst there is provision in this particular contract for a representative to act on a persons behalf, there appears to be no specific stipulation regarding nominations.'

Maurice Bainbridge paused briefly to catch his breath and to make sure Charles Pinkney was following what he was saying. Despite much frowning on Pinkney's brow, the solicitor continued with his summary.

'So it is my view that a representative can be *anyone* who merely represents the interests of *'The Claimant'*, which in your case is quite obvious. You are a blood relative and therefore represent an interest.'

Charles Pinkney allowed the words to digest. As he did so, his mood shifted from pessimistic to optimistic. After a short pause, time spent ordering his thoughts, he eventually asked his question.

'So if I understand you correctly, Mr. Bainbridge, I can be that representative you have just talked about … and that being the case … I could make the claim under the *'Agreement'*. Is that what you are saying, Mr. Bainbridge?'

'I see no reason why not, Mr. Pinkney. However you are overlooking several important points.' The solicitor shifted his posture.

'Firstly in order to fulfil the stated requirements you would, by necessity, be required to produce *'The Trophy'* to which the *'Agreement'* refers … a Tom Morris putter I believe. Secondly the putter would need to be authenticated and a further document we possess here …,' he raised the sealed envelope into the air, '… is designed to do just that. And thirdly, you would need to make that ahead of the other interested party.' Maurice Bainbridge left that last comment hanging, waiting on the reaction.

Charles Pinkney's expression quickly reverted back to one of default pessimism and his mood darkened in an instant. He had failed, before that moment, to properly acknowledge that others could equally present themselves as representatives. The comment triggered a thought process as he began to put two and two together.

'This other interested party … I take it you mean the *Erskine's.*' His phrasing had been more of a statement than a question.

'That is correct and I have to advise you that this is the second appointment I have undertaken concerning this matter in the last few weeks.' The solicitor's words were chilling.

'The second appointment! You mean the Erskine's are also aware of the *Agreement* … and all that it signifies?' he asked frantically.

'Precisely so, Mr. Pinkney. In fact I had this very same discussion with Mrs. Elizabeth Erskine, in this very office, not so very long ago. She demonstrated the same surprise, I might add.'

'Did she make the claim?' Charles Pinkney asked, even more frantically this time.

'She did not. Like you, she also had a copy of that same print with the very same inscription, although I recall it was numbered one of two.' The solicitor removed his reading glasses once more, 'Yes, Mr. Pinkney, she finds herself in precisely the same position you find yourself in, and I think I'm obliged to inform you, without any *'Trophy'* also, it would also seem.'

'Are you *absolutely* sure she doesn't have this *'Trophy'* ... the golf club I mean?'

'Oh yes. I've spoken to her subsequently and she is convinced she does not possess the club either,' he said, noticing Charles Pinkney was beginning to regain some of his colour, '... which suggests to me, although this is pure speculation on my part, that you or your family may have it, or perhaps should I say more precisely, once had it, Mr. Pinkney?'

Charles Pinkney thought about this for a while and was almost certain he did not have the club any longer. It was probably in the collection he sold to the now elusive dealer, and he could simply not comprehend his misfortune if that were the case. Nevertheless, he probably had a reasonable chance of getting it back if he acted quickly. It was even more critical he get in touch with that dealer now. It was a little disconcerting, however, that he had not been able to get through with his earlier attempt. The message had been left, but he would need to follow up with another as soon as he left the solicitor's office. He would certainly avoid haggling over the price now, with so much at stake. It would be folly to worry about the odd pound or two. He was also relieved to learn the Erskine's had not produced the club either which perhaps meant they too cannot make the claim at this time. But that situation might now be short-lived. Without doubt, they would be on its trail that very minute and if Elizabeth Erskine had had her meeting with the solicitor a few weeks earlier, it meant she was now well ahead of him in the chase.

'*Elizabeth*?' he wondered, the name beginning to ring bells in his mind. It was all beginning to make sense now, he thought.

But he was in utter turmoil at that moment with so many different scenarios seemingly possible. He knew he was in no position to make a claim and it was entirely probable the Erskine's could not do so either. Both families had, quite clearly, only recently learnt of the *'Agreement'* and would now be set on making a claim ahead the other. He knew the Esrkine's did not have the club, the solicitor had just told him, but do they know he is without it either, he wondered? Probably not he decided, in which case they will be equally concerned that they were about to lose everything over this too. It was all very confusing and he was in no frame of mind for calculating all the various permutations.

'Do you think you may have the club, or believe you might be able to re-acquire it?' the solicitor patiently enquired, attempting to infringe into Charles Pinkney's deliberations.

Charles Pinkney was lost in his thoughts and appeared to ignore the question. This could be a blessing in disguise he was thinking, an opportunity to clear his debts forever. The solicitor had just told him he had a chance to snatch the Erskine's entire estate from under their noses, legitimately as well. He doubted the wisdom of the contract his ancestor had created and he wondered what could have prompted it in the first place. But that was immaterial now. He was perhaps on the threshold of acquiring an entire estate, and all for the price of a golf club. He was starting to feel much more buoyant, relishing the prospect in fact.

Checking himself for the moment, conscious he had just been asked a question, Charles Pinkney switched his attention back to the solicitor.

'I'm not too sure. I'll need to take a good look around,'

he replied cautiously.

The solicitor, noting some reticence in the gentleman's response, concluded little more may be accomplished by continuing the meeting at length, so he attempted to close proceedings with a generalised summing up.

'I realise this is quite a shock for you, Mr. Pinkney, but I can assure you the situation is exactly the same for the other party. Despite the passage of time, the *'Agreement'* remains current, awaiting resolution. As I explained to the other party, the two original protagonists, for motivations known only to themselves, had entered into a contract to resolve an issue by contest. The stakes were clearly high, winner takes all in fact, with their respective estates offered up, to be wagered on the outcome of a golfing challenge. Both men agreed to this and applied their signatures to an agreement that formed the basis of their contract. We can only speculate why, but nevertheless that contract now exists in law and has validity as far as I can determine. As far as we can ascertain, both gentlemen died before any resolution could be affected and as such that resolution remains outstanding. It is not clear who is the rightful *'Claimant'* and we have no real way of determining this other than by presentation of *'The Trophy'*, a Tom Morris putter it seems, duly authenticated. In which case, it would be equitable to assume, and there is no alternative provision as far as I can ascertain, that whichever party could present the putter would be regarded legitimately as the rightful *'Claimant'*; claimant indeed to the other party's entire estate in fact. That is my assessment of the situation and it would seem that you and the Erskine's are now regrettably pitched into a contest of your very own, a race to acquire the putter ahead of the other. I wish you both good luck in your pursuit and expect sometime soon, to be asked to draw this to a conclusion.'

Maurice Bainbridge closed his file on his desk.

Sensing the interview had just been irrevocably concluded, Charles Pinkney thanked the solicitor, gathered his belongings, then headed out into the street. Pausing on the steps and taking several deep breaths, he checked his mobile phone but there were still no message from the dealer. He was on the brink perhaps of solving all his problems at someone else's considerable expense and he prayed for good fortune in his quest.

Returning to his car, he found it clamped and immobilised. A bad omen, he mused.

Chapter 5

'Robert, I can't believe you did that,' she screamed at her husband, 'I can't believe you messed up like that!'

'I've said I'm sorry haven't I?' Robert Erskine pleaded whilst sitting beside the telephone impatiently dialling over and over again. Each time the same repetitious message frustrated him.

'I'm sorry the office is closed at present. Our opening times are 9.30am to 4.30pm Monday to Friday. Please call between these hours.' It was now 9.37am, the message was relentless and Robert Erskine was becoming increasingly agitated.

Since returning home the previous evening with a second belated copy of the day's local newspaper, his quiet life had become awkward and difficult. Elizabeth Erskine had still not forgiven her husband for leaving the first newspaper in the bank that previous morning, the newspaper which had printed MacIntyre McBride's final announcement of their sporting auction and the very one which, if it had been read as expected, would have granted them the opportunity to attend. The second copy was no use at all. It was already too late to take action.

'Have you got through yet?' Elizabeth Erskine called through from the Drawing Room.

'Still getting that blasted answer machine. It's not a bank holiday is it my dear?'

'Just keep trying!' came back his curt instruction.

On about the thirtieth attempt, the phone finally began ringing continuously. It rang and rang, but eventually an apologetic voice addressed him.

'Sorry for keeping you waiting. Stuart MacIntyre speaking.'

'Good morning, Mr. MacIntyre, so sorry to bother you so early,' he said timidly. Elizabeth Erskine had wandered through to stand beside her husband by this time and rolled her eyes in astonishment at his unnecessary humbleness.

'No problem whatsoever, how can I help you? Please call me Stuart by the way,' the auctioneer politely offered, indirectly seeking a name in response.

'I'm interested in the auction that took place yesterday. I'm sorry I wasn't able to attend, but wondered if you might be able to provide me with some information?'

'I will if I can. What exactly are you wishing to know, Mr...?' He was still fishing for a name but Robert Erskine was being equally evasive.

'I wonder if you could tell me if you had a *Tom Morris* putter in your auction yesterday, Mr. MacIntyre?'

Stuart MacIntyre was absolutely certain he had sold a Morris putter the previous day, but was not quite willing to divulge that information quite so readily without first checking out the credentials of the caller and the purpose for his enquiry.

'May I ask who's calling?' the auctioneer asked bluntly.

'Oh, simply an avid collector who's kicking himself for having just missed your auction.' He was staring to sound a little cheesy and well he knew it. Elizabeth Erskine rolled her eyes once again.

Robert's reluctance to offer a name was becoming all too apparent and he began to think it may end up being detrimental to his cause. He decided, therefore, that if pressed he would provide a false name. For now, however, he would try and steer the conversation in a different direction.

'I'm only really interested in a Tom Morris golf club, I have to say. Did I miss one by any chance?' he asked innocently.

Stuart MacIntyre thought for a few seconds and decided, he too, would be moderately unhelpful with his reply.

'I'm a little confused. You asked a moment or two ago about a Morris putter, but just then you mentioned clubs. Is it just Morris putters you're interested in, or any Morris clubs?' the auctioneer asked.

The question threw Robert Erskine slightly. He knew absolutely nothing about golf so wanted to avoid going down any road that would make it abundantly apparent he was not the 'avid collector' he purported to be.

'Err, sorry … just his putters, I think,' he stated awkwardly. Perhaps now, though, he would get the information he was seeking.

But Stuart MacIntyre was of a mind to tease his anonymous and hesitant caller. 'Long-nose, duplex, gunmetal, brass or steel?' he playfully enquired.

Robert Erskine was starting to wish he had been more honest from the start, but his true identity had to be guarded and his intentions kept secret. Unfortunately, he was now digging a hole for himself and sensed, from the tone in Stuart MacIntyre voice, that suspicions were being raised. He needed to start thinking on his feet and turn a little more convincing. From what he recalled his wife telling him about her meeting with Bainbridge, he knew the golf club was 'old, long and wooden', but that was about all she had said. He chewed momentarily over the options he had just been given.

'You said long-nose … yes I'm interested in long-nose putters by Tom Morris,' he declared with some relief. 'Do you still have one?' he asked, desperately hoping the auctioneer would come back with a positive response. He prayed for a '… yes we do because no-one wanted to buy it'.

Stuart MacIntyre, on the other hand, was thinking the caller was overly defensive for some reason, offering much too little by way of information. Quite unusual, he thought, as most collectors were generally over generous with their irrelevances. Many a time he has taken calls from collectors or dealers who had literally occupied a good hour of his time, offering exaggerated explanations about how they first got started in collecting, recollections of how they were kicking themselves for letting things go at give away prices, casually name dropping or searching out complimentary valuations, so on and so forth. Not this caller though, a very guarded individual in fact. Stuart MacIntyre was becoming a little tired with the call, after all he knew there had been only one genuine Tom Morris putter in the sale and that had been sold. There would be no harm in letting that information out, but he was a little disappointed not to have been able to extract some personal details for his database, especially one who appeared to have an interest in what could be described as the connoisseur clubs. One last try he decided.

'Yes, there was a Morris putter in the sale yesterday,' Stuart MacIntyre declared, with the use of the past tense not escaping Robert Erskine's notice, 'but I'm afraid that particular club was sold. Not very surprising as they rarely come up for sale. Would you like me to take your details and keep you advised of any Morris putters that might be entered into future sales?'

Robert Erskine was cursing their misfortune. Only a day or two earlier and they would have had a real good chance of getting their hands on the club, quite convinced it was the one they had been seeking. But it now appeared gone, perhaps for good, which may turn out to be a blessing in disguise. Perhaps they would be safe now, no longer at risk of losing everything. He was beginning to think the news was not at all bad in the circumstances when his wife abruptly cut in.

'Well, did they have one?' she asked impatiently, her husband seemingly having drifted off in thought. Robert Erskine placed his hand over the mouthpiece and turned to his wife, a little hesitant at sharing his news, especially given her current disposition towards him.

'No, they had one in the sale yesterday … but they sold it,' he said cautiously.

'*Who to?* … Find out to *whom!*' she ordered.

'Does it matter who to?' he asked her, 'The Pinkney's don't have it any more and that's all that matters surely?' Elizabeth Erskine yanked the phone from his hand and raised it to her own mouth.

'Who am I talking to?' she demanded firmly. Stuart

MacIntyre was a little taken aback with the change in voice but more perhaps with the change in tone.

'Stuart MacIntyre, senior partner,' he responded quite guardedly, 'And whom am *I* talking to?'

Ignoring the question entirely Elizabeth Erskine set out her stall. 'It's vitally important we contact the buyer. Would you be able to give me a name and telephone number please?' There was obvious tension in her voice which she could not be disguise.

The conversation was turning peculiar thought the auctioneer and there was absolutely no way he was going to divulge customer information, particularly to a complete stranger, a person who was behaving in such an irregular and impolite manner. He detected, in the women's voice, there was some great importance attached to the enquiry, perhaps a degree of desperation and under normal circumstances he would have been more the willing to oblige. But they had disappointingly been a little too clandestine for his liking.

'I'm sorry madam, but that is completely out of the question. My business would soon flounder if my customers knew I was disclosing their personal details without their prior permission. I can note your interest in seeking the purchaser and if you are willing to provide me with some of your own details, then I will attempt to contact the purchaser myself and pass on your interest. What he chooses to do thereafter is entirely up to him. Would that be satisfactory?'

Elizabeth Erskine was now in a quandary. The auctioneers offer was extremely tempting and it was entirely possible the buyer could be persuaded to sell the club to them. This was an opportunity too good to miss and an offer which could not be refused. The stakes were too high to consider anything else, but it would be a huge risk as she would have to declare her identity. She paused for time to think.

Knowing the club was in the hands of a third party was simply offering insufficient security for her as literally anything could happen to it from that moment on. It was also possible that Pinkney may even get onto the trail himself, especially now she had practically pointed the print out the day before. It might only be a matter of time before their adversary was riding with the hunt also.

No, the club had to be secured, she decided, at least then she could prevent Pinkney using it against her and her family. If it could be bought from the new owner she would be able to sleep peacefully once again knowing her house and home were no longer at risk. The stakes were indeed high, but it was now necessary to gamble a little.

'That would be very kind of you, thank you very much indeed, Mr. MacIntyre,' she said, graciously accepting the auctioneers offer. The auctioneer was relieved he had, at last, managed to steer the conversation towards some form of conclusion.

'Perhaps then you might be kind enough let me have your name and contact number?'

'My name is Elizabeth, and my phone number is Shipston 863245.' The auctioneer was aware she had avoided offering a surname, but he was too much of a gentleman to push on that particular point. A Christian name and phone number would be sufficient for the time being.

'Thank you. I will pass your interest onto my client ... Elizabeth,' he said, '... and may I also go on to advise my client how much you would be prepared to offer for his putter?'

Elizabeth Erskine was completely thrown at this point having no idea whatsoever. She could hazard a guess at what might be a reasonable sum. A hundred pounds, perhaps even two hundred, would be a price worth paying for what was, after all, only a golf club. It was her turn to cup the mouthpiece. She turned to her husband.

'He wants to know how much we want to pay for it!' she announced, 'What should I say?'

'I've no idea,' he confessed, 'What do you think?'

Stuart MacIntyre was getting a touch impatient on the other end of the line, but idled his time by flicking through his records to see for himself what the club had brought the day before.

'How the hell would I know?' she remarked.

'Three hundred maybe?' Robert Erskine's offering was a pure stab in the dark and it didn't help her in the slightest. That was a stupid figure she thought. How could a golf club be worth three hundred pounds? She decided to employ a different tactic and removed her hand from the mouthpiece.

'Mr. MacIntyre. Are you still there?'

'Yes, I'm *still* here.'

'Mr. MacIntyre, my husband and I think the equitable thing to do is to offer something in the region of twice what the buyer paid for the golf club in the first place. We would of course be agreeable to pay you a small commission for your troubles, perhaps something in the order of ten percent. How does that sound?' She was sure that would be tempting enough. Stuart MacIntyre found the entry he was looking for.

'Elizabeth, I hope you don't mind me calling you by your first name?' he enquired having no other choice in the matter, 'I'm sure my client would be most interested to learn of your offer. This is abnormal practice I must add and usually I wouldn't be encouraging such activity. However your offer is most generous. If we take the buyer's commission into account we can work out the true cost,' he said reaching at the same time for his calculator, 'so I shall let my client know you are prepared to offer something in the region of ...', there was a short pause whilst he completed his calculation, '... something in the region of four thousand five hundred pounds.'

He waited for a reply but none came forth. 'In which case I'll be in touch should my client wish to proceed further. Thank you and good day to you.' Stuart MacIntyre carefully replaced his receiver.

Elizabeth Erskine had, by that time, already dropped hers.

Chapter 6

They were well into France before Anne Hudson found it palatable to have any sort of conversation with her husband. Tom knew, before they had set off, that it was going to be a difficult first few hours following his confession, but he was prepared to ride it out. There was no point whatsoever in trying to clear the air with an argument. That simply would not work. He knew his wife preferred the silent routine to display her annoyance. After all, it had worked so effectively in the past. But he hated it and always felt a little cheated when denied a chance to shout and ball. Her silence always made him feel uncomfortable, but that was exactly what she wanted from him just then, although it was now persisting much longer than normal. She was beginning to soften a little he decided, relying entirely on body language for evidence. So the time had come to start chipping away at the ice. The correct choice of subject was going to be a difficult one; his over-spending or the holiday itself? He elected to go for the much safer option.

'I think we should start looking for a place to stop for the night … somewhere nice. What do you think?' He was treading carefully and hoped he had pitched his introduction wisely.

'If you think we can afford it,' came back the cutting remark. Tom bit his tongue hard, his blood beginning to boil. Surely he had been made to suffer long enough? He was feeling uncharacteristically humble and apologetic whilst there remained tensions between them, but that particular remark was just begging for an argument.

'Okay, I've said I'm sorry,' he said, almost shouting, with more than a hint of irritation, 'So I spent a bit more than I said I would ... It doesn't mean we can't enjoy ourselves though.'

'It's not the money Tom ... You're missing the point.'

'Well if it's not the money, what are we arguing about?' he asked, more than just a little perplexed. He was also a little apprehensive now, given that he had only mentally rehearsed the *'money argument'* responses.

'I didn't know we were arguing,' she said. That stumped him and he glanced quizzically across at his wife, displaying the deepest frown he could muster.

'Tom,' she said softly, 'I have every confidence in your judgement on these things and if you believe it was money well spent, then I'm fine with that.' His frown faltered, but the body blow was inevitably coming. Tom braced himself, just a little unsure what form it was going to take.

'It's just that you promised me you would not go mad ... and just look what you've done.' She flicked her head in the direction of a group of clubs on the back seat. 'I'm worried Tom. I just think you're getting a bit carried away with this idea of yours. I think you're building yourself up for a big fall, a big disappointment. It's becoming a bit of an obsession. You're placing too much importance on this. I think it's time you got a grip and got back to doing it just as a hobby ... instead of spending thousands of pounds.' She said without pausing at all for breath.

The punches had landed hard, but he was relieved she had finally come out with it, sharing what was actually bothering her. He found himself secretly agreeing with his wife, her carefully chosen words designed to make him stop and think. She didn't do it very often but when she did, it was usually for the right reasons. Anne was more pragmatic than her husband, the love of her life who had a tendency to throw himself into something without first thinking through the implications.

The dressing down, he realised, was well deserved but he was also able offer some reassurances in return.

'You're right my love. I've not to get carried away with all of this and I promise you I won't. This is just a little experiment.' He also flicked his head towards the back seat, 'If it works we might make some money out of it. If it doesn't, then a least it'll be out of my system and we can get back to normal. But if you don't try, you never know.'

Tom's words were having the desired effect and he saw her relaxing, but to comfort her further he added, 'Not only that, my love, there's no way I wouldn't be able sell them again, for at least what I've paid anyway. I've got a very strong feeling though, something special is about to happen.'

'I'm sure you're right,' Anne said, not entirely convinced, but happy she had at least got her point of view over. She decided to let it drop and get on with enjoying the holiday. 'What was that you said about somewhere to stop?'

The rest of the trip to the South of France was much more amiable. As a concession, he rearranged his first planned meeting with Jean-Pierre from Dijon, the pair agreeing to meet during the return leg. The time instead was used to venture off the beaten track from time to time and wind their way through the beautiful French countryside, stopping off in small hamlets for refreshment and generally making sure they made the journey part of their holiday as well. In one village, they came across a small market, a table top sale in fact and were able to pick up a few bits and pieces for their home. A small silver pill box was bought for pennies and despite being a little grubby, they were convinced it was worth considerably more than they had paid. Strangely they also bought an old chimney pot which, seemingly, had spent its previous fifty years on the rooftop of the local primary school. Reclamation was big business back home so a suitable space was created in the car for its journey, down by the front passenger's feet in fact. They were finally beginning to relax and enjoy themselves with all the earlier traumas now well and truly behind them. Tom was also quietly confident his business meeting scheduled for a couple of day's time, was going to be well worth his time and effort.

The telephone call Charles Pinkney had so anxiously been waiting on had finally come through earlier that day, but it had taken a dozen more attempts on his part before the dealer had eventually responded. His growing desperation for an acknowledgement of any kind had been exhibited in his calls, as consecutive messages were left during the proceeding six hours, each one rising in pitch and shortening in length as his frustrations had grown.

During their conversation, one which had tested his patience to the limit, the dealer had either been overly guarded or just frustratingly playful, as extracting anything useful had proved very difficult indeed. Some quick thinking on Charles Pinkney's part and some well chosen words of reassurance about the dealer remaining his '*first choice when it comes to selling more of the family heirlooms*,' had unsurprisingly untied the mans tongue. He had learnt how the dealer had recently placed the entire collection into auction, MacIntyre McBride in fact, after first managing to negotiate some concessions and secure himself preferential terms, it had been revealed. The dealer had then drifted into some unnecessary over elaboration, offering more information than Charles Pinkney was eager to hear; particularly a long winded tale about past auction successes. All very interesting Charles Pinkney had thought, but completely irrelevant to his immediate needs, especially as he had, by then, extracted all he had wanted from the man.

But an innocent question dropped into the conversation at the end, had changed his mood entirely.

'Sorry, to interrupt,' he had said attempting to stem the flow, 'but I would be more interested in knowing when and where MacIntyre McBride intended holding their auction.'

'You're too late, Mr. Pinkney,' the dealer had announced, 'it took place a couple of days ago. Made me quite a bit of money,' he had added. Charles Pinkney had been taken aback, but had still managed to hastily express his thanks and end the call despite the dealer having been in mid sentence.

Sitting alone now in his drawing room, the gravity of his situation was becoming ever more apparent as he began to consider the cost of his earlier eagerness to sell those clubs. And in particular the Morris putter, one which had acquired an importance well beyond its worth.

So it had been sold at auction just a few days earlier he reflected and he cursed his bad luck for the hundredth time. *But who might have bought it*, he wondered? The situation was posing him a great problem with no way of knowing if the Erskine's had actually nipped in just ahead and stolen it from under his nose. His dejection grew by the minute as he allowed a feeling of helplessness to wash over him. Never before in his entire life had he ever felt such weakness. It was a novel sensation for him and one he was finding insufferable. Always in charge, always ahead, forever dominant, he had enjoyed success and good fortune in the main, so it was of little surprise that he managed to promptly come back to his rightful mind when he realised how desperately uncomfortable it was making him feel. Somehow he would retrieve his position he convinced himself. As an alternative to speculation and a drift into despondency, he was going to establish his actual circumstances with a couple of phone calls.

'Knowledge leads to power and power converts into control' he reminded himself as he searched for his address book.

Charles Pinkney's first call was placed with Bainbridge & Bainbridge who were able to confirm they had received no further communication from the Erskine's since their earlier meeting. For Charles Pinkney that was encouraging and reassuring news as he felt certain they would have been hammering on the solicitor's door if they had acquired the club.

He thanked Mr. Bainbridge and requested a call should that situation ever changed. The solicitor assured him that he would be the first to know.

His second call was to the auction house which had

recently sold his collection. It had taken three or four attempts for his call to be answered, but he was eventually invited to speak to a gentleman called Stuart MacIntyre, the senior auctioneer and the person who had conducted the recent auction.

Introducing himself and apologising profusely for disturbing Mr. MacIntyre, Charles Pinkney then explained he had been the former owner of a good number of golf clubs which had been sold recently in Mr. MacIntyre's saleroom. Notwithstanding this, he was seeking some assistance in tracking down one club in particular, one which he had regrettably released by mistake. Confessing he was no expert, he went on to describe the club as best he could, simply recalling it was an old Tom Morris putter, one which held particular sentimental value to his family. He requested a name from the auctioneer, the name of the buyer as he was most anxious to trace that person in order to make an offer for its prompt return, thus alleviating an embarrassing predicament. Going on to explain how he would be most generous in his appreciation of any assistance Mr. MacIntyre could offer, he then finished his tale with a further apology and waited for the senior auctioneer's response.

When it came, it was not one he had been anticipating.

'Mr. Pinkney, I have to say yours is not the first call I have received regarding the Morris putter and I am beginning to find it most curious. It's not uncommon to receive calls from collectors asking if a particular item has remained unsold, but I've received this call and another concerning that one particular club in the last day or two, both from persons who wish to contact the buyer for differing reasons ... and I'm beginning to ask myself why?'

Stuart MacIntyre had not been entirely satisfied with the tale he had been just been told. It had seemed implausible given the earlier call. Being careful to protect his professional integrity and the confidentiality his client's would expect, he was eager to understand the true reason for the extraordinary interest the putter was now attracting, and certainly before he was prepared to divulge anything commercially sensitive. He was calling Mr. Pinkney out on this issue and was expecting, at the very least, an honest response to his question.

But Charles Pinkney had just been told the one thing he least wanted to hear. The Erskine's were clearly trying to trace the buyer as well, asking the very same questions it would seem. *Who else would possibly want to discover the buyers name, if not them,* he thought? No wonder the auctioneer was being guarded.

Wanting to find out if any details had been passed onto the Erskine's, he reminded himself of the need to choose his words thoughtfully so as not to antagonise the auctioneer. The pair of them had opposing objectives he had quickly realised, himself seeking the *'who'*, Stuart MacIntyre apparently more interested in the *'why'*. He swallowed hard and stuck his neck out a little further.

'Mr. MacIntyre, please forgive me. I understand I've put you in a difficult position with this and I would understand fully if you chose not to divulge confidential information,' he said, attempting to sound contrite. He paused deliberately, hoping the auctioneer would follow up with a signal of some sort, something at least to indicate he had played his cards right. When nothing was volunteered though, he had no choice but to carry on blind.

'I was wrong to ask for a name, please forgive me.' The apology was not even acknowledged and the auctioneer was giving him absolutely nothing to work with, clearly irritated over the caller's reluctance to answer a simple question. Nevertheless Charles Pinkney needed to discover if the Erskine's had been told anything at all, anything that may lead them to the whereabouts of golf club.

'Perhaps you might then be prepared to let me know if the buyer's details were passed onto the other party?' he enquired, a hint of desperation in his voice.

Stuart MacIntyre was prepared to do no such thing. In his twenty odd years as a reputable auctioneer he had never divulged confidential information to a third party without first seeking expressed permission to do so. There was an unwritten code of professional conduct that was understood by both buyers and sellers alike. He had been true to that code throughout his career and had contempt for those who were either ignorant of, or oblivious to its existence. Trying to retain his composure he decided he would bring this particular conversation, just like the previous, to a swift conclusion.

'Mr. Pinkney … all I'm prepared to do for you at this precise moment is pass your interest onto my client … just as I intend to do for the other enquirer. Theirs happens to represent a significant interest in the Tom Morris putter and they have asked me to make this known to my client. I presume your interest is similar. I will transfer you shortly to my receptionist who will take your details, and I will be back in touch if my client wishes to take the matter further. Thank you and good day, Mr. Pinkney.' Stuart MacIntyre ended the call abruptly, replacing the receiver and returning to his business.

Charles Pinkney was bewildered over the auctioneer's attitude. A little too defensive he thought. Nevertheless he had discovered some interesting things during those last few minutes, enough to make him feel decidedly more positive about his prospects for recovery. He knew, or at least suspected, the Erskine's had also missed the auction and had also attempted a retrospective offer, an offer that had yet to be accepted it would appear. *But what precisely had their offer been*, he wondered? *How much had they actually placed on the table?* He knew he could simply not afford to be outbid on this one. Securing the club was critical to his survival.

Despite his many reservations about calling back, infuriating the auctioneer and risking outright rejection, he knew he had to phone MacIntyre's once more and let it be known he was prepared to improve on any other offer under consideration. Hesitantly he dialled once again and asked for Stuart MacIntyre himself. After several minutes being kept on hold and for reasons the receptionist was not willing to divulge, Stuart MacIntyre was seemingly unavailable to take his call, leaving him with no option but to dictate a message.

He asked the receptionist to read it back to him afterwards, so she duly obliged;

'Could you let Mr. MacIntyre know, that not only am I prepared to offer his client a sum significantly more than he paid in the first instance, I am also prepared to top any other offer lodged for the Tom Morris putter. I would be grateful if you could make sure Mr. MacIntyre understands this fully and passes this information onto his client without delay'.

Charles Pinkney was assured his message would

receive the appropriate attention.

Although not entirely sure quite what commitment he had just made, he felt nevertheless confident it would be too attractive to decline. It was simply a case now of waiting the whole thing out and seeing what emerged.

Yet Charles Pinkney was not tolerant man and both sitting and waiting were not in his nature. In his own mind he was confident that in a straight race he would normally end up the victor, because he was usually able to design it that way. And a straight race this now appeared to be. Any uncertainty over the club's whereabouts were now diminishing, so keeping it clearly in his sights was all he needed to do from now. Provided he could keep tabs on the club and ensure his offer continued to be the most attractive, then the outcome would be assured. Having convinced himself he was capable of engineering the success he sought, Charles Pinkney was, nonetheless, beginning to think his offer might end up having to be quite a considerable sum. And that prospect worried him. Cash was currently not his strong suit.

Later that day, Stuart MacIntyre eventually found time to sit down, read his messages and contemplate the two offers on his client's putter. It was most unconventional, but the seriousness of those offers placed a responsibility on him to forward the information onto his client. What happened thereafter was not really of any interest to him he decided, although he would prefer to avoid being drawn into the role of broker, at least not without some form of consideration for his efforts. He searched through a database on his computer and promptly found what he needed; a name, an address and phone number, all of which he noted down on a scrap of paper. Picking up the phone he dialled the phone number, only to hear a fairly mundane and unimaginative answer phone message on the other end.

'Anne & Tom cannot take your call at the moment, but if you'll leave your name and number, we'll call you back as soon as possible. Thank you'.

Stuart MacIntyre duly complied, simply introducing himself and encouraging a return call. He avoided any mention of the specifics, preferring instead to pass that information on first hand. Having fulfilled his obligations, he then returned to his normal day to day business.

Charles Pinkney was in a reflective mood, later that evening, as he sat in front of a blazing log fire in his sitting room. He began to wonder if there was some way of gaining an unfair advantage in all of this. Although he did not know the Erskine's personally he had learnt, through idle gossip, a little about his adversaries over the last day or so. They had emerged as being a particularly inert couple, rather straight laced, conventional and quiet, polite and unassuming in all respects. Pretty non-descript in fact, he was deciding. Certainly not risk takers as far as he could ascertain and no doubt frantic, like he, at the prospect of losing all that they owned.

'Ripe for manipulation perhaps,' he contemplated before dwelling on that particular thought for a moment or two longer. Drumming his fingers on the arm rest and drawing on his favourite cigar, he coldly considered his options.

'Yes, I think it's time to pay them a little visit,' Charles Pinkney finally decided.

Chapter 7

The holiday had been at risk of ruin by the atmosphere which had developed during those first few hours on foreign soil, but like all couples who were close, the moment had soon passed and all was right with the world once again. A couple of days in the sun, nice hotels, the change of scenery and some amusing contortions with an unfamiliar language had started to relax them both. They were enjoying each others company and they had agreed to say no more about it, although Tom Hudson was praying his meeting with the man called Philippe was going to be worth the effort, pay dividends and prove him right after all. It was a huge imposition on their enjoyment, an unwelcome disruption to the otherwise relaxing and indulgent routine that was evolving, but the rendezvous was a one-off opportunity to reinforce his trading aspirations. He had attempted to sell the idea that, if successful and profitable, these trips could become a regular thing but his wife was proving a difficult nut to crack on that score. She was convinced that, at best, this whole business could only be short-lived. After all they had little or no savings to make it successful anyway. Nevertheless, she wanted to support her husband and had sensed his apprehension at meeting this 'Philippe' person. She tried that morning to encourage him as best she could, even though he recognised it for what it was, very much a half hearted attempt with no real conviction behind it. His belief was obviously not shared. Perhaps it was all pie in the sky, but ideas were being turned into fortunes each and every day, so why not him with this, he wondered?

They had arrived in Menton on the French Riviera the previous evening after a punishing motorway drive the day before. Close to the Italian border and looking across the Mediterranean Sea, Menton had been a haven for the rich and wealthy during the late Victorian era, but had handed the mantle over to its more illustrious and younger neighbours of Cannes and Monaco many years ago. Nevertheless, it was a beautiful town with baroque architecture, a renaissance feel and retaining still much of its Victorian charm. It was a perfect place to spend a week eating seafood galore, drinking champagne and generally pretending to be one of the jet-set. A trip to a casino was definitely part of their itinerary, especially as Anne who, with her degree in statistical analysis, had devised what she called her *'can't possibly lose'* formula for playing roulette. They were determined to put it to the test later that week and were even prepared to risk some cash in the process. But business always comes before pleasure.

Tom kissed his wife goodbye that morning, hesitated in the doorway of their room, promised he would be careful and sensible, before departing somewhat reluctantly. If he was going to be an entrepreneur and if fate had thrown up this one and only chance, then he had better get on and do it. He was a little disappointed his wife had chosen not to come with him that morning, preferring to stay in the hotel and go for a swim, but maybe that was for the best. If he should end up embarrassing himself, or if his contact failed to appear, at least she would not witness it. Avoiding the *'I told you so'* was vitally important to him, so her absence was perhaps welcome. At least he would have a chance to invent some plausible excuse on his way back to the hotel.

Yet despite all the preparations, he was feeling tense and apprehensive. Their car had been conveniently parked round the side of the hotel the evening before, and after checking it was still safe and sound, he pulled a couple of clubs from the boot to take along with him. The Tom Morris putter was nestling at the back with others he had acquired at the auction. With no time to clear the boot before setting off on holiday and being unsure exactly what to bring along by way of example, the whole lot had been pushed to the rear and brought along for the ride. Uncertain still what to show Philippe, he picked up the Morris putter but replaced it immediately. Too precious, he thought, to risk walking around with such a valuable commodity. He had another similar, the reproduction club, bought unintentionally but which looked for the world like the real thing. Less risk in taking that along, he thought, pulling it free along with one other club.

Approaching their meeting point, a small café in the centre of town, he knew straight away his contact had kept his promise. A rather large gentleman, with a handlebar moustache, swept back flowing grey hair, pink short sleeved shirt, vivid checked plus-fours and pink knee length stockings, had jumped to his feet and was striding to meeting him halfway with what had to be the most welcoming smile imaginable. They met and shook hands enthusiastically.

'Tom, Tom you made it. Well done!' he bellowed in excellent English but with a distinct French accent nonetheless. He continued with his greeting.

'But your lovely wife is with you, no?' he asked, 'I expected you to bring her also my friend. Maybe she is watching from a distance safe?' Without seeking a reply, the large pink shirted man laughed at his own remark. 'Never mind. Come with me Tom and I present to you, a friend of mine.'

He was ushered towards a table in the shade, just off the pavement. Conscious he had not yet been given a chance to speak he was nonetheless introduced immediately to a second person.

'Tom, please allow me to introduce my good friend and my partner in golf, I must add,' he said amiably, 'Tom this is Bertoise …. Bertoise this is Tom.'

Bertoise, a slender chap and much more conventionally dressed, rose to his feet and they shook hands, inviting their guest to take a seat. Again in very good English, the second man spoke.

'Tom, can I order you a drink? I know it is early in the day, but Philippe and I often like to be good to ourselves,' he explained, winking at Philippe, 'And also we must have a few beers to welcome such a beautiful day. You like beer Tom?'

This was Tom's first chance to say something.

'Thank you. Yes a beer would be just perfect. How did you know it was actually me you were waiting on?' His question was greeted with laughter.

'Tom, look at yourself!' Philippe was smiling as he spoke. 'Look what you have in your hand. We can't take our eyes off them,' he added, pointing down at the clubs. There could have been no mistaking who he was. Two golf clubs were firmly clutched in his left hand and he felt a little embarrassed and self-conscious. But at least the ice was now well and truly broken.

The trio got to know each much better other over a few beers and a camaraderie developed between them. In conversation Philippe admitted he was not French at all, but in fact Belgian. Tom was surprised and apologised for any earlier presumptions he had made, apologies that were dismissed as unnecessary by his jovial host. The beer was affecting them all and the conversation grew ever more cordial, but after a short while Bertoise called proceedings to order. Although addressing his partner, he spoke in English for everyone's benefit.

'Philippe, perhaps we should do some business now. Tom has left his wife waiting on his return and they are on holiday are they not? You and I have our match this afternoon and I need much more preparation, as you know.' The pair laughed once more at what must have been a private joke.

'You are right my friend. Tom, please excuse my friend's impatience. We are partners in golf and we have a game this afternoon. It is a very important game, especially for Bertoise here … not so much me though.' Philippe looked at his friend and laughed once more. 'You see, I have won many trophies, but today, my good friend here is hoping for his first. How many years has it been now Bertoise?' he asked teasingly.

'I have been playing for 17 years Tom, but I am not improving. In fact, I think I am getting worse. We are in the final of a competition Tom, and Philippe here has finally let me into his secret,' he said raising his glass of beer, 'The only way to win is to relax I am told, that is why I am here with you today, enjoying your company and having beers to calm my first tee nerves I hope.'

'Bertoise is not being entirely truthful with you Tom,' said Philippe smiling after he had spoken, 'You and I have done some business have we not Tom? I am always happy with what you sell me. You and I have also been corresponding and you know I am interested in buying more from you. I do not like the competition and I think we can do business together.' Philippe paused for an acknowledgement which came without any hesitation.

'Thank you Philippe,' replied Tom. The Belgian nodded his head in appreciation and then continued.

'It is such a coincidence you take your holidays here so why not make an opportunity I think. We meet, we discuss business. I will come to the point now Tom. I like you very much and I would like to buy about fifty golf clubs from you every month but only regular clubs, hickory clubs in good condition, but not aficionado clubs if you know what I mean Tom. I have good customers round here and most are wealthy but very busy if you understand me. They are very interested, but also very lazy. So they ask me to do everything. You know what I am looking for Tom, many more the same as before. I can pay you with no problem, we just need to agree the price. I think I mentioned the price I am happy to pay, did I not Tom?' Philippe finally paused for breath. There was so much there to digest.

'Yes you did Philippe. It's a good price for you and me both. It makes it worth our while, for everyone. The price does not include shipping, I need to remind you.' He avoided any comment concerning the quantity, instead choosing to contain his excitement for now.

'I understand Tom, this is understood. I pay for the shipping on top. I am happy with this and that is why I ask you for so many clubs, it makes it cheaper for me.' Philippe was being true to his word and Tom was beaming, desperate to share the good news with his wife.

'But Tom, we can make the final arrangements later this week and we can meet another day,' Philippe added, causing Bertoise to interrupt at that point.

'For goodness sake Philippe, Tom is on holiday is he not? Let him have some peace. You can talk later when Tom gets home, surely?'

'Forgive me Tom, Bertoise is right. I was being selfish as usual, much too interested in myself when I should be telling you all about my friend here. I asked you to bring some special clubs Tom and I see you have not disappointed us.' He nodded in the direction of the clubs.

Taking his cue and lifting the two clubs onto the table, Tom went on to describe the first club in great detail, mainly to Bertoise as Philippe had, by then, taken a back seat. It was a small headed dish faced rut iron from about 1870 made by Tom Stewart of St. Andrews and one which he had purchased privately about a year earlier. He was particularly proud of this club and was able to describe its purpose, a club designed to strike a ball out of deep cart tracks, a hazard all too common on golf courses in those days. He was in his element and his audience were captivated.

'Tom, this is exactly the kind of club I was hoping you would bring. It is scarce, it is special, it has a character and it has a life of its own. You have brought it to life with your words and I see it more than just an old golf club now. It had a purpose and it would have used by many golfers over the years. It is a curious thing, but I now try and picture these people in my mind ... but now my friend, tell me about the other one?' Bertoise enquired eagerly.

The second club was not quite what it seemed. It was

the reproduction Tom Morris putter he had mistakenly bought at the auction a few days earlier, but it would be a useful example nonetheless. It was placed in the middle of the table and before any declaration or confession could be made, Bertoise had lifted his hand to silence any preamble. Picking it up for inspection, the Frenchman scrutinised the golf club at close quarters.

'Tom, please let me take a look at this club for a minute or two and I will then impress you with my knowledge this time. Agreed?'

'Be my guest,' Tom replied whilst at the same time nudging Philippe under the table to attract his attention. Philippe lent forward. 'It's a reproduction, a copy,' he whispered in the Belgian's ear, who in turn tapped his nose. A few moments later, Bertoise spoke.

'I am thinking I might be about to upset you Tom, or perhaps even insult you.' He paused to observe any reaction his comment may have caused before continuing, 'and that is why I am a little troubled about saying what is in my mind.'

'No, please carry on Bertoise. I am very interested in what you have to say.'

'Very well, Tom. I will try and be kind.'

Bertoise cleared his throat before continuing.

'I am very much thinking that the man who made this club is not perhaps the same man who has put his name to it, my friend.'

It was now Phillipe's turn to do the nudging under the table. Interrupting the conversation, Philippe looked at his partner and spoke.

'What are you saying Bertoise? Please explain yourself. I fear you may be upsetting our guest.' His voice was raised in false indignation. The Frenchman briefly looked across at his Belgian colleague before returning his attention to Tom.

'I can see in Tom's eyes that he knows what I am saying, *n'est pas*? But I will explain myself for your benefit, my good friend.' He glanced over at his pink shirted colleague. 'What you see here is a copy ... yes a very good copy indeed ... a copy of a golf club that would have been made many years earlier than this one my friend,' he announced knowingly. 'But I see you are smiling Tom.'

'Bertoise, you are a very perceptive man and you certainly know your golf clubs. Yes you are quite right and Philippe here was just pulling your leg because he also knows you are correct.'

'Tom, please do not misunderstand what I am about to say. I do not wish to be discourteous, but I was unsure whether you were testing me, trying to deceive me or just unaware it was a copy. I was worried you might have paid more than you should. It is a very good copy and made by a master craftsman I have no doubt, but not the craftsman whose name is seen on the head,' Bertoise said apologetically. 'But what is this leg pulling you describe? It is an expression I do not understand.' Everyone laughed.

More beers were ordered and Tom shared his tale about how the repro-club had come into his possession by error. Bertoise listened courteously and with interest, but soon tapped the table with his glass to call order.

'Gentlemen, time is precious and there is something I

have to say before we depart. You see Tom, I have more discerning tastes than Philippe here. He has no finesse, he is just interested in the common people, the masses. On the other hand I am a collector of only the best. I enjoy owning objects that are perhaps not always easily come by.' He left the statement hanging for a brief while to create an impression. It appeared to work as Tom obediently pulled his chair closer.

'Please do not misunderstand me, I am not a rogue. When I say '*not easily come by*', I do not mean stolen, I simply mean exclusive. There is great enjoyment in owning such things, as you can imagine.' Tom was beginning to tingle by this time and the next few moments went much better than he could possibly have imagined.

'I want you to be my agent in England Tom. I want you to look for special clubs for me and buy them on my behalf. It is not always possible for me to be everywhere at once you see, so I need someone I can trust to do that for me. I have met with you, Philippe has spoken of you, we have enjoyed some company together and you like beer. All these things are good Tom and I am happy to say these things. You have a passion which is obvious, you have knowledge and you have access to what I seek. It seems to be a perfect marriage for both of us.'

The arrangement certainly was a perfect one for Tom, much better than he could have ever imagined. The discussions progressed onto specifics as Bertoise made it clear were his particular interest lay, authentic and collectable clubs with pedigree and vintage, the sort of clubs that rarely surface onto the open market without causing a bit of a stir. The Frenchman also outlined his price band, broad enough to allow his new agent considerable latitude. He also outlined his proposals for reimbursement, all of which sounded more than acceptable for all concerned.

'This is all very good Tom, and we will leave you now to enjoy the rest of your holiday,' Bertoise said politely, 'But first let me take those clubs off your hands as a gesture of my good will and to recompense you in a small way Tom for sacrificing some of your vacation to meet with us.'

Tom thanked the Frenchman and insisted there was no need for him to feel obliged in anyway. The Frenchman simply smiled and disregarding the last comment, removing, instead, a thousand euros from his wallet and placing them down in front of Tom. Raising a hand to halt any objection, Bertoise politely sealed the deal.

'Thank you Tom. We can do much business together, I'm sure.'

Meanwhile, back in England, a potentially much less convivial meeting was imminent.

'Will he be expecting something to eat then?'

'How would I know?' Robert Erskine replied defensively.

'You mean you didn't ask him?' countered Elizabeth Erskine, her hands gripped tight.

'Why would I ask such a thing? All I know ...,' he paused briefly whilst recollecting an earlier conversation, '... is that he wants to come over and see us this evening. He said it was in our interest. What else was there to say?' he pleaded.

'What else was there to say?' Her cry was one of complete exasperation. She paced back and forth across the living room.

'What else was there to say? I don't believe I'm hearing this.' The tension is her voice was all too apparent. '*Not on your life*, would have been my immediate rebuttal,' she screamed back at him.

And that was the root of the problem as far as Robert Erskine was concerned. It should have been his wife Elizabeth taking the call from Charles Pinkney earlier, yet it had been he who had been forced to speak instead. She was making him very uncomfortable indeed and he felt a huge sense of injustice with it all. He had taken on the responsibility under protest he recalled and was now living with unwelcome consequences.

They had been arguing now for almost an hour and Robert Erskine was beginning to lose his patience. The phone had rung earlier that evening and he had been brow beaten into answering it, even though his wife had been sitting just a few feet away and he being across the other side of the room. She had made some excuse about 'her hands being full', and he had been ordered to pick up the receiver despite his protests. If his wife had spoken to the man instead, then the persecution he was now enduring would not have been cast in his direction. It had been his misfortune and now he was being made to take on the full and absolute responsibility for agreeing to the callers' request without first consulting his wife.

'*But how could I have consulted her*', he asked himself rhetorically? As soon as he had picked up the receiver, she had announced she was going upstairs to sort out some laundry, sweeping out the room leaving him isolated to make the fateful decision on his own. He had been placed on the spot and had responded with politeness to what seemed to be a sincere request to meet. His curiosity had been heightened with a suggestion it would benefit everyone, although he now concedes he never thought to ask what that might actually be. He was now at a complete loss to understand why he should have done anything other than agree to the suggestion and was bewildered why his wife should now be acting in such an indignant fashion.

'I don't want him in *my* house!' she declared venomously, 'It's a simple as that, Robert. I don't want that man in *my* house … prying …indulging in our hospitality … imagining himself sat in front *our* fireplace.' She pointed towards the fireplace in question as if believing her husband was unaware of its existence. 'And, and…'

Unable to find more words, her eyes filled with tears and she broke down slightly. Robert put an arm round his wife, gave her shoulders a gentle squeeze, kissed her on the cheek, led her to the sofa and they sat down together, still embracing. Elizabeth was the first to speak again.

'I'm sorry, my dear, it's not your fault,' she said softly and reassuringly, her head slightly lowered, 'You were right to say yes, I would have done the same in all honesty.' She was now looking straight into her husband's eyes. After a brief pause she added, '… so we'll stand firm together on this Robert and hear what he has to say before we make any judgements.'

'Thank you, my dear.' He was grateful and relieved, in equal doses, to be off the hook once more.

'Did he say what it was all about?' she enquired with a clear mind now.

'Gave no clues at all I'm afraid, although he did sound very upbeat and keen to talk to us. All he said was he wanted to see us both, about you know what, and asked if it would it be convenient to come round at about 8 o'clock this evening.'

They both looked across at the mantelpiece in unison where the clock was telling them there was only five minutes to go. Somewhat unexpectedly, they heard the sound of a car turning on gravel right outside, causing the Erskine's to grip hands and curse simultaneously.

'I'll get the door,' announced Robert Erskine, ashen faced.

'Wait,' his wife said, 'I don't want him to see me in such a state. Can you keep him occupied for a few minutes whilst I freshen up?' she asked, her voice sounding a little despondent.

'Of course, my dear,' he said comfortingly, 'And cheer up for goodness sake, how awful could this possibly be?' he asked. Seeing a doubtful look appear on her face, he went on to add by way of reassurance, 'I'll not say anything I shouldn't … well not at least until you join us'. They each smiled, drawing sharp intakes of breath to control their mutual apprehensions.

'And if he's got that blasted golf club with him, I swear I'll take your gun, Robert, and *shoot him dead*,' she responded expressionless, before racing out the room.

Robert Erskine struggled with that concept for a second or two, not knowing precisely what his wife had intended by the comment. *Did she have intentions or had she been merely joking?* It was something he was incapable of fathoming out right there and then. So putting the thought to one side, he headed for the front door as quickly as possible even before the doorbell had actually rung, being keen to avoid inconveniencing his guest by causing him to wait. He straightening his tie and tidied his hair en route.

Charles Pinkney had chosen to dress casually for his appointment with the Erskines. He was not entirely sure why but had instinctively felt it was the better approach, designed to put his hosts at ease, making them less cautious he hoped. He was extremely thankful Robert Erskine had answered the phone earlier and not Elizabeth.

Two quite different 'scripts' had been rehearsed before making the call and he was amply prepared for both eventualities. Being a meticulous man and knowing he would only have one opportunity to secure a meeting, he could ill afford to squander his chance through lack of preparation. Robert Erskine's voice on the other end of the line had come as a relief making it much more straightforward for him. From his discrete enquiries he learnt Robert Erskine was the softer target of the two Erskine's, much less likely to risk offence by probing intentions. So that had been his approach with Robert Erskine, a suggestion made, implying some benefit for all by meeting. Believing not too many question would be asked, he had been confident an invitation put to Robert Erskine would be accepted without any deep inquest.

Elizabeth Erskine, on the other hand, would have been quite a different proposition entirely. From their brief encounter a few weeks earlier he had sensed a shrewd and sceptical person, one much more inclined to be defensive in response, especially given she had met him in person and suffered first hand as a consequence. Almost certainly, she would have formed an opinion of him, and formulated some preconception in her mind, one which would now be difficult to break down. Quite simply, Elizabeth Erskine would be suspicious and mistrusting of him and he would have needed to be uncharacteristically tactful and charming.

Thankfully Robert Erskine had answered his call and so his task had been made all the easier. Agreement to meet at short notice had been extracted with consummate ease and he now felt in complete control, looking forward with relish to the prospect of manufacturing a favourable outcome.

It was all going to plan and he was feeling relaxed and confident as he stepped out of his car and advanced towards the arched entranced. Pausing briefly to absorb his surroundings, he cast an envious eye over the building in front of him. It was grand and imposing, a monument to Georgian architecture, unequivocally magnificent he decided. He turned on his heels to steal a look at the panorama that extended behind him. The landscape was formal and well manicured with a mixture of neat topiary, mature shrubs, classical stone features, ancient yews and bowling-green quality lawns. In the distant there were outbuildings, stables perhaps and what looked like a walled garden beyond. He looked back down the bordered driveway along which he had just travelled. It was nearly a quarter of a mile in length and almost as long as his own he determined.

He was impressed, very impressed indeed. In his mind he was already starting to plan the changes, but his musings were disrupted by the sound of the front door unlocking. An outstretched arm and a welcoming hand invited him inside.

Chapter 8

Although it was a Saturday afternoon, Maurice Bainbridge was unofficially working, albeit not behind his office desk. In fact he was on the second floor of a large industrial building which, in its former years, had been a highly productive textile mill. But having lain empty for decades, a consequence of recession, its vast floor space was now being put to alternative use as a document archive facility, one of those ever growing establishments that so many businesses now rely so heavily upon to ease their acute storage problems. Ever growing commercial rental in town have forced businesses to discard the convenience of on-site storage and place greater emphasis on converting the available space into a profitable concern. With storage and overheads needing to be cheaply and effectively managed, low cost solutions, such as the building Maurice Bainbridge had just entered, were a practical solution, albeit not a particularly convenient one.

Maurice Bainbridge had promised his wife he would amuse their fourteen year old son that day whilst she went on a shopping spree with her friends. So what better way than rolling up their sleeves and embarking on some private detective work, he had decided. That at least was how he had sold the idea to his son Jonathan, or Jon as he preferred to be called. Jon, realising he was holding all the cards and typical of most cash minded teenagers, had employed his best negotiating skills before agreeing, thus managing to extract for himself some significant concessions from his father into the bargain. Firstly, an increase in pocket money by a pound a week, secondly, some money to buy a CD he had been saving hard for, and thirdly that his pal Oliver be allowed to come along to help. Truth be known, the extra eyes and hands were going to be a blessing the solicitor had realised. He knew the search was going to be troublesome so his acceptance of the terms was practically automatic, leaving his son momentarily downcast for not having bargained harder.

Standing in front of row upon row of dust covered boxes, all of similar size and appearance, and holding a solitary piece of paper in his hand, Maurice Bainbridge called the boys to order so he could relay his instructions.

'First things first, boys … this is not a playground and you shouldn't really be here,' he said with a serious look on his face, 'The man in the office downstairs has said you can help me … but no climbing or fooling around, understood? This is a place where people work and there are rules to be obeyed.'

He was trying to impress on the boys the importance of behaving sensibly. The inclination to drift into solicitor mode and start quoting from the Health and Safety at Work Act was almost too tempting to resist, but he managed to contain himself and settled for something much more likely to create an impression on the boys.

'So if I catch either of you running around … or acting the goat … then all deals are off … understood?'

'Yes, Mr. Bainbridge,' responded Oliver almost immediately. What an obedient and well mannered child the solicitor thought. But there then followed a prolonged silence and Maurice Bainbridge found it necessary to look his son squarely in the eye.

'Okay then!' came the reluctant acknowledgement everyone had been waiting on. Maurice Bainbridge continued with one eye now fixed firmly on his son.

'Right boys, here's what we have to do. In here, somewhere in this row...,' he pointed down a long aisle of identical looking storage boxes stacked on shelves, '... in *row D, stations 1009 to 1237* it would seem ... there is a box ... inside a much larger box ... and we have to find it'.

The two boys looked at him quizzically, clearly expecting much more to come But, when nothing further was offered by way of instruction, they turned to each other and shrugged shoulders.

Maurice Bainbridge looked up and down the row once again and began to wonder if it was going to be an impossible task. The briefing had been short and sweet and the boys were clearly bemused. Was that all they were going to be told? The question was clearly crossing their minds.

The solicitor was gazing into space, lost in thought it appeared, so his son interrupted him.

'Is that it then?' Jonathan asked incredulously, 'There must be *ten thousand* boxes down there,' he added pointing down the aisle. Like all teenagers, he had a tendency to exaggerate. The solicitor's attention was hauled back into line.

'Right boys, between here ...' he said placing his hand on the container closest before moving along the aisle about twenty paces and touching a second, '... and here ...,' he announced, his hand patting a large container, '... there's a box with a code number on its side which looks like this.' He took a piece of chalk out from his jacket pocket, referred once again to the piece of paper in his hand, then knelt down.

The boys gathered round to watch Jonathan's father scramble around on the floor whilst writing out *KNG77896BB* with his piece of chalk.

'Have you got a pen dad?' his son enquired not in the least bit impressed with his father's efforts. Maurice Bainbridge took a biro from his inside pocket and handed it across. Jon took the pen and nonchalantly copied the number onto the back of his hand before offering the pen to his friend Oliver, who duly followed suit. They were then off in a flash even before the solicitor had chance to issue his final instruction.

'And be careful ...,' he called out ineffectively in their wake.

Within seconds the boys were climbing all over the racking and shelves like a pair of monkeys. Boxes were being hurriedly dragged out from position, rotated and turned upside down to reveal their hidden coding. Hands were being consulted simultaneously before each box was pushed back into place after rejection. Although he suspected there may be over two hundred boxes to inspect, he was now confident the boys would rip through them all in no time. But that would be just the beginning of his search, he realised sombrely.

'*What were we actually looking for?*' he asked himself. He could not be entirely sure he decided, but was hoping for his grandfather's day files perhaps, personal records kept by the proprietor of Bainbridge & Bainbridge back in the twenties and thirties. It was practice folklore that Edward Bainbridge, sole proprietor between 1917 and

1937, was a meticulous man who kept comprehensive records of all his appointments and interviews. In the form of hand written diaries, he knew they had been prepared and kept by his great grandfather as an aide-memoir for future reference. But it occurred to Maurice Bainbridge that his grandfather could never have contemplated a need for those particular records so far into the future.

The Erskine and Pinkney contract had been relatively easy to unearth in the office, having remained classified as current despite the passage of so many decades. The files had never been closed down and consequently remained active, albeit pushed into some dusty recess in the basement of their office. Having been rescued from the sentence of archive by his father several years earlier, they had fortunately been on hand and Maurice Bainbridge had been able to demonstrate professional efficiency by producing the original documents quite readily for the first of the two interviews. But not so his grandfather's day files it seemed and all the hundreds of closed cases, old wills, probates, land registries and so forth. They had all been gathered together long ago, stuffed into boxes, referenced and transported to their present surroundings, destined to reside there for the rest of eternity perhaps, or at least until someone stopped paying the rentals.

Maurice Bainbridge continued to troubled and intrigued by the *Agreement* however, ever since he carried out his preliminary analysis and offered his advice to the parties concerned. Its bespoke nature, the elaborate provisions, the strange reliance on authentication, the very terms of the *Agreement* and the monumental stakes, altogether added up to something quite peculiar. It was, for all intent and purposes, a wager between two eccentrics who clearly distrusted each other to the point of obsession. But it was a formal wager nonetheless and one which seemingly remained unresolved still. Its unwelcome emergence after so many years was going to have serious repercussions for at least one of the two families now embroiled in its provisions.

He had earlier scrutinised the terms to the point of exhaustion, but his conclusion always remained the same. It appeared to have a genuine legal status and therefore binding on those who fell within its reference terms. But for his own piece of mind, especially as it appeared he may very shortly have to play an integral part in the destruction of someone's security, he wanted to satisfy himself that he was placing the right interpretation on the spirit of the *Agreement*. It was essential he was absolutely sure of his ground on this one and certain in his own mind he was acting correctly and fairly, after all there existed the possibility the whole business may have been retrospectively revoked somehow. But that was looking unlikely he thought, given an extensive search of their premises had subsequently revealed nothing further in connection.

It worried him that he knew little about the circumstances that had driven the signatories into their reckless action in the first place. *What possible compulsion could there have been to create such an elaborate contract in the first place*, he wondered? He desperately needed some guidance and understanding on this and Edward Bainbridge, he instinctively knew, was going to help him achieve it.

A little too engrossed in his own thoughts he was completely oblivious to what was engaging the boys until that was, the inevitable happened. The crashing of boxes and young voices yelling made him realise it was time to start paying more attention to what was going on. Oliver was buried beneath a pile of files, books and papers of all descriptions along with the empty box that had, until very recently, contained them all. Jon was standing by his friend's side, unable to control his laughter.

'*Get them off me!*' young Oliver was demanding. He was thankfully not badly hurt, but clearly much less impressed and amused by the whole incident than his friend appeared to be. Jon was of no use at all, preferring to poke fun rather than help, so it fell to Maurice Bainbridge to initiate the rescue.

'You're in for it now dad … Oliver's mum will sue you,' the solicitor's son dramatically announced, 'Look he's bleeding.'

Oliver's forehead had a slight graze which, like most head cuts, appeared much worse than it actually was. Even so, Maurice Bainbridge knew his son was right and questions would be asked later on. But for now he was only interested in getting Oliver back on his feet. Whilst he was doing this, it dawned on him that his son's first thoughts had been one of possible litigation. The future of Bainbridge & Bainbridge was going to be in safe hands he reflected proudly.

It turned out the boys had succeeded in locating the very box they sought, but it had been placed annoyingly high on the topmost shelf. Instead of asking for assistance, they had tried to pull it out themselves only to discover, too late, it weighed much more than either had expected. Jon, quickly realising they had no chance of keeping hold as it slipped from their grasp, had jumped out of the way leaving his friend to cushion its fall alone. Maurice

Bainbridge had no way of knowing this of course and the boys took advantage of him, wasting no time in re-negotiating the terms of their own particular *agreement*. In promising some further concessions, Maurice Bainbridge had guaranteed their silence for later on that day.

As fate would have it, Maurice Bainbridge found amongst the pile of documents that were now spread across the factory floor, some of the diaries he hoped still existed. A quick thumb through a couple of pages of one leather clad volume in particular, quickly reassured him their efforts that day had been worthwhile. The adjacent boxes each held similar contents so he knew his search was practically complete. He gathered a small collection together and placed them to one side before helping the boys put everything else back into the box. Declining offers of assistance, he hoisted the box back onto the top shelf himself, scooped up his spoils and ushered the boys towards the main office on the ground floor. They all then headed back to the solicitor's home, Oliver in tow having been granted a sleep-over as part of the renegotiations. Everyone, it seemed, had profited in some individual way that afternoon.

That evening, with peace and quiet having finally descended on the household and with time and a glass of wine to himself, Maurice Bainbridge embarked on his voyage of discovery, wading through his grandfather's day notes. He was looking for particular references to particular meetings, knowing the appointments, if indeed there had been any at all, would have taken place sometime during 1921. This deduction came simply as a result of knowing both the *Pipeshank* prints and all the documents were dated

August of that particular year. On his desk lay five volumes, all very grubby and a little ragged, but nevertheless of consecutive dates spanning September 1920 to January 1922. Five volumes of what must have been nearly thirty in all discovered that day.

Although Maurice Bainbridge had carried out only a cursory browse, sufficient to identify the dates he was looking for, the diaries had nonetheless revealed a fascinating account of day to day business in the practice. If for no other reason than just idle curiosity, he was determined to find time over the coming months to read each and every entry. Being an accomplished and popular after-dinner speaker, with a reputation for amusing anecdotal commentary on misleading and peculiar cases in law, it also occurred to him there could be no shortage of material here, enough perhaps for a further five years on the circuit. He leant back in his chair for a moment or two, lifted his glass and drank the entire contents in one before setting about to leaf through the first of several volumes.

Each entry appeared to follow a similar format. A new page for each day, left margin, right margin, entirely hand written in ink with a good quality fountain pen it appeared. Transcripts had been kept of all his grandfather's interviews it seemed, with no apparent mistakes being made, no errors or corrections. The transcripts were supplemented with summary notes and comments along with occasional footnotes which appeared to have been added retrospectively. References to statute or precedents it seemed that presumably had a bearing on the issues or case in question. And then there were the more interesting and enlightening entries, brief notes written into the margins, personal comments concerning clients who, from having read just one or two examples, appeared to be highly libellous. Edward Bainbridge was beginning to emerge as a most intriguing fellow, his grandson was quickly discovering.

It took nearly a full hour of meticulous and sometimes tedious reading, but finally the solicitor came across an entry which gave him much encouragement. He had never been entirely convinced there would be a reference of any kind to either Sir Giles Pinkney or Sir Randolph Erskine, but there in front of him were some words which confirmed he was on the right trail. Amongst the day notes for the 11th June 1921 was a brief entry;

'3.22pm: Appointment confirmed by telephone. 15th June at 9am prompt. Two gentlemen in dispute who wish to provide instruction, arriving separately. Lodgement of particulars will be the business. No advices offered except insofar as neither profess to be plaintiff or defendant. Settlement by regulated contest undisclosed!! Two hours allocated. Fees; 10/- per hour or part thereof verbally advised and verbally accepted by Sir Giles on behalf of both parties.'

Marvellous, thought the solicitor as he quickly thumbed over a couple of pages to the 15th June. And to his amazement, it was all there, a complete account of the meeting that morning, a considerable entry in fact that would make fascinating reading he was sure. There, before his very own eyes, was his unique opportunity to gain an insight into the mindset of those two intriguing gentlemen. The entry might give him a chance to understand the reasoning behind the dispute in the first place and perhaps some guidance that might lead him to conclude the whole contract was based on a mistaken premise at the time, perhaps even rendering the contract void. If he could find a flaw in the basis of the *Agreement*, or indeed the provisions in common law that were applied, then he might be able to ease the burden for his new clients. Perhaps Edward Bainbridge himself may have added his own comments about its integrity. He had been, after all, a businessman and would probably have complied with most instructions in the first instance if a fee had been suggested. But by way of safeguarding his own professional integrity Edward Bainbridge may have offered the gentlemen some subsequent words of caution, words that if recorded, may present grounds to have the agreement retrospectively quashed or invalidated. It was a long shot he conceded, but worth investigating nonetheless.

And that was what was really lying at the heart of his disquiet. He harboured a desperate need to somehow find a way of resolving this business with no harm being inflicted upon anyone. Since that first meeting with Elizabeth Erskine he had endured many sleepless nights, cursing the fact that he Maurice Bainbridge, the sole practitioner of a family business spanning decades and generations, had been handed the responsibility and burden of disclosure following so many years of ignorance and innocence. It had now fallen to him to be a reluctant participant in its resolution and he resented the fact. Yet despite this and without obvious complaint, he now shouldered the duty of care to those who sought his advice and guidance. The extraordinary circumstances however, were taking their toll on his well being and he was not at all convinced he had yet exercised that duty of care diligently. He felt solitary and vulnerable at that moment requiring some reassurance that his interpretations were sound, but looking once again at the dairies he was somewhat comforted in the belief they were going to help him in some way. Edward Bainbridge, even from the grave, was sure to guide him through all this.

Concentrating once more on the notes, he spied an abundance of entries for the 15th June 1921, all very neat and legible, unusually spanning several pages. It must have been a busy day he thought. He was tempted to go straight to the 9am appointment, but other entries caught his eye and he was curious to read those as well. Just like all the previous entries, these too were comprehensive and copiously written in Edward Bainbridge's own hand. The art of dictation appeared to be something his grandfather had not then embraced and he was grateful for that. Before diving into the entries, he took a short break for a few minutes to refill his glass and then returned to his desk to carry on reading.

8.05am: Telephone call taken from Mr. Bradley concerning Thomson's continued refusal to pay for the vehicle. Drafted letter to Jerome Saunders Solicitors advising of our clients intention to raise further actions against their client within a fortnight should the settlement remain unsatisfied. Copy letter to file EB/123/19

8.15am: RSVP to St. Mungo's WI. Enclosed note expressing my sincere apologies for not replying sooner but added my delight in accepting. Note 11am 17th July, dress informal, lunch thankfully provided.

8.20am: File ref: EB/034/21. Researched Court Summaries Moscroft vs. Hinchcliffe 1883, and Williams v. Dobson 1841 for definition of 'A Reasonable Man' in connection with the Sneddon case. Contention being, 'was this or was this not the conduct of a reasonable man'? Further contention being proffered is the novel proposition to be argued by Sneddon's counsel, that the defendant was not in fact a 'Reasonable Man' in that a reasonable man is always thinking of others, prudence his watchword and safety first his rule in life. Contrast with the 'Economic Man' whose every action is prompted by the spur of selfish advantage and directed to the single act of monetary or positional gain. This contention, if successfully argued, mitigates Sneddon's obligation to have acted in a reasonable fashion in preventing the collision of the two motor launches. Equally in pursuant of their defence, there is no legal recognition of the 'Reasonable Women' in English Law and as such the conduct of Miss Sneddon was not required to come up to the standard of a reasonable man, sufficient in this case to be only that expected of a women as such. There is merit in this unorthodox defence, however unpalatable. Schedule time next Thursday to research more thoroughly.

Removing his reading glasses, Maurice Bainbridge once again leant back in his chair and reached out for his glass. Having a legal mind of his own, he was finding the entries extremely interesting, adding a new perspective to his own insights into the application of law. Without the benefit of an experienced colleague for so many years, having only just recently taken on a junior partner, there had been little or no opportunity to consult with others. For the most part, he had worked in isolation throughout his career and as such had to rely entirely on his own interpretations of English Law and precedents. But by reading these diaries he was beginning to sense that for the first time he was being granted a different perspective, affording an opportunity to become a more versatile and knowledgeable solicitor. His grandfather had been a respected member of the Law Society and he was beginning to comprehend why. These diaries were going to be the most important single source of reference for his practice in the future and he made up his mind there and then to recreate all the many hundreds of entries in modern format. He decided he would investigate the possibilities early next week and obtain some cost estimates.

In the meantime, it was back to the business in hand. He read the 8.20am entry once again with a combination of astonishment and amusement. *Was it possible a case had been considered, arguing that a woman had no obligation to act reasonably? Could this first entry be the source of his next after-dinner speech,* he pondered? He would have to examine the cases quoted in much more detail and perhaps there may be subsequent entries in the diaries that undermined the principle, but the thought that a women could successfully argue in law that her perceived status in society placed no obligations on her, implied or otherwise, was most fascinating and most alarming. He rubbed his hands before moving onto the entry that interested him much more.

9.00am: The two gentlemen arrived separately but within minutes of each other. The first introduced himself as Sir Randolph Erskine and the second gentleman as Sir Giles Pinkney. Neither men shook hands and each displayed a quite extraordinary distain for the other. I established that both gentlemen were in agreement, however, on the substance of their business and my instructions were simple; a requirement to carry out their instructions as stated. The pair expressed an expectation that I should challenge these instructions should I, at any point, form the opinion that their proposed arrangements could not satisfy examination, leading either party to legitimately default without recourse. All that being accepted and having laid out my fees, the business of the day was established. To summarise a lengthy discussion, which at times had both gentlemen raising their voices in a most disagreeable and inappropriate manner, it transpires the two men are adversaries for reasons not immediately apparent. Both were common in the desire to finalise an agreement with exceptional terms and conditions, with specific provisions to form the basis for a full and final settlement of their disputes.

My enquiries into the nature of their disputes were met with reluctance by both to offer any explanation, suffice in their own words, simply to know that dispute existed. I advised the responsibilities placed upon me earlier demanded explanation for I had no wish to associate my services with matters criminal. It was made plain that without satisfaction in this regard I could not act on their behalf. After a long silence, Sir Randolph Erskine intimated it had been a culmination over many years, starting in India over twenty years earlier. They had been competitors in a trading venture over which both men had each been mistakenly granted equal mineral rights to certain territory deep within the Indian subcontinent. This had been an irreversible administrative error it was stated. When a lucrative discovery was eventually made, both men had claimed exclusive title to that resource despite knowing the other was entitled to an equal share. At this point the interview degenerated as Sir Giles Pinkney voiced his objection and accused Sir Randolph Erskine of manipulating the facts, placing an insincere misinterpretation on events. After allowing the pair time to exhaust their arguments, I called the interview to order inviting Sir Randolph to continue. The dispute, it seemed, could not be reasonably settled to either man's satisfaction and the judgement of Indian magistrates had been one of equal share. The resentment this caused in each man, I was advised, manifested in several ways over subsequent years, despite both men acknowledging they had enjoyed considerable benefit from these shared trading rights. It was the undisguised opinion of both men that each had stolen from the other.

Maurice Bainbridge was fascinated with the account which was exactly what he had been hoping for. A footnote had been added to the bottom of the page;

> *(Note for file: Enquiries to be made with the British Consulate in Delhi to seek transcripts of the ruling. Sir Randolph undertook to provide Session details).*

He turned a page and continued reading.

The men, thereafter, took further exception to each others company and in my presence, proceeded to recall a catalogue of misdemeanours perpetrated against the other. In the main, these were fairly inconsequential, but for interest I note a few examples.

   i.   A dispute over machinery patent rights

   ii.   A dispute concerning public 'rights of way' over Sir Giles's estate.

   iii. A dispute concerning car-parking privileges at the golf club.

This last issue seemed to aggravate feelings even further. It is clear both regarded retention of status at the golf club as paramount, so the car park incident had resulted in an inflammation of their mutual distain. A further incident at the golf club had quickly ensued and it was that which now brought these two gentlemen to my office. To protect their respective standings within the club and their positions of respect within local society, their affairs would now to be settled in a way which, having now heard the detail, is most peculiar and quite without precedent in my opinion.

My curiosity led me to ask a direct question, asking for a full explanation of the incident, a question which I now freely admit came with a less than honest preamble, but I needed to learn the substance of the incident, in case it had a bearing on future proceedings.

Maurice Bainbridge could hardly contain his excitement as he scribbled down his own notes. The entry was much more comprehensive than any other read previously and he presumed the extraordinary nature of the circumstances had also captured the imagination of Edward Bainbridge. Inquisitively, he flicked through the dairy to see how much remained. Pleasantly surprised he saw it went on for several more pages.

The incident had taken place three weeks earlier, although the two men were in disagreement over the actual date, an immaterial fact but one which sparked a heated debate. It was finally agreed to be some time between the 14th & 21st May 1921. The occurrence took place at the Royal Stratford Golf Club where both had been members for nearly ten years. On the morning in question, neither man had been partnering the other. An innocent question on my part left me in no doubt they had been playing in separate groups. The events of that day were relayed by both men who seemed, at least on this, to be agreed on the detail, settling quickly into a rhythm of alternating recollections. My attempt at sensible dialogue with the two gentlemen soon degenerated once more into argument and I had no option but to gather further explanation from each separately. The following is an amalgam of both men's tales, painstakingly taken in shorthand by my clerk and subsequently transcribed.

A certain amount of commotion from the bedroom above caused a brief interruption to the solicitor's concentration, but the sound of his wife running up the stairs and insisting the boys stop fighting soon settled things down again. Choosing not to be drawn into that particular dispute, he continued with his study into a much earlier one. Edward Bainbridge was still going strong, but his grandson had learnt one thing, the notes having not been written during the interview, but subsequently it seemed.

Play had apparently been slow and frustrations had grown. Sir Giles, I was told, had been following Sir Randolph for the entire round and had noticed, with some satisfaction he now confessed, that Sir Randolph was becoming ever more agitated with his game. On one occasion, he witnessed Sir Randolph throwing his club down the fairway, a claim which was denied when posed to Sir Randolph. When the players came to the eighteenth hole, their rounds had already taken over four hours and being keen to finish playing, Sir Randolph had attempted to play a shot well beyond his capabilities it seemed, only to send his ball into an unplayable position, deep inside a quarry to the left of the fairway, about 150 yards from the tee. Admitting now he should have taken his penalty and played another ball, he proceeded to try and recover his first attempt with several shots from deep within the chasm, all of which failed to gain sufficient height to clear the escarpment in front of him. On each occasion, his frustrations grew I was told. By then, a small number of people had gathered on its perimeter to witness his distress including Sir Giles who, in the absence of a 'wave through' and no prospect he thought that the player would ever emerge, had played his ball safely from the tee to a point adjacent the quarry. From here he had been able to join the assembled grouping, along with his playing partner and their caddies. All were now witness to Sir Randolph's un-gentlemanly conduct, although Sir Randolph denies adamantly his behaviour at that point had been questionable. It was claimed by Sir Giles and not denied by Sir Randolph that for nearly ten minutes he lashed his battered ball against the cliff face before it finally emerged. And before, during and after every stroke he uttered a number of unrepeatable expletives which were carefully recorded by Sir Giles and his grouping. In all, Sir Giles claimed to have counted over one hundred utterances and that only whilst being close by to witness. Clearly the quantity would, in all honesty, have been considerably more he had attempted to imply. Sir Randolph did not deny this but was keen to stress, with a little shame it seemed, that a few of the expressions used that day had never been used before by him and that it was a shock to him also to hear them coming from his own lips. He had apologised publicly to those around him, but it seems that was insufficient for Sir Giles. The two men confronted each other after their game, beside the clubhouse and Sir Giles announced he was going to take the matter further. Not only was he intending to report the misconduct to the Captain, he was also sure it was a common law offence to swear so profoundly on a golf course, claiming he had read a recent article the previous day (I would wish to investigate the inference that an offence in common law had occasioned. I will add my retrospective comments hereafter). The pair admitted they were both then locked in confrontation with Sir Randolph threatening retaliation by publicly revealing some unpleasantness that Sir Giles had hoped would remain secret. Neither gentlemen were prepared to discuss this with me, although I suspect Sir

Randolph may well have been tempted if time had permitted.

Maurice Bainbridge had been picturing the three men sitting there in his very office so long ago. Even the furniture would have been the same as there had been very little change to his surroundings since that day back in May 1921. His mind was conjuring up all sorts of images, whilst he carried on reading, all the time making more and more notes. His grandfather had clearly been very meticulous in his recordings. Maurice Bainbridge wondered whether his grandfather had merely been a very diligent fellow, or whether the entries were deliberately detailed, intended for some future reference perhaps. He could only speculate.

The diary entries went on to describe how the two gentlemen had brought some articles with them, along with some documents for the solicitors review and comment. It became apparent from the descriptions the two men wished to enter into a contest to settle their differences, but not a contest in the traditional way, certainly not *pistols at dawn* or the like. No, this was to be a golfing contest, not a *'one off'* event, but a tournament, an annual match in fact that had no stipulated end date in mind. The match, or matches would continue indefinitely until one or other conceded the tournament, not in words, but in deed. Verbal concession would be disregarded, with concession only being recognised by non appearance on the first tee on the stipulated date at the stipulated time. And the stakes were high, very high indeed. The notes had gone on to record a festering resentment growing in the two men over many years, a resentment of their respective wealth, along with the position and influence that followed suit. Edward Bainbridge had noted this fact, referencing an earlier entry concerning their dispute over mineral deposits in India. It was abundantly clear to the interviewer, that the hatred each now bore for the other was a consequence of that original dispute. Clearly, both had felt cheated and being at their wits end with each other, were finally demanding satisfaction, winner literally taking all.

The contest was to be represented by the two framed prints they had brought with them, pictures that Maurice Bainbridge recognised from the description, the very ones brought recently to his office by both Elizabeth Erskine and Charles Pinkney, neither of whom recognising the significance of the narrative and instruction on the reverse. Those particular words had been given to Edward Bainbridge on a piece of paper for his review, and his notes recorded his satisfaction over the wording, being both plain and adequate for the purpose. His only comment had been a preference to identify each print separately with each man keeping his own copy by way of reference.

The second item had been a document the men had drafted, forming the terms and conditions of an agreement. Again, Maurice Bainbridge was familiar with this, having read the contents out loud on two occasions recently. Edward Bainbridge had undertaken to review this document later that day and his footnotes had proposed some minor amendments. He had also noted the trophy referenced in the document was to be a golf club of specific description and a third item brought along was designed to verify the specification of the golf club.

This third item had, not surprisingly been a sealed envelope with no one, other than the two gentlemen, knowledgeable of its contents. The words it contained would remain concealed and both had signed and sealed the envelope for security, with instruction contained in the actual agreement as to the circumstances which would warrant its opening. Again this item was to be left with the solicitor.

By now, Maurice Bainbridge was exhausted with the extent of the commentary and was unsurprised to see that no further appointments had been recorded for that particular day. Clearly the interview had extended well beyond the two hours allotted and the painstaking notes were a testament to the importance attached to the session. And with them, Maurice Bainbridge had discovered all he needed to know about the original circumstances and was taking comfort from the fact that Edward Bainbridge had added nothing to suggest the *Agreement* may be dubious. Gaining his own satisfaction was going to be of little comfort, however, to the Erskine's and the Pinkney's, but at least he had passed on sound advice.

Within the few sample diaries he had retrieved that day, these particular entries appeared to be the only references to '*The Morris Men*' as far as he could ascertain. There was no explicit commentary on how long the contest had lasted, if it had concluded, who perhaps emerged the eventual victor, nor indeed if it had actually ever commenced on the first place. Nevertheless he had a better insight now into the background of the dispute and he was certainly much better informed now than three hours earlier.

There was, however, one final entry for that day, linked back to the earlier interview with the gentlemen, concerning the suggestion that an offence in common law *may* have taken place on the golf course. It was written in different ink and with a broader nib, so perhaps had been added at a later date. Edward Bainbridge had written;

Rex v Guthrie 1919: Sheffield: 'Are Golfers to be

regarded as Gentlemen?'

Mr. Reginald Guthrie charged under the Profane Oaths Act 1745 with swearing and cursing on a Kentish golf course no less than 206 times, as recoded by witnesses. Penalty under the Act, a fine of one shilling for a labourer, soldier or seamen, two shillings for every other person under the degree of gentleman and five shillings for every person of, or above, the degree of gentleman. Fine to be imposed for each and every profanity -- A golfer was generally regarded as a gentleman and the defendant faced the prospect of a considerable fine. Defendant maintained a golfer was in fact, not a gentleman and forwarded many arguments, in particular a claim that golf may well be included in the category of 'intolerable provocations' which may legally excuse or mitigate behaviour that is not otherwise excusable, and that under provocation a person may reasonably act as a lunatic or lout on the golf course. The Stipendiary, giving judgement, was not satisfied the arguments had any real substance, but the case is pending Appeal.

'And the after-dinner material just keeps on coming!' Maurice Bainbridge amusingly thought to himself.

Chapter 9

'Please, come through. My wife will be joining us shortly,' invited Robert Erskine, '… and please take a seat. Can I get you a drink?' he enquired being his customary courteous self.

The two men, having shaken hands firmly in the entrance hall, had then ventured slowly through to the drawing room, all the while Charles Pinkney casually taking in his surroundings. Their introductions had been pleasant enough with Robert Erskine having been thanked for his willingness to meet at such short notice, although there had been a blatant attempt on his host's part to avoid any real eye contact, keeping his head lowered throughout their greeting. This curious behaviour had not gone unnoticed and Charles Pinkney wondered if Robert Erskine had been chastised in someway, perhaps as punishment for accepting his invitation so readily. Yet despite drawing considerable amusement from the odd behaviour, it confirmed his earlier suspicions that any real challenge to his plans would come from the lady of the household.

Charles Pinkney was in no doubt what his objective that evening must be. He needed to create a significant advantage for himself and was quite prepared to be extraordinarily deceptive to achieve his goal. The fact that he was capable of contemplating such a reprehensible act, he found a little inexplicable. But for reasons beyond his comprehension, he had formed the distinct impression it was coming quite naturally from within. He had been aware for some time, particularly in business, that he rarely suffered from pangs of conscience. Winning at any cost was his natural way, so it was unusually disturbing that he now had to acknowledge a kind of failure on his part. Allowing so much of his wealth to slip away, albeit unpreventable, he regarded as a slight on his ability to retain an upper hand on practically everything.

Worst still, his sense of inadequacy had been heightened of late with the *'Morris Men'* disclosure and the pending prospect of total loss that came along with it. That disclosure had been the proverbial final straw as far as he was concerned, demanding immediate rectification. Whilst he had few doubts that his money problems could otherwise be successfully managed in the longer term, the insecurity and added burden the *'Morris Men Agreement'* had introduced was disturbing him greatly. He was experiencing vulnerability and he hated the sensation.

But he was determined to frustrate the 'set rules' that had been imposed by the *Agreement*. They did not suit him, so they needed altering; it was as simple as that in his mind. The time had come for him to re-establish himself in pole position, no matter how unsavoury others may subsequently judge his actions. And his creativity earlier that day had presented an opportunity this evening which he was unwilling to fritter away, even if that meant selling his soul in the process.

But Elizabeth Erskine was not a business acquaintance and as such, presented an unfamiliar challenge. Charles Pinkney had always prided himself on his accomplishments at the expense of his fellow man, as generally he had the measure of most of his male counterparts. But dealing with a woman, and a strong minded woman at that, was a different proposition entirely, a situation for which he had little or no experience to draw upon. The outcome that evening was by no means in the bag. Elizabeth Erskine had the potential to be a real fly in the ointment, he decided.

His short walk from hallway to drawing room had given him a chance to briefly absorb his surroundings. The house was just as impressive on the inside as outside. The entrance hall was oak panelled which extended through into the drawing room, an imposing space with high ceilings and all the accoutrements of wealth. Fine objects adorned the room, mostly inherited, passed down through the generations he presumed, creating a fine blend of functionality and extravagance equal to his own home, at least until those enforced disposals. To say he was resentful would have been a gross understatement. Practically all his family heirlooms and virtually all his available cash had disappeared before his very eyes in a few short weeks. And in the process, just to rub salt into his wounds, he had let slip the one thing that may have replenished his fortunes; an insignificant golf club that was now long gone. It was proving difficult for him to come to terms with that realisation and he was not coping too well. After all, he had sold it for less than the price of a fine bottle of vintage wine.

Despite this, he was back on its trail, perhaps. The status quo might yet be reinstated. Of course, he would have to trip up the opposition before they got too far ahead but that, after all, was the master plan. He was reluctantly prepared to pay a handsome price for the clubs' return but he also knew the Erskine's could ill afford to let that happen. They too, he was convinced, would be committed to paying whatever proved necessary to secure the club for themselves, although he was unsure if they intended to actually use it *against* him. Nevertheless, he could neither risk nor afford a straight contest. His cash was all but gone and his credit was no longer attractive to lenders. A poor position to find himself in, particularly when the Erskine's were clearly capable of mounting a considerable challenge. They could easily see him off in any head to head should that ever be allowed to happen, of course, the evidence for which was all around him.

So he knew he had to somehow turn this free for all into a cast iron certainty for himself, and preferably without the Erskine's ever realising he had achieved it.

The two men were now standing in the centre of the drawing room exchanging pleasantries and small talk. Polite enquiries had been made about each others health, which had prompted some commentary on the state of the health service. Lots of idle window gazing had followed, coupled with the inevitable discussion about the poor weather England had been experiencing of late. Awkward pauses frequently punctuated the muted conversation, which prompted plenty of sipping time. Robert Erskine had fully charged a couple of glasses with his finest malt whisky, but the pauses meant the contents were draining quickly. Sensing his wife's continued absence was delaying Charles Pinkney from getting to his point, Robert Erskine introduced her into the conversation in a hope it would initiate a more purposeful discussion.

'My wife will be with us in just a minute or two,' he announced, optimistically. Charles Pinkney said nothing, but instead pressed his glass tight against his lips and peered over its rim at some expensive porcelain adorning the fireplace.

'She's been working in the garden all day. Probably

just changing into something more comfortable,' he added, simply for something to say.

Charles Pinkney was well aware Elizabeth Erskine's attitude would be the difference between his success and failure that evening. It had briefly crossed his mind to take advantage of her absence and conclude matters with her husband instead. Although that notion offered him a line of least resistance, it would also be pointless, he quickly realised. Elizabeth Erskine had the power of veto and to exclude her would simply be inviting trouble. There could be no room for error on his part as he would only get one chance at this, he reminded himself. So, best play it carefully and allow her to participate, he decided. But he would have to be on his toes and anticipate the unexpected. This was no ordinary deal he was attempting to close here, so he needed to be on top form.

Not that Charles Pinkney ever doubted his own abilities. Throughout his business life he had always been an excellent negotiator, capable of closing out just about anything, particularly if it served his purpose more than his employer's. Yet, despite that, he was standing on unfamiliar turf on this occasion and having to work blind into the bargain. If the stakes had not been so high, he was convinced he might have otherwise enjoyed the challenge.

He was pre-occupied with his own thoughts and beginning to find his host both a distraction and a nuisance. Nevertheless he remembered it was his turn to speak. Without giving any proper thought to his choice of words, he simply said the first thing that came into his head.

'Do you play golf Robert?' he enquired with obvious detachment.

'Err…no, I'm not a golfer …,' said Robert Erskine, caught a little off guard by the question, '… Are you by any chance, Charles?' he asked politely in return.

'Err … no … me neither …, never played in my life,' Charles Pinkney replied, feeling somewhat foolish and kicking himself for asking such an awkward and inappropriate question in the first place. Both men knew exactly why they were standing there together, a delicate situation that warranted some discretion. So he was annoyed with himself for having raised the subject of golf at such an inopportune moment. It would simply serve to put Robert Erskine on the defensive and make the whole exchange much more awkward than it otherwise needed to be.

The silences lengthened from that moment, both men trying desperately to avoid eye contact by keeping their heads lowered and examining the bottom of their now empty glasses. Despite the absence of whisky the sipping continued regardless as the tension in the room grew and grew.

Robert Erskine was starting to feel extremely uncomfortable in Charles Pinkney's company. He knew the pair of them had been avoiding the real issue whilst waiting on his wife's arrival. This made him feel a little inadequate and a somewhat superfluous, if truth be known. He felt her delay was quickly shifting from regrettable to inexcusable, and he was convinced she was doing it deliberately. Was she trying to make him suffer for allowing the meeting to happen in the first place, he wondered, or was it simply intended to send a strong message to their guest? It must have been nearly twenty minutes since Charles Pinkney had first entered their house and the man's impatience was becoming evident. The delay, he could see, was now infuriating the man, so he took the decision to kick things off for himself, with or without his wife's participation.

'*Do you have the golf club, Mr. Pinkney?*'

The voice came from behind the two men. Elizabeth Erskine was standing in the doorway on the far side of the room, silhouetted, intentionally perhaps. Charles Pinkney could see she was dressed quite formally.

Her question had caught both men by surprise and there had been no casualness in her tone. It had been a direct question aimed at signalling an uncompromising intent from the outset. Robert Erskine, relieved he was no longer centre stage, seized the opportunity to fade into the background. Charles Pinkney, on the other hand placed his empty glass down on an adjacent table, cleared his throat and stepped marginally forward to greet her.

'Good evening, Mrs. Erskine,' he responded politely, 'or can I call you Elizabeth?' He was thankful she had finally joined them, so at least now he could start engaging his plan.

'You have not answered my question, Mr. Pinkney. So I will ask you again … *do you have the golf club with you?*' She remained static in the doorway.

'For goodness sake, Elizabeth. Charles has something he wants to discuss with us. Please come here and sit down my dear. We've been waiting for you to join us for the last twenty minutes.' Robert Erskine was attempting to avoid any confrontation she may have in mind. 'I'm sure Charles would like us to start discussing his proposal. After all, time's getting on and it's beginning to get dark outside.'

'I have absolutely no intention of entering the same room as Mr. Pinkney until I have my answer.' Her response had been directed at neither man in particular, but the intended message was loud and clear with no chance of misunderstanding. 'And I see you two are getting on like a house on fire … first name terms no less,' she added derisively, before anyone else had a chance to speak.

'Elizabeth, please come through. I'd like us all to sit down and talk,' Charles Pinkney said offering out his hand. He was more than a little concerned, however, over the obvious hostility she was displaying.

She deliberately hesitated and delayed her response, leaving the two men guessing what her next move might be. She waited until Charles Pinkney was left with no option but to lower his outstretched arm.

'Mr. Pinkney,' she eventually said, 'this is not our first encounter, is it?' Her question was intended to be rhetorical. 'Indeed much has happened since our last meeting,' she stated. 'If I recall, you were particularly unpleasant to me on that occasion … isn't that so, Mr. Pinkney?'

She was attempting to place him on the back foot and when she saw his head lower, she suspected she had been momentarily successful. Continuing slowly and deliberately, she pressed home the small advantage she perceived she had been gained.

'I've also been informed by Mr. Bainbridge that you have visited his offices recently and are equally acquainted with the terrible circumstances threatening our livelihoods. It would seem we are all now reluctantly engaged in some ridiculous race to lay our hands on something that will literally mean the difference between peace of mind and certain ruin.'

She was being overly dramatic her husband thought, but he allowed her to carry on uninterrupted.

'And for all I know, you might have already succeeded in re-acquiring that golf club which seems to be regarded now as the *be all and end all*.' She was staring at Charles Pinkney with venomous eyes. He opened his mouth to speak, but she had not yet finished.

'So I will ask you for the third and final time, Mr. Pinkney … do you have that golf club with you?' quickly adding, 'And please don't address me as Elizabeth once again.'

Rocking a little at her blatant hostility, he was reluctant to answer straight away. Instead, he looked pleadingly over towards Robert Erskine who, believing it was signalling his cue to interject, unwittingly sprung to the man's defence, not really understanding why, but nevertheless doing so, much to the obvious surprise of his wife.

'Charles …,' he said hesitantly, before correcting himself, 'I mean Mr. Pinkney, came here empty handed as far as I understand.' All eyes were now upon Robert, so he attempted to assert himself for the first time, 'So please come and sit down Elizabeth.'

Elizabeth Erskine maintained her silence, crossed her arms and contemptuously stood her ground, completely ignoring her husband's request.

Having gained a few moments to gather his thoughts, Charles Pinkney decided it was now time to be assertive himself, particularly if he ever expected to gain the upper hand.

'I noticed you used the expression *re-acquire,* Mrs. Erskine. It's reassuring for me to hear you acknowledge the club had rightfully belonged to me in the first place ... before I foolishly let it slip from my possession that is.'

He watched for some reaction to his deliberate baiting, but none surfaced. 'So, that can mean only one thing, of course ... that my family, my great grandfather, had in fact been the final victor in the contest and that the honours should rightfully go to me.' He tilted his head to one side and with an expression close to smugness and raised his eyebrows, inviting her concession.

If his thinly disguised challenge had thrown her, it did not show. In fact not a flicker crossed her face. Starting a slow advance towards him now, she finally emerged from the shadows of the doorway. Charles Pinkney straightened himself in readiness. Allowing the man just a brief moment to bask in his cleverness, Elizabeth Erskine responded quickly.

'I accept nothing of the kind, Mr. Pinkney.' She deliberately changed direction whilst speaking and wandered over to the window, her back kept constantly turned towards him. She spoke again, this time softly and contemptuously.

'Firstly, none of us have any way of proving that to be the case. Indeed, from what I've since learnt, both these *'Morris Men',* as they seemingly wish to be called, died practically simultaneously.'

'That's just pure speculation on your part,' Charles Pinkney countered.

'Not so, Mr. Pinkney. It's a simple fact quite easily confirmed with a little visit to the local Registrar of Births, Deaths and Marriages,' she patronisingly informed him before turning around. 'So there is every possibility ... would you not agree ... that either could have been victorious on that final day with that club simply awaiting presentation to the winner?' Charles Pinkney screwed up his eyes, quietly analysing the possibility. Elizabeth Erskine continued uninterrupted.

'Secondly, none of us have any way of knowing, nor indeed proving, the matches indeed ever took place. If that were the case, there could be no winners or losers, could there?' She was sneering slightly now. 'These are real possibilities, are they not, Mr. Pinkney?'

He avoided her direct gaze, but was quick to respond.

'It's possible, I'll grant you that,' he said nonchalantly, 'but unlikely we'll ever find out one way or the other.' He was attempting to be conciliatory, but he could not resist the opportunity to be mildly patronising in the process. 'But that's immaterial isn't it? You and I both know that.'

Robert Erskine noted the choice of words, '*you and I*' and was a little indignant that *he* was no longer considered an active participant in the discussions. Charles Pinkney continued.

'But possession, as we keep being told, is nine tenths of the law ... would you not agree, Mrs. Erskine?' After asking his question, he raised his eyebrows for the second time.

'So it would seem, Mr. Pinkney,' she replied moving a little closer as she spoke, 'And that's precisely what all this is about ... isn't it?'

'You're absolutely correct Elizabeth and neither of us can claim to possess the club … can we?' He was feeling a little more confident now over the use of her first name.

'It would appear not,' she replied engaging eye contact once again, apparently ignoring his attempt at over familiarity. He had flagrantly disregarded her earlier request, but she was not inclined to make a scene.

Charles Pinkney defiantly maintained his gaze as it was fast-turning into a battle of wills. He was searching for signs she was beginning to soften, but he could see none. Their meeting had started off confrontationally and appeared to be continuing in the same vein. This was not at all what he had been expecting, nor indeed planning. None of this was helping his cause.

Yet despite the obvious ill feeling towards him, the pair of them had at last agreed on something, offering the prospect of a less hostile dialogue from here on in. His hopes were quickly dashed, however, when Elizabeth Erskine went straight back on the offensive.

'So I take it you have not had your offer accepted through … that auctioneer fellow?'

Charles Pinkney's disappointment at the lack of conciliation in her words must have been evident. Elizabeth Erskine had clearly done her homework. He was moderately impressed and replied amiably.

'It would appear not, and I take from your question, neither have you.' he remarked, 'It's been nearly two weeks I believe … we both know that … and like me, I expect you've never been off the phone trying to find out. I even considered raising my offer I might add … quite significantly in fact, but decided that would be unethical.'

By suggesting me was a man of principle, he hoped this tactic would start paying better dividends.

'Quite so,' she replied dismissively, not at all convinced Charles Pinkney was accustomed to moments of ethical dilemma. Nevertheless, it was hugely encouraging for her to learn that he too had not heard from the auctioneer. Attempting to keep her relief disguised, Elizabeth Erskine altered tack slightly.

'But tell me, Mr. Pinkney ... if you had managed to *re-acquire* the club ... and I use the expression very cautiously now ... but if you had managed to get your hands on it again, by *fair means or foul*, ... and I emphasise those particular words deliberately, just in case you might mistakenly think I'm trying make polite conversation here ... but if you had ... what would your intention now be?'

'I'm sorry, what do you mean?' he replied a little taken aback by the directness of her question.

'No need to apologise, Mr. Pinkney ... not yet at least.' She moved a little nearer to close the gap between them.

' I asked you quite a simple question but you seem to be having some difficulty understanding, so I'll ask you more slowly this time,' Elizabeth said mockingly, '... I asked you what would your intention might now be?'

Not waiting for a reply, she offered some suggestions to help him out.

'I see you are struggling with that,' she said as a matter of fact, 'so I'll help you a little with your choices.' Turning away now and walking slowly around the room, she had cleverly elevated her status to that of principal player.

'Can we perhaps expect you might simply throw it away and spare us all this sufferance? ... I think not. Why would you go to all the trouble to gain it in the first place, if that were so, I ask myself?' The mood in the room was thoughtful.

'Or perhaps you have blackmail in mind, Mr. Pinkney ... prepared to torture us indefinitely whilst you extract your pound of flesh little by little ... each morning my husband and I waking up wondering what fresh demands you might be contemplating,' she speculated. 'There is perhaps a sadistic streak in you Mr. Pinkney that is not necessarily being exhibited here ... Am I not right?'

Her animosity towards him was palpable, but Charles Pinkney assumed it was borne simply out of apprehension. If that were the case, then maybe the hard exterior she was displaying may be more brittle than it appeared. It might well be worth tapping a little harder, he thought to himself.

Whilst he pondered, Elizabeth Erskine made it abundantly clear she had not yet finished with her conjecturing.

'Or perhaps you would simply go running to that Mr. Bainbridge fellow, triumphantly claiming your prize and having us cast onto the pavement without so much as a second thought.' She paused for effect before asking her question. 'Which would it be, Mr. Pinkney?'

The room fell silent. The metaphorical guns had just been primed and cocked ready to fire. But who would be tempted to pull the trigger first?

Charles Pinkney found himself in a weak position, placed on the spot and expected to answer the very question he wished to avoid. The initiative was with

Elizabeth Erskine. The tide needed turning somehow.

He noticed she had casually glanced at her watch shortly after asking her question, so he guessed his audience time may well be fast running out. But how could he quickly gain some ground here, he wondered? If Elizabeth Erskine was expecting something from this conversation, it figured she must be willing to trade. Those were the rules, certainly in business, anyway. You rarely achieve something for nothing in this world, everybody knows that.

But her attitude, so far, had been uncompromising and there had been no obvious signs she was in a trading frame of mind.

He decided it was time to test the strength of her resolve.

'And if I were to ask you the same question, Mrs. Erskine … what would *your* answer be?' He had spoken a little too tentatively for his liking, but was confident his question would shift the initiative his way. How would she like being placed on the spot for a change, he wondered? From her changing expression however, he realised immediately that turning the tables had been foolhardy.

She took her imaginary aim and pulled the imaginary trigger. Her tone hardened instantly.

'My husband told me you had some important business to discuss with us, something that simply couldn't wait I was told, something that demanded our immediate attention. Without my consent, you should know, we stand here face to face and I have to say I am more than a little disappointed. All I've learnt, so far, is that you are a very deceptive man Mr. Pinkney. You have worked your entry into our house on a false pretext it seems, and instead of being open and forthright, I find you to be nothing but evasive. In fact I don't believe you have answered a single question I have put to you this evening.' Her eyes were now blazing, '... So what am I to make of *that*, Mr. Pinkney?'

She paused briefly, which Charles Pinkney mistakenly interpreted as an invitation to speak. He opened his mouth, but was interrupted before he could draw breath.

'Take a good look around you, Mr. Pinkney, because ... believe you me ... this will be the one and only time you ever get to set foot in *this* house, I can assure you of that.' Without waiting on a response, she turned to her husband and issued her orders.

'Robert, please show this gentleman to the door.'

Charles Pinkney's plan was taking a vertical nose dive, so desperate measures were now called for. Robert Erskine was advancing towards him, humiliated it appeared at being instructed to handle the expulsion.

Nothing left for it, he decided. He would have to play his trump card to avoid an undignified, premature exit. Charles Pinkney took one step back to buy just enough time to get his words out.

'For your information, Elizabeth ...,' he said, again skirting danger but with nothing further to lose, '... and you Robert ...,' deliberately now involving his other host, '... it had been my intention this evening to come along and propose a truce between us.'

The statement was left hanging in the air. But it appeared to grab their attention, so he pressed on quickly.

'Yes, I can't deny I have been trailing the club ... seeking its whereabouts just like you ... expressing an interest in buying it back ... again just like you. But believe me when I say this,' he paused to make sure they were paying attention, '... believe me when I say ... it's only because I want to protect myself ... protect what I have ... save it falling into someone else's hands ... *your* hands in fact.'

Robert Erskine was the first to react.

'Elizabeth, did you hear that? Charles thinks just the same way as we do ... There's us thinking he's come here to do us harm, when all the time ... he just wants to protect himself ... just like we do.' Without waiting for his wife's endorsement of his sentiments, Robert Erskine was striding forward to shake the man's hand. 'We're so sorry Charles ... please forgive our earlier rudeness?'

Charles Pinkney could not believe his good fortune. The bait had been well and truly swallowed, certainly by Robert Erskine at least, and from the man's expression, it was already digested. Elizabeth Erskine, on the other hand, was clearly still chewing, trying it out for taste, it seemed. She was not responding in the same manner he noted, seemingly more interested in boring holes into her husband's forehead with her now piercing eyes. Perhaps he needed to lay it on a bit thicker.

'Like you, I could only speculate what your intentions might have been. Without knowing this, I had no choice but to get the club back. Getting it back meant I would've neutralised the threat ... nothing more than that ... no sinister intentions from me I can assure you.'

Laid on just a little too thick perhaps, he scolded

himself. Nevertheless he was delighted with the new direction he had established, and especially with Robert Erskine's unforced confession. If only he had been able to deal exclusively with this man, it would have been ever so much easier, he concluded. The Erskine's had, quite rightly he conceded, always perceived him as a threat. And that would certainly have accounted for Elizabeth Erskine's hostility from the outset. But their own intentions had clearly been benign and in learning that, he had been gifted the one advantage he needed to now close things out in his favour. Whilst his hosts were pre-occupied exchanging sideways looks, he seized the opportunity to continue talking uninterrupted.

'Turns out we're all of a like mind ... that's marvellous isn't it? ... we'll all sleep much easier tonight ...no enemies here it seems ... just friends ... who'd have thought? ... eh Elizabeth? ... eh... Robert?'

Elizabeth Erskine, irritated by the over-familiarity that was being expressed in unwarranted abundance, once more turned her full attention back to their 'guest'.

'Firstly, Mr. Pinkney, my husband was perhaps a little too hasty in offering *our* apologies.' She threw her husband at scornful look. 'Secondly your sentiments are admirable. But we all know there is a world of difference between words and actions. You surprise me somewhat and I concede I may possibly have misjudged you ...,' she noticed Charles Pinkney beginning to grin, '... but we all know that despite the best intentions, temptation often prevails,' she added, needing to deflate the man slightly.

She straightened herself then said, 'I have no reason to doubt your self control, Mr. Pinkney ... but our dependence on that alone, is perhaps a little too much for you to expect of us.'

She was not prepared to trust him without further safeguards and Charles Pinkney was becoming aware of this. He was beginning to greatly admire this woman. She was shrewd and sceptical, wishing much more from him than had so far been offered.

So, more he would provide. He began edging towards her, a movement that was so discrete it went practically unnoticed.

'Well if the risk is in the possession, then why don't we all agree, here and now, to withdraw from the chase together … seize the moment and agree to *let sleeping dogs lie* … figuratively speaking of course.'

He was within a couple of feet of her now, holding out his hand, inviting the agreement.

The gesture took Elizabeth Erskine by surprise. He noticed she was looking down at his hand and suspected his proposal was being given serious consideration.

It was all now perfectly teed up for him.

'I'm only going to do this once, Elizabeth,' he said emphatically, 'If I leave without your handshake, then there's simply no chance of an end to all of this … it'll run and run until one of us loses everything. Are you prepared to take that gamble?' His ultimatum was clearly having an effect, with her own hand edging out ever so slightly.

She was now in a quandary and looked towards her husband for help. She knew they both wanted this situation resolved ever so badly. And neither of them could be regarded as risk takers. They were both panic stricken at the prospect of losing everything and had discussed endlessly what they might do in that event. The thought was beyond contemplation and chilled their souls whenever the prospect was considered. So, if an olive branch is now being offered, then it might be worth grasping with both hands.

Robert Erskine, recognising the dilemma his wife was facing, took the initiative with a reassuring and discrete nod of the head. But the gesture had not gone unnoticed by Charles Pinkney, and believing his offer was close to acceptance, he held his nerve and kept his arm invitingly outstretched.

'Very well, Mr. Pinkney,' Elizabeth Erskine finally said, 'I'll shake your hand on that ... and you have *my* word.'

Her agreement had been secured with a firm handshake and Charles Pinkney could not help himself. A broad smile covered his face, a smile that was not reciprocated.

'And you have *mine*,' he replied somewhat shiftily.

Elizabeth Erskine held onto his hand just long enough to perform the act, before releasing her grip with impolite haste. She swept past her husband and straight out the room without uttering a word.

Charles Pinkney, now feeling very content with himself, and having no need to linger unnecessarily, took the opportunity to make his excuses. The last thing he needed was a prolonged departure, affording his host's an opportunity to change their minds.

'Robert, we've done a brave thing here this evening, all of us ... I can tell you. I for one am very much relieved ... but it's getting late, so I think it's best I'm on my way.' He quickly turned towards the door, Robert Erskine by his side as he advanced.

'I'm so pleased we've all agreed to this. Let sleeping dogs lie …and that's precisely what I meant,' he added as they neared the front door.

'No need to wave me off Robert,' he said sardonically, '…and pass my best wishes onto your wife for me, will you?' He grabbed the door handle and turned it impatiently.

'Good evening to you Robert.'

And with that Charles Pinkney was gone in a flash, the front door having slammed firmly shut in his wake.

Robert Erskine stood alone in the hallway, somewhat bemused at the turn of events. Everything had happened so quickly in the end. One minute they were at each others throats, the next an impromptu reconciliation. It was almost too much to comprehend and he was not entirely sure he understood how it had come about.

But could it be true? Had they all just agreed to call a halt to the chase for that golf club? Did this mean the matter was now at an end? He was not entirely convinced it was, but nevertheless he had to talk to his wife. She had seemed quite distressed as she had ran out the room a few moments earlier and he felt the need to not only comfort her, but also to find out what she thought of the whole affair.

His wife was not easy to find however, with no sign of her throughout the house, upstairs or downstairs. She was not in any of the obvious places, so he started calling out her name. There was no reply. Becoming a little anxious about her well-being, he decided to look outside, eventually finding her standing on the veranda, just off from the dining room. She was looking out across the moon lit gardens, arms folded and motionless. He rushed over and placed his arm round her. She responded by titling her head in order to touch his arm with her cheek, then turning towards her husband and taking his hand, she spoke softly.

'Tell me I did the right thing just then Robert.'

Robert Erskine squeezed his wife's hand. 'Of course you did my dear. What choice did we have?' She smiled, his words an obvious comfort to her, but he sensed it was simply masking her true feelings.

'I'm not sure Robert, and that's the problem. I'm not sure I did anything right back there.'

'It wasn't just you my dear, it was both of us. We did it together, just like we said we would. I'd have done exactly the same.' He was trying to reassure but it appeared to be having little or no effect. She was looking helplessly into his eyes.

'I know you would have Robert, but that's not the point.' She took a moment or two to gather her thoughts then said, 'I feel we conceded something needlessly just then, a concession that was perhaps unnecessary at this moment. And, I feel I've just painted us into a corner without really understanding why I did it … and I'm not all that sure I needed to either.' Her eyes were betraying a great sadness. 'But he was there in front of me and I was being put on the spot. I felt I had no choice but to accept his offer … I was frightened Robert, I was frightened I might have thrown away our one and only chance to end it all if I'd refused him … do you understand what I'm saying Robert?'

'Elizabeth, please? Of course I do … and I'll say it again … you did the right thing … I'd have done exactly the same.' He was not convinced she was accepting any of it.

'Look, he wouldn't have come over here if he hadn't been thinking along the same lines as us, I'm sure of that,' he said. 'Couldn't you see it in his face … he's just as worried about losing everything as we are.' Robert was looking for some acknowledgement from his wife, but she was lost in her own thoughts. He carried on regardless, trying to sound as upbeat as possible.

'It was really quite bold of him to come over here and see us like this. We don't know much about him, but he does seem to be a reasonable sort of fellow … don't you agree?' There was still no reaction coming from his wife, although a slight frown was developing.

'Anyway, from what I can make out, the chase is off now … we don't need to worry about that retched golf club appearing any more and forcing us to hand over the keys … do we?' Still no reaction. He was beginning to think she was beyond counselling, but carried on nonetheless.

'In fact, I'm pleased he came over to see us … at least we can all sleep much easier now.' He deliberately halted at that point, giving his wife no option but to say something in return.

'*Let sleeping dogs lie*,' she finally said, more to herself than her husband however.

'I'm sorry, my dear?'

'Let sleeping dogs lie. That's what he'd said, hadn't he?'

'That's right my dear and a jolly sensible thing too, if you ask me.'

'But that's the problem, Robert. That's precisely what's bothering me.'

'What do you mean, my love?'

She thought a little more before answering. 'Dogs and lying … interesting choice of words wouldn't you say?' She turned to look at her husband closely.

'So I can't help wondering if he's just uttered a harmless platitude … or whether he's just cryptically announced a statement of intent ….'

The suggestion got Robert Erskine thinking but being, on occasions, an over-trusting character, he decided his wife was simply being overly theatrical.

'I think you're being at bit too dramatic my dear,' he said. However, the possibility was clearly starting to ferment in his mind.

'Am I, Robert?' she asked, 'I'm not so sure.' She was clearly beginning to think the worst. 'It worries me Robert, because I've just given my word … something that might not mean much to others, but it's important to me … I never go back on my word.'

'Of course you don't, Elizabeth. You never would.'

'So that's why I think I've painted us into that corner. If he goes back on his word … and for all we know he might … I'm not sure that I could do the same.' She gripped his hand harder.

177

'I think I've placed us in a weaker position, Robert. I can't help but think I've just thrown all our options out the window, for no reason at all ....,' she said despondently, '.... and that's the bit I'm feeling really sick about.'

Robert Erskine was feeling much less upbeat now as he dwelt on his wife's words. Could she be right? Had they been duped perhaps? He knew that his wife could be frustratingly proper at times, to the point where she would rather be disadvantaged than act dishonourably. She was a gentle person in the nicest sense of the word and he was ever so proud of her for that. But it also made her vulnerable and he could see in her eyes that she was feeling she may have been exploited. She looked resigned to a fate that was now beyond her control, morally obligated to a man she hardly knew, a virtual stranger who could so easily turn from friend to foe in a whim. *She* had given her word and he knew that would be forever binding. There would be nothing in this world that could possibly persuade her go back on that, no matter how catastrophic the consequences might knowingly be. The outcome of their meeting that evening, far from offering peace of mind, had only served to add to their worries, at least in his wife's mind, it seemed.

But, it was beginning to dawn on Robert that perhaps he was under no such obligation. After all, it had not been his hand the man had shaken that evening, something Charles Pinkney had perhaps overlooked in his haste to depart. Indeed, the man had deliberately excluded him from participating, and *his* own agreement had not been sought. Robert had been aware of this throughout, and whilst it had caused him considerable embarrassment at the time, he was now quite content to have been a mere spectator. He was not an unobservant man and he had not been completely oblivious to the possibility that Charles Pinkney may be untrustworthy. So, it had crossed his mind early on that evening, that maybe his withdrawal from the discussions might be a sound tactical move.

Nevertheless he now had a dilemma. Robert could see his wife's obvious distress, but was very reluctant to share his current thoughts with her. She would only make him promise something foolhardy after all, binding him to that same moral obligation she had now committed. Desperately wanting to reassure his wife that all may not be quite as bleak as she imagined, he had to settle instead for a simple act of comfort, an arm placed lovingly round her shoulders.

It was going to be a difficult time for him, keeping his counsel all to himself. He looked upwards to the stars and thoughtfully started working on their insurance policy … just in case holding one in reserve might prove beneficial one day.

Chapter 10

Tom Hudson was back at work, but only in body. His spirit and mind were very much elsewhere.

The holiday was now well and truly over and the inevitable tread mill beckoned him once more, or more precisely, the offices of a small time advertising company. For the most part, that day had been spent gazing blankly into his monitor. His dream of independent trading was beginning to look a distinct possibility, and as such, warranted its elevation in status from harmless distraction to full blown fixation. Being now incapable of thinking about anything other, it was going to be a difficult time at work over the next few weeks, with his long standing aspiration to make the leap from *Editor's Assistant* to *Assistant Editor* having now dissipated completely. Planning what now seemed his overdue escape from permanent employment, had become his number one priority. But first he had to be convinced his prospective venture could be turned into something viable.

Consequently, every spare minute of that first day back at work had been spent browsing the internet or reading the *Antiques Gazette*, seeking out auctions, fairs or car boot sales. In no time at all, he had peppered his diary with entries, practically one for each day if time permitted. The seemingly unlimited opportunities to seek out antique golf clubs was making him nervous, as the probability it could just about work out began to materialise. The buyer's were already in place and from what he could gather, the prospective supply chain might even have the potential to satisfy the demand. '*Imagine that,*' he thought, just about as close to the perfect economic model as any budding entrepreneur could ever hope for.

It would mean getting up with the larks, of course, and heading out in all weathers, but he had absolutely no doubt that would appeal to him. The clubs were definitely out there waiting to be found, he had proved that in the past, so it simply boiled down to effort and leg work on his part. The impetus was certainly there and, evidently, so were the rewards. A perfect match in anybody's book, he decided.

But did he have the courage he kept asking himself? That was a difficult one for him. Could he make a living out of it, he wondered? He was very keen to convince himself he could, but even keener to convince himself he should. Having been back from holiday only two days, Tom was once again drifting headlong into that other world of his ... the one which provided him with so much comfort ... but the very same world which also frightened the life out of his entrusting wife.

Sitting at his desk that afternoon, unable to stir up any enthusiasm to add the finishing touches to an article applauding the virtues of purchasing '*your new sofa from Bob's New Sofa World*', and seeking something more interesting to occupy his mind, Tom pulled a piece of folded paper from his shirt pocket. Written, in his own hand, was the telephone number of MacIntyre McBride, sporting auctioneers. A message had been left on the answering machine whilst away, inviting him to call back as soon as it was convenient. The caller had been Stuart MacIntyre himself, advising he had information of interest, and wished to pass it on. Presuming it was no more than advice concerning some upcoming auction, Tom had been unable to raise his interest sufficient to phone before then. But the day had been dragging its heels so what better time to return the courtesy call. MacIntyre's had to be applauded, he thought to himself, at least they made efforts to keep their preferred clients informed. Considering he might now be regarded as a preferred client, he was secretly proud of his apparent acceptance into the 'inner circle', but at the same time not in the least bit surprised given how much money he had spent with them recently.

Finances, however, had taken a bit of a beating in recent weeks making it hard for him to envisage getting any sales momentum up and going. His new Belgian acquaintance, Philippe, might just have to wait a while for his first consignment of clubs, but there was still Bertoise to consider. Stuart MacIntyre must have some connoisseur clubs in his next sale. Why else would he be bothering to call, he asked himself?

Having been pulled up once already that day, for missing an important deadline, Tom was keen to be much more discreet with his personal business. Despite this, when a quiet moment presented itself, he quickly grabbed his mobile phone and headed for the relative privacy of the office foyer. He placed his call, whilst keeping a watchful look out for any approach by his boss.

The phone was answered promptly and after taking his name, the receptionist at MacIntyre McBride politely placed him on hold and checked to see if Mr. MacIntyre was available to take his call. Within a few seconds, he was speaking directly to the principal auctioneer.

'Ah, Mr. Hudson, I've been expecting your call. How are you?' the auctioneer enquired.

'Kind of you to ask. I'm very well thank you. Just back from my holidays, so feeling a little down in the mouth if you know what I mean … back to work and all that.'

'I know, it's such a nuisance,' the auctioneer said making polite conversation, 'Thought you must have been away because I left a message on your answering machine quite some time ago if I recall. Anyway, I have some good news that might cheer you up.'

Whilst the auctioneer had been conducting the introductions, Tom had pulled a notebook and pen from his pocket and found himself a vacant seat in the foyer. Expecting a list of clubs to be reeled off shortly, he flipped open the notebook and found a clean page. He was grateful Stuart MacIntyre had seen fit to call him personally, but felt a bit of a fraud having only made one purchase of any real significance to date. But that alone must have been enough to promote him into the top division, so he was eager to sound professional, business like and responsive.

'It's very good of you to take the trouble to call me, Mr. MacIntyre. It's very much appreciated.' He was now ready to start writing. 'I take it you have some clubs that might interest me. When exactly is the next auction?'

'We'll be holding it two weeks on Thursday. But that's not the reason I'm calling, Mr. Hudson, although you're right, there'll be clubs in the auction that I'm sure will interest you. I'll arrange to have a catalogue sent to your home address.'

He was a little taken aback, but thanked Stuart MacIntyre nonetheless for his generosity. Auctioneers are not renowned for being liberal with their free offers, so to get a courtesy catalogue was a triumph in itself. Definitely now part of the in-crowd, he decided.

'No, I wanted to inform you of some unusual third

party interest in one of the items you purchased at our last auction; the Tom Morris long-nose putter in fact. If you'll just bear with me just a second I'll pull out the lot number.' There was a short pause during which time Tom's curiosity began to grow.

'Yes here it is … *lot number 195* … originating from a collectors estate, if I recall correctly,' continued the auctioneer.

'I'm sorry?' Tom had been caught momentarily off guard.

'Rather unusually,' the auctioneer continued, 'I've taken a couple of calls following the auction, almost straight after if I'm not mistaken. Both callers seemed somewhat keen to acquire the putter you had purchased, Mr. Hudson. Naturally I told them it had been sold, but I didn't say to whom of course.'

'Of course not.' He was listening intently now. 'Please call me Tom, by the way.'

'Curiously, one of the callers was linked to the estate from which it originated. But I have to say I found his manner to be a little objectionable. The other was a lady, a little more respectful but still quite abrupt. I have to confess I was a little annoyed with their attitudes, they were quite demanding you see, although I would say the lady did sound a bit more desperate than the gentleman.' Stuart MacIntyre stopped momentarily, presumably to allow some digestion of his words.

'In any event,' he continued, somewhat keen to get everything off his chest in the one go, 'I was less than enthusiastic about engaging in long conversations with them. Having said all that, they have been pestering me ever since. I've stonewalled them of course, but I'm now quite relieved I've made contact with you at long last.'

Tom Hudson was pleasantly surprised with the announcement, yet eager to find out much more about these mysterious callers. He pressed the auctioneer for more. Stuart MacIntyre was seemingly very willing to off-load his information, wholesale and speedily.

'Yes, it's safe to say they are both very keen to purchase the club from you …Tom … and asked if I could pass their interest directly onto you, which I am now doing of course. I have to say, they both appear to be willing to offer you considerably more than our records show you paid in the first instance. I have their telephone numbers if you wish to contact them yourself. I did say I wasn't prepared to act as a broker in all of this. What you decide to do is entirely up to you of course, Mr. Hudson, and I have to confess I'm really quite relieved to have passed the problem over to you, if you know what I mean?.'

There was quite a lot of information there to absorb in a single go, but Tom did pick up on the *considerably more* bit of the conversation without too much difficulty.

'Thank you very much indeed, Mr. MacIntyre. It was very kind of you to take these calls on my behalf and pass the information onto me. You've taken me by surprise I have to admit,' he confessed, desperately wanting to go straight to the 'precisely how much?' question. But that would have appeared impolite, after all, Stuart MacIntyre's only obligation had been to transmit the interest. So to come straight out and ask him *how much* would appear somewhat cheeky, especially as the responsibility to find out, now rested firmly with himself. All that being said, inquisitiveness got the better of Tom and he asked his question nonetheless.

'Did they, ...,' he was treading carefully now, '... did they by any chance happen to mention how much they might be prepared to pay, Mr. MacIntyre?' Getting his words out into the open was a relief, but he cringed in readiness for the reply.

However the question came as no surprise to Stuart MacIntyre and far from being irritated or outraged at the impudence, he was more than pleased for the invitation to oblige the caller. Somewhat businesslike, Stuart MacIntyre obligingly divulged all he knew without any hesitation.

'I know for certain one of the parties, the women I believe, offered something in the region of four thousand five hundred pounds and asked this to be made known to you. The gentleman, it seemed, was even prepared to improve on that offer further, and has emphasised this repeatedly ever since ... It must mean something to them both ... certainly their interest is considerably more than the club's worth. Not bad if you can get it, wouldn't you agree Tom?'

Tom's mouth had dropped wide open and without any regard for those around him, started pacing quickly up and down the foyer. A young office girl had to swerve to avoid contact and practically lost hold of the tray she was carrying. Cups full of steaming coffee slid across the surface and but for some comic manoeuvring on her part, the whole lot would have tumbled to the floor. She looked at him in astonishment.

'Sorry, Mr. MacIntyre ... could you just hold on a second or two whilst I think about all of this.' Tom removed the phone from next to his ear and checked to see if the girl was alright. Affronted, she turned her back on him and disappeared quickly down the corridor. Feeling a need to be overly excessive with his apologies, he chased the now fast disappearing girl, managing to overtake just before she reached some double doors. Standing inanely like some clown, he held the door open which she passed through without comment, throwing him a sideways glance that left him feeling even more ridiculous.

But at least he had bought himself some thinking time. Tom raised the phone to his mouth once again.

'Sorry about that, Mr. MacIntyre. Are you still there?'

'Yes, I am Tom,' the auctioneer patiently replied, 'Would you like me to give you their telephone numbers?'

'You've taken me by surprise, Mr. MacIntyre. I'm a little stunned to say the least. I can't imagine why they want it so badly. It doesn't seem to be anything special to me.'

'Me neither,' came the auctioneers considered reply, 'I'm sure we would have noticed something for ourselves when we catalogued the club. Still, you should never look a gift horse in the mouth,' he said encouragingly. 'I take it you still have the putter?' he enquired.

'Yes, it's at home.' Tom spotted an opportunity was presenting itself to show off a little and reinforce his growing 'stature' within the trade. For the next minute or two he spoke of his recent expedition to the south of France, the contacts he had made and the likelihood that he would be making significant purchases in the future. All very interesting the auctioneer had pleasantly acknowledged.

When finally Tom stopped, he waited for some indication the auctioneer had been impressed. A silence enveloped the conversation, a silence which grew and grew to embarrassing proportions. Stuart MacIntyre was clearly indicating a little impatience, believing nothing more could be achieved from encouraging the recitals. Realising the auctioneer had so far gained nothing in return for his efforts, Tom took a moment to consider his options. Perhaps in response to a feeling of modest obligation, he was prompted to make a spur of the moment offer.

'I have an idea which may benefit us all,' he proudly announced.

'Oh yes, Tom. And what might that be?' The auctioneer's attention had now been recaptured.

'I know you're a busy man, Mr. MacIntyre, so let me quickly explain. I'm thinking on the hoof here, so bear with me. I very much appreciate you acting in this way and it was good of you to let me know about these offers. I also appreciate that you had no real obligation to do this and the fact that you've taken the trouble to advise me makes me want to compensate you in some small way.'

The auctioneer was a little offended with what appeared to be a prospective offer of payment for his troubles. 'Not necessary, I can assure you, Mr. Hudson,' he said dryly, 'All in a day's work.'

'Please call me Tom.' Failing to recognise his words had created an awkward moment, he pressed on obliviously. 'I'm thinking I might like to do some business with you, Mr. MacIntyre. It could also get me out of a knotty situation here. I have to confess I'd feel rather uncomfortable about phoning these people and getting into that whole horse-trading thing. So embarrassing, if you know what I mean?'

'I know what you mean, some people are cut out for that sort of thing ... others aren't,' came the auctioneers immediate reply anticipating a more conventional commission heading his way. 'Please, call me Stuart.'

At last, he thought, first name terms with the auctioneer. He punched the air in celebration, narrowly missing the same young office girl who was attempting to sneak past him for a second time. Ducking instinctively, her approach had clearly been a cautious one. She widened her berth whilst passing, then picked up her pace before Tom had any chance to offer his apologies yet again. Quickly returning to the matter in hand, he carried on with his conversation.

'Well, Stuart, here's the deal,' he said with new familiarity, 'If it's not too late, we'll put the club back into auction and see what happens. You contact the interested parties and let them know it's on offer again and with a fair wind, we'll get a good price. If they want it that badly, then we might even get a little more than the four and a half grand.' He paused to punch the air once more, this time checking out his vicinity well beforehand.

'We'll protect it with a reserve of course,' Tom continued, 'say two and a half thousand. That way I get the sale, you get your commissions and the buyer gets his club ...or her club so too speak.' Proud of his impromptu plan, he asked, 'How does that sound, Stuart?'

'I have to admit the thought had crossed my mind, but I couldn't have prompted you of course,' the auctioneer said with some satisfaction, 'Yes that sounds perfectly equitable … and the beauty of it all is no one need get their hands dirty.'

'Your right Stuart, it suits everybody doesn't it?' Entry into the 'inner circle' was clearly beginning to pay dividends.

'And thank you, Tom, for recognising I've assisted you in some small way.'

'No need to thank me, Stuart. It's the least I could do. I'll bring the club round to your office in the next day or two. I suppose it's too late to catalogue now, but I'm not that bothered really. We only need our two callers to turn up, don't we?'

'You're right Tom, it's too late for the catalogue, but I'm issuing an addendum anyway, so we'll include it within that,' the auctioneer offered helpfully, 'It'll get a mention on the website also.'

'That'll be great, Stuart. Many thanks.'

'And no need to worry about bringing the club over just right now, we've got the description and photographs from last time, so we can use them. Just make sure it's here for the pre-sale viewings, say the Tuesday before the sale.'

'No problem, it'll be there in good time.'

'Anyway Tom, it's been nice doing business with you. I'll make those telephone calls early this afternoon. All the best … and bye for now.'

'Thank you Stuart. Looking forward to seeing you at the auction in a couple of weeks. Thanks again for all your help … cheerio.'

It had got a little too sycophantic towards the end, Tom

decided, but at least the arrangements had been confirmed and everyone was content.

At around the same time, in an office across town, Maurice Bainbridge was clarifying his requirements with a young man in a sharp suit. A definite triumph of image over substance the solicitor was realising.

'Well, this is about the extent of it, although, I've no doubt one or two others might appear out of the woodwork over the next day or so.' His hand was passing over four piles of antiquated books neatly stacked on his desk, all uniform in size and appearance, about twenty in all. The young man standing before him nodded very attentively but without passing comment.

'I have already discussed my requirements with your colleague over the phone,' the solicitor said as matter of fact, 'What was his name again?'

'Jason,' the young man responded with somewhat disengaged interest.

'Yes, Jason that's it. Very helpful chap was Jason. Seemed to understand exactly what I'm looking for.' Maurice Bainbridge was not quite sure why he felt the need to prolong the conversation, other than an underlying need to reassure himself he had made the right selection.

'Yeah, he's been with the company the longest, getting on for two years now. He knows his stuff and I'm learning a quite a lot from working with him.' The sharp suit was saying the words but was also looking blankly into one corner. 'He reckons we can have all these catalogued onto disk in next to no time.' He noticed the solicitor was scrutinising his every word. 'We've done this sort of thing loads of times before, sir.'

'Very good!'

Maurice Bainbridge was looking at the young man over the top of his glasses, somewhat unconvinced by the reassurances he had just been offered. 'Anyway, I've discussed my requirements with Jason and he's quite confident you can have the whole thing done and dusted in about ten days. Is that right?'

The young man consulted his clipboard.

'Yeah that's right. Say's here ten days. That's what it says. The whole thing copied onto disk, everything referenced like you wanted sir…' he checked his clipboard again, '…everything indexed with that coding you mentioned to Jason.' The young man straightened himself at that point and attempted, somewhat unconvincingly, to look businesslike, 'All you need to do is type in a few words, something that you're looking for, press the button and hey presto … it'll search the whole lot and throw up everything your looking for, if you know what I mean. Is that okay sir?'

The solicitor felt a little dismayed with the young man's apparent over-simplification, but nevertheless he tentatively offered his agreement.

'Just perfect … exactly what I'm looking for.'

With fixed smiles they stood there looking at each other, neither choosing to speak first. The young man was making no move to gather the books from the desk and this confused the solicitor. Realising the young man required prompting of some kind, he asked a question.

'Have you brought something to put them in by any chance?'

'Yes, I have.'

'That's good.'

No movement followed, so the solicitor took the initiative.

'Well, if you don't mind, I'm quite busy.'

The young man finally got the message and with a flurry, pulled his mobile phone out from his pocket, pressed a couple of keys and raised it to his ear. The phone was clearly ringing for longer than the young man had expected, so he supplemented his wait with gestures, the meaning of which were completely lost on the solicitor. Finally, the young man spoke into the phone.

'Hi Jeff it's me. How close did yer get parked?' He winked at the solicitor for some reason, 'That's a shame mate, can't wait to see your face when you see all these. Anyway, get a move on. They're ready here to pick up. Bring that extra sack out the back of the van will yer mate?'

Maurice Bainbridge was stunned as he considered the prospect of something disastrous happening to this grandfather's unique legacy. His reliance on them had grown considerable over the last few weeks and he was now beginning to seriously doubt the wisdom of his choice, secretly regretting his decision to offer out the commission in the first place.

But theirs had been the most attractive proposition. So anxious was he to have the diaries converted into a database, that time had been the deciding factor in his choice of company. With the exception of this particular company, all other bidders had quoted something between three and six months to complete the task, engaging a small army of technicians in the process. The costs other sought were considerable. Thankfully, the company this young man was representing had promised completion in a fraction of the time and for a fraction of the cost. Seemingly, they had uniquely developed a process capable of scanning handwritten notes and no doubt had peppered their sales pitch with exaggerated claims. But a brief demonstration and testimonies from satisfied customers had sealed the deal for them.

Waiting for their safe return would be an anxious few days for Maurice Bainbridge, but well worth it, he hoped. The database, if it turned out as expected, would enable him to literally travel back in time to an era when values differed, to a time when actions in law and their interpretations often bordered on the ridiculous. There, gathered in front of him on his desk, was a reservoir of knowledge and expertise that was irreplaceable, a collection of diaries which could so easily have been lost forever in some careless clearance many years earlier.

His grandfather had apparently been meticulous in his recordings and Maurice Bainbridge could only speculate as to the mouth-watering treasures and treats that awaited his scrutiny. His chosen profession, he had recently contemplated, clearly had a different perspective on things back in those pre-war days. Frivolous litigations were discouraged, with efforts being concentrated more on the maintenance of standing and status. There appeared to be far less inclination to sue for trivial accidents or omissions with much less emphasis on financial gain at another's expense. In Edward Bainbridge's day, certainty of success was not always a pre-requisite for a solicitor's involvement, which probably accounted for some of the more off-beat cases that had found their way into the courts. Actions to preserve personal integrity and save face were more commonplace it seemed, Maurice Bainbridge had noted, designed to punish dishonourable conduct, to publicly humiliate or to extract simple apologies. The whole world gave the impression of being more ordered and structured back then, he had thought, a much more equitable and charming period in which to have lived. Much could be learnt from those diaries, he had concluded, and he was getting quite excited at the prospect of it all.

Elsewhere, Charles Pinkney was entertaining a few 'associates' at his home.

'Gentlemen. Thank you for accepting my invitation at such short notice,' he said by way of introduction, 'I have some serious business to discuss with you.' His announcement was addressed to them all but, courteous though it had been, was really only intended for one person in particular.

The assembled group before him, three in all, were clearly of mixed pedigree. The first, an older gentleman, appeared well travelled given the depth of his leathery suntan. He was smartly dressed and had adorned himself, quite deliberately Charles Pinkney deduced, with gold trimmings of every description. He had positioned himself to sit directly in front of Charles Pinkney.

The second 'gentleman' was standing expressionless to the older man's right and was clearly employed for his stature and menacing demeanour. He was dressed much more casually, presumably for increased mobility, Charles Pinkney had imagined. The third, a smaller man with darting eyes dressed in a smart suit, was sitting to the left practically off-stage, a closed brief case resting on his lap.

The older man replied on behalf of the group. 'Mr. Pinkney, it's our pleasure ... How can we help you?

Charles Pinkney was considering taking a few risks.

Being reasonably confident he had hoodwinked the Erskine's into withdrawing from the chase, he needed now to secure some finances, just in case the putter should miraculously re-surface. Assuming that happened, he may only get one opportunity to get his hands on it, so had to be ready with cash in hand, something he was unable to do at that particular moment. Despite the persistence of his calls to the auction house, none had yet paid dividends, but here may be good reason for that. He maintained the belief that his bait would soon attract some interest, therefore a meeting, such as this, had now become essential. If he could secure a loan of some sort, by whatever means, he could place himself in a position to substantially increase his previous offer for that elusive club, an increase anyone would be foolhardy to disregard.

Arranging a conventional loan would be problematic and time-consuming. A serious credit problem was hampering his ability to move on, a situation made even worse with the Inland Revenue growing increasingly intolerant over his inability to pay the inheritance tax which was now considerably overdue. And just to add to his problems the banks had eventually got wind and seeing his risk rating climb up the scale, had, not unexpectedly, withdrawn their previous support. Otherwise dependable lenders were now disregarding his enquiries and his ability to secure short term finance was proving impossible by conventional means. Mortgaging his property had been something he had considered recently and might normally have offered a suitable solution, but some anomaly concerning the title deeds needed resolving first. Although, not a problem in itself, the fixing of such a discrepancy would be somewhat protracted he had been advised, effectively shutting off that particular avenue to him.

The gentlemen that were now settled comfortably in his home, did not represent any established or respected institution, but they did at least offer some prospect of guaranteeing his ability to purchase the golf club at very short notice. It was not his preferred choice and he was extremely apprehensive about it all, but once the club was secured, all his debts could be cleared in full. There would even be a considerable surplus in the bank he had calculated, enough to start enjoying life once again, free from the stresses and burden of pending bankruptcy.

'Well this is the situation Mr. ..?'

'*Smith*'

'Mr. *Smith* … yes, I see. Well, Mr. Smith, I'll come straight to the point. I'm sure you and your colleagues here have other important business today, so I'll keep it as brief as possible.' Charles Pinkney was nervous and it was all very apparent. His eagerness to conclude the transaction swiftly had absolutely nothing to do with any concern over the gentlemen's busy schedule. The sooner he could get them out his of house, the better it would be.

'I need to borrow twenty thousand pounds, and I'm told you might be able to help me.' He impressed himself with his directness. Twenty thousand was considerably more than he needed, but the extra cash would permit him some recreation.

'Yes, we do have other business, Mr Pinkney, and I'm grateful you've come straight to the point, so I'll come straight to the point as well.' The older man nodded to the other man seated off to his left. In an instant, the brief case lid flipped open revealing a vast amount of cash, all crisp notes and all neatly bundled.

'There's fifty thousand pounds in that case, Mr. Pinkney,' the man called Smith casually announced, 'Would you like it all?'

Charles Pinkney was mesmerised with the sight of so much cash and a little taken aback with the generosity of the offer. Tempting as it was, he had no need to borrow that amount. It would have been foolhardy and he knew it.

'Twenty will be more than enough,' he replied, delighted with the effortlessness of the negotiations. The older man looked him up and down before replying.

'Mr. Pinkney, twenty five grand is a nicer, rounder figure would you not agree?' he said firmly and deliberately.

Charles Pinkney thought about this for a while and began to think his celebrations were perhaps a little premature. Twenty five was far more than he would need, but it seemed he had no choice. *'Take it or leave it',* was the distinct impression he was forming, judging by Mr. Smith's body language.

'Then twenty five it is, Mr. Smith.' What would an extra five thousand matter, he asked himself? After all, he expected to be very rich, very shortly.

'That's good, Mr. Pinkney, you've made a wise choice … but are you sure that's going to be enough, though?' the older man, enquired, not missing a trick.

'As I said, Mr. Smith, twenty five should be just fine.'

'Very well, Mr. Pinkney … don't ever say I didn't offer you the chance,' Mr. Smith responded, somewhat menacingly. 'And for how long would you be wanting to borrow the twenty five thousand pounds, Mr. Pinkney?'

'About two months…,' Charles Pinkney declared '…three at the most.'

The older man was looking at him strangely and the larger man to his right was now smiling.

'But Mr. Pinkney, that's not in the slightest bit attractive to me.'

'How do you mean?' Charles Pinkney looked a little puzzled, '… It might be possible to pay it back sooner … I just can't tell at this stage.'

The larger man was now laughing out loud.

'You misunderstand me, Mr. Pinkney, and please excuse the impoliteness of my colleague here.' Mr. Smith gave the larger man a quick look, causing him to quickly change his expression and take one step back. Mr. Smith continued, the whole atmosphere in the room having become much more intimidating.

'If all my customers settled their accounts so quickly, then I'd go out of business. Do you know understand what I'm saying, Mr. Pinkney.'

'I think I'm beginning to get your drift,' he replied cautiously.

'Good, I think we understand each other perfectly well, so here are my terms, Mr. Pinkney.' He waited until Charles Pinkney had given him his undivided attention.

'You take twenty five grand from me right now. All you need to do is sign a few pieces of paper my friend is holding over there in his hand ...,' he gestured to the man with the brief case, '...and then my other friend here....' he pointed to the larger man, '...*he* will come and see you in about six months and you will give him forty thousand in cash. Nice and simple. Would you not agree, Mr. Pinkney?'

It was extortion, pure and simple. The interest rate on that had to be phenomenal. But he was clean out of options. When it came down to it, he was only risking fifteen thousand pounds, the difference between the loan and the repayment, a large sum of money but small beer compared to the returns he could make from it. The 'loan' would give him the means to settle things once and for all. He was unlikely to ever have such an advantage over the Erskine's ever again. He had no choice but to accept it.

'I take it the papers you just mentioned are a contract ... and one not necessarily negotiable.' Charles Pinkney, despite his personality failings was, nonetheless, a worldly man.

'That's right, Mr. Pinkney. Nice and clear ... no misunderstandings ... just a few things we need to know about you and just a few things you can expect from us, just in case you should find it difficult to keep us informed of your whereabouts ... if you know what I mean?'.

The papers were handed over and Charles Pinkney swallowed hard before reading. The conditions were worse than he had expected and the consequences over default were clear to see. No room had been left for any misunderstanding.

'You are a shrewd businessman, Mr. Smith. Your terms are quite explicit … I don't think anyone could get hold of the wrong end of the stick with these,' he said with a touch of sarcasm in his voice as he waved the papers aloft.

'You're absolutely right, Mr. Pinkney. I have to protect my interests,' said the older man, 'But the way I look at it … you get your money no questions asked and I get all the assurances I need to help me sleep easy at night.'

Charles Pinkney nodded and permitted himself a wry smile.

'Now Mr. Pinkney, it's time for you to decide.' Mr. Smith announced as he examined his Rolex.

Charles Pinkney granted himself a moment for a final contemplation.

'Very well, Mr. Smith … hand me that pen.'

Chapter 11

'I'll only be a couple of hours, Robert. Is there anything you need whilst I'm out?' Elizabeth Erskine enquired as she prepared to leave the house, 'Are you alright for cigars?'

'I'm fine, my dear. You just go and enjoy yourself. No need to rush back.'

'Okay, my love, I won't be long,' she confirmed, '... and phone me if you think of anything. I promise not to spend all our money.'

And with that, Elizabeth Erskine climbed into her Mercedes, gave her husband a quick wave and then sped off down the dusty driveway, towards the gatehouse. He watched from the front door as his wife's car reached the exit and after pausing to indicate, it turned sharply left onto the main road and out of sight.

Since shortly after her meeting with Bainbridge & Bainbridge she had become a recluse, withdrawing completely and not wishing to commit to anything long term. And their meeting with Charles Pinkney had not helped improve matters either. It was plain to Robert that his wife had become worse still for a short while afterwards, having given her promise and not at all confident the man could be trusted. Yet despite all this, he had managed to calm her fears, not with words or actions but with something much more intangible, a reassuring presence which had inexplicably lifted her gloom.

Thankfully within the last few days, he had noticed her

outlook on life had turned decidedly more positive, even to the point where and she had felt sufficiently invigorated to organise a trip into town with a couple of her friends. He was pleased she was finally making an effort to cheer herself up.

Hearing the telephone start to ring, and being a little distance away, Robert turned on his heels and dashed inside to grab the receiver. He managed to reach it in time.

'Hello, Robert Erskine speaking,' he said, breathlessly.

'Mr. Erskine, good morning to you, my name's Peter Harrison,' a young man's voice confidently announced on the other end of the line, 'and I'm calling from MacIntyre McBride, the sporting auctioneers. You spoke to my colleague Stuart MacIntyre a few weeks ago I understand.'

The introduction had been short and precise and Robert Erskine realised immediately the significance of the call. A little surprised and a little apprehensive, he gathered his wits together.

'Good morning to you too, Mr. Harrison,' he drew in a deep breath then continued, 'I take it your call is about that golf club …err… the putter, I mean … I'm so sorry.'

'That's right Mr. Erskine, Stuart MacIntyre asked me to call you. He would have made the call himself, but he's getting ready for his vacation. He's going to be away for three weeks or thereabout, so I'm left in charge,' the caller declared proudly. Being eager to hear the words, Robert Erskine crossed his fingers and asked the obvious question.

'Well, Mr. Harrison, perhaps you might put me out of my misery. Is it good news or bad?'

'A bit of each actually.' The caller's voice was upbeat.

'Which would you like first?'

Robert Erskine instantly became irritated. With such a life-changing issue at stake and so much riding on the outcome, he was in no mood for the whole good news, bad news thing despite having encouraged it in the first place. His nerves were already shot to pieces and the caller was only responding to his invitation to tease him. Not the young man's fault of course. How could he possibly be aware of the true significance of the call?

'Not wishing to be rude, Mr. Harrison, but if you'd just get to the point, I'd very much appreciate that,' he pleaded.

'Yes of course,' but insisting on playing the game nevertheless, he went on to say, 'The good news, Mr. Erskine, is that the Tom Morris putter has turned up at long last. It's taken us a little while, but we've managed to contact the buyer and I'm pleased to inform you, he is willing to sell.'

Robert Erskine's heart was in his mouth. ... 'willing to sell' ... did that mean sell it to him? He hurried the caller to elaborate further.

'Go on please,' he urged.

'That's the good news, Mr. Erskine. But I take it you'll want the bad news as well?' he enquired innocently. If the caller had been within arms length, he would have been throttled at that point. With fortitude of character however, Robert Erskine was able to control himself sufficiently to utter a passive reply.

'Yes please, Mr. Harrison ... If you don't mind, that is?'

'Well, the bad news I'm afraid, is there's someone else

who is seriously interested in the putter also.'

'*Tell me something I don't know,*' Robert thought to himself before responding to the statement. 'I'm aware of that … so what does that mean exactly?' he asked, beginning now to fear the worst.

'It means, Mr. Erskine, that the seller has been placed in a quandary. He knows there's some serious interest in his putter, but he doesn't wish to enter into any negotiations with either of you … he would find it a little too awkward and embarrassing, so I'm told.' The young man paused to allow his words time to sink in. 'Basically, he doesn't want to barter.'

'But you said earlier he wanted to sell,' Robert Erskine responded hastily and a little confused.

'And that's why I'm calling. The seller has decided to place the putter up for auction once again.'

'Up for auction! What exactly does that mean?' Robert belatedly realised his question would sound somewhat absurd, especially to an auctioneer. The caller mulled over the question for a brief moment, then replied.

'What happens is this. … Bids are invited for an item which we call *'a lot'* … If there is a reserve on a particular *lot*, the auctioneer usually starts the bidding just below the …' He was stopped in his tracks.

'Forgive me please, but I think I phrased that badly,' Robert Erskine interrupted, '… I think I know how an auction works … what I meant to ask,' he said impatiently, 'was whether the other interested party had been told yet.'

'No not yet, I'll be making that particular call next. Can I take it you're still interested sir?'

Robert Erskine was not sure what to say and was uncertain how to react to the news. He decided to seek out more information.

'Could you tell me when the auction is likely to be held, Mr. Harrison?' he asked the caller politely.

'Certainly, Mr. Erskine. It's on the tenth of August starting at eleven in the morning, at Treddington Town Hall, where we normally hold our larger auctions,' he said before adding, as if from script, '…with viewing from nine on the morning of the auction and between ten and four the day before. We'll send you a catalogue which has all the details inside including a location map. The Tom Morris putter will not be in the catalogue itself, but you'll find it on the addendum sheets, *Lot 127a* I believe. Did I say, I'll be handling the auction myself that day.'

'No, I don't believe you did,' Robert replied politely, yet somewhat detached in thought. He was still unsure what to say at that point and was reluctant to disclose anything without first giving it some serious thought. He could easily weaken his position if he were not careful. There was every possibility anything he said may be passed onto Charles Pinkney, albeit inadvertently, but something, nonetheless, that might encourage the man to negotiate a private arrangement with the seller through the auction house, despite all the earlier promises that had been given.

Robert now had a real dilemma on his hands as he conjured with all sorts of permutations inside his head. Should he express a lack of interest? He was not sure that would be wise, it might grant Charles Pinkney a free reign. On the other hand, he could not risk Pinkney thinking for one moment that he was contemplating bidding for the club, especially now a fragile truce of sorts had been established between them. To declare an interest might panic the man into a reaction, sparking off the whole contest once more, placing everything into turmoil once again.

Now was definitely not the time to reveal anything, he finally decided. He still needed to weigh up his options, so there was no benefit in disclosing anything at this point. Robert desperately needed to digest privately the information he had just received, perhaps not even telling his wife about the call. No, he would keep his cards close to his chest for the time being, he decided. Let Charles Pinkney do all the speculating, just for now.

'Mr. Harrison, thank you very much. I'll look forward to receiving the catalogue. Do you have my address?'

After a further brief exchange, the phone was back down on its receiver, yet Robert Erskine was unsure how the take the news. Standing silently alone in his hallway, he had a sense of real isolation which was seriously alarming him. Should he share it with his wife? Dare he share it with his wife? His thoughts danced between the two, failing to settle on either.

Moving without conscious thought, he found himself standing in the drawing room facing the gilt framed *Pipeshank* print. Standing there motionless, simply staring at the picture, studying its every detail more closely than ever before, he wondered why he had been drawn to it.

It looked no different, just the same as always, just an ordinary picture hanging on the wall lost amongst all the others. Having seen it a thousand times and given it little or no regard, it had always been of no consequence, at least not until very recently, that is. Having been part of the furnishings requiring no special attention, and having practically disregarded it for his entire life, Robert would have found difficulty in describing the print, if ever quizzed. Having never taken the trouble to study the subject matter before, and having no cause to do so, he now found himself looking inexplicably deeper into the image than ever before.

Stepping a little closer, he began to experience a strange affinity, one never felt previously. Robert knew little about golf and cared even less, but the images were rousing something within. A casual look showed no more than a mere game of golf between two anonymous gentlemen. And that had certainly been his only impression before now. But this closer study was prompting thoughts that it may be depicting something much more significant. Those two golfers, in the very act of swinging their clubs, were perhaps playing for stakes greater than just the celebration of winning. The expressions etched on the faces of the spectators alone gave credence to the notion. But much more clearly, it was being transmitted by the two principle players. One golfer was waiting his turn, looking conceited and confident, as if knowing the outcome was already assured; a foregone conclusion perhaps. The other golfer was grimacing with determination, contorted in stature as he attempts to force a few extra feet onto his tee shot. A successful outcome seemed to be of much more importance for that particular individual, the concentration on his face much more intense.

Robert Erskine could not take his eyes away from that second gentleman, recognising a strange familiarity of some sorts. It was not so much the golfer's appearance; there was certainly no resemblance there; but it seemed associated more with his predicament, his circumstances, his perseverance and endurance. Was the man symbolic in some way, perhaps? He was unsure, but it was, nevertheless, difficult to dismiss the possibility out of hand. The print was definitely encouraging him to examine his own character for some reason, to reflect on his own ability confront adversity. Was the print representative of their present struggle? He was beginning to believe it was. For the first time ever he was looking with purpose at the picture.

Standing there alone and silent, he interrogated his thoughts and scrutinised his own personality. Mesmerised by the image hanging before him, he dwelt on his current circumstances and felt utterly dejected. Quite inexplicably, and very suddenly, a peculiar sensation hi-jacked his entire being without the aid of conscious thought. Robert's instincts sharpened in an instance. He felt somehow different, spiritually supported and strengthened from deep within. Robert was no longer doubtful which course he should now embark on.

In the office of MacIntyre McBride, Peter Harrison finally placed his own phone back down onto the receiver and then drew a line through a further two of the twenty or so actions he had listed in his notebook. A cup of coffee was placed on his desk, so what better time to sit back and relax for a few minutes and reflect on his day so far.

Responsibility for organising the upcoming auction had been entrusted to him, a young man in his mid twenties, nicely spoken and a knowledgeable sporting expert, particularly of cricket and football memorabilia. The auction house employed many specialists across the sporting spectrum, each supporting their colleagues, enabling Stuart MacIntyre, a renowned expert on golf himself, to provide a full and professional service to his many and varied domestic and international clients. Peter Harrison had been nominated to act as auctioneer for the next sale for several reasons, but mainly because it was going to be a general sporting sale. The emphasis would be on cricket, football, rugby and tennis memorabilia, in all, around seven hundred lots plus a hundred or so golfing items, mainly those remaining unsold from the previous auction. The fact that Stuart MacIntyre himself was going to be out the country for an extended vacation made the selection of auctioneer a straight-forward one, but in any event he had felt it was time the young man made his mark with the gavel.

Reclining in his chair, Peter Harrison lifted his notebook and scrolled once more down his list of tasks. Most had been accomplished without any real complication. Catalogues had been dispatched, payment made to Stratford Council for the hire of the hall, porters had been selected, stock transfer arranged, an account reminder issued to one particular client who appeared to have developed amnesia, collection itinerary completed and sent out to the couriers. He was beginning to enjoy the responsibility. There was more to organising an auction than he had appreciated, but the true gratification would come shortly with his chance to stand on the podium, gavel in hand, conducting proceedings all on his very own.

But he still had a difficult call to make that morning and he was prevaricating. It was to a dealer in town, whose goods had been deposited for the sale in a damaged condition, rending them worthless in effect. He strongly suspected, however, they were in that state when packaged for collection. Not all dealers were completely trustworthy, he was discovering, and this particular gentleman had developed a bit of a reputation for being awkward in the extreme. Nevertheless, it needed confronting and it would be his next task.

For now though, he just needed some time to himself. His last call had been a little challenging to say the least, to a Mr. Pinkney in fact. Objectionable fellow the young auctioneer had concluded. That Tom Morris putter was turning out to be more trouble than it was worth, he had decided.

The earlier call to Mr. Erskine had been both courteous and polite, just as one would have expected. But Mr. Pinkney's reaction had been unwarranted and unnecessary he thought. After all, he had only been doing his job and that was limited strictly to advising this potential customer of the clubs' availability in the upcoming auction. He had followed through with a polite enquiry into Mr. Pinkney's continued interest, which had generated a less than ethical proposition. What had the man been thinking? The auctioneer's duties did not extend to acting as broker between buyer and seller. Peter Harrison was quite perturbed by the audacity of the man, especially the inappropriate questions regarding the possible intentions of Mr. Erskine, the other interested party.

But the novice auctioneer had stood his ground resolutely when challenged, refusing to entertain any offer of direct negotiations with his seller, even though it appeared Mr. Pinkney was intimating a considerable sum could be placed on the table and palms could perhaps be *crossed with silver* in return for special treatment.

No, he had dealt with it very professionally he reassured to himself. The abuse he endured, after his refusal to facilitate an offer, would not affect him. He had carried out his responsibility to the seller, compliant with the expressed wishes it would seem, and the principal buyers had been informed of both the time and the place. He had acted professionally. What happened after that was not his concern. Mr. Pinkney would have to take his chances along with the rest of the world and express his willingness to buy in the time-honoured fashion. No special favours, no dubiety over the outcome. Highest bidder wins. It was as simple as that.

Peter Harrison drained the coffee from his cup and lifted the receiver. He hoped his next call, to the belligerent dealer, would be much less confrontational.

Chapter 12

With all his holidays now exhausted for the year, coupled with a realisation that any further days off work would place him on a collision course with his line manager, Tom Hudson resigned himself to the fact that he would not be attending MacIntyre's' auction that day. He had no choice in the matter. If he wanted to keep his job, he would need to be at his desk that morning and be clearly seen to be putting in some effort. Tom's recent behaviour had attracted some unwanted attention from his superiors and had been the topic of much debate. Only his exemplary record was now protecting his hide. Having sailed pretty close to the wind for the last week or so, he had, in no time at all, frittered away all his previously hard earned credits.

The Tom Morris putter had been safely delivered to the auction house, registered and appraised a few days earlier. Peter Harrison had taken charge of it personally, and after a brief exchange noting the clients' wishes, a fixed reserve of two thousand five hundred pounds had been agreed. The auctioneer confirmed the club was being featured on their website, previous photographs being utilised, and already several enquiries had homed in from overseas. At least two proxy bidders had expressed interest and several telephone lines were being reserved for the benefit of absent bidders. Peter Harrison had been very upbeat and was confident some serious bidding would happen on the day. He had also made a particular point of confirming he had made contact with the two principle customers neither of whom had seemingly withdrawn their interest. All in all, a good day was to be expected, the young auctioneer had predicted.

All the more reason why Tom now felt utterly frustrated. There he was, shackled to his desk, destined to miss all the excitement, miss all the bidding and denied the chance to witness all the thrill of the occasion. For him, it was a huge disappointment and for his office colleagues it was a sufferance they had to endure. The message radiating out was loud and clear for all; *'Approach with caution!'*

Thankfully, he had managed, at least, to view the auction sale the previous evening and had left commission bids with one of the porters. He might not be there in person, but at least Tom would still be in with a chance of purchasing something. For a small consideration, the senior porter had agreed to act on Tom's behalf. The man had been handed a list of wants along with the fixed bidding limits. Interest was focused mainly on the cheaper clubs as he needed bulk on this occasion, to satisfy the needs of the Belgian Philippe. From bitter experience, mainly as a result of being stung at some of the less reputable auction houses, he believed that commission bids, left on the books, only served to encourage some less scrupulous auctioneers to start the bidding unreasonably high. Tom had made a study this over several months and considered the practice to be commonplace amongst the fly by night outfits. He had no reason to suspect such manipulation would ever be entertained at MacIntyre's. They were, after all, proud of their professional standards. Nevertheless, it had now become habitual for him to use the porters when unable to attend in person. In return, the porters usually tipped a wink should a few sleepers find their way into catalogues. The system suited everyone.

Settling down to his work, the clock on the wall became a constant distraction.

Robert Erskine had completed some final adjustments to his attire. Tweed suit, three piece naturally, brown brogues, white shirt with cuff-links, silk handkerchief and regimental tie; the standard uniform of the landed gentry and the old boy network; tried and tested over many generations; guaranteed to open most doors. But on this day, it was being worn as a masquerade and not to generate a favourable impression. For his wife had been told a little white lie; an unscheduled meeting at the Rotary Club requiring his urgent attendance. And the suit was on parade by way of affirmation.

Yet Robert Erskine was scheming to head in a quite different direction altogether, to a rendezvous that would necessitate the wearing of neither suit nor tie. He had been deceitful, but for good reason he had decided. It was crucial his wife should have no prior knowledge of his intended trip to MacIntyre's that morning. If she had become aware of his plans, then no doubt his attendance would have been prohibited. Elizabeth Erskine had given her word and there could be no retraction, even to the extent of demanding that others respect her wishes. So, if she had asked him to change his plans, then he would have had no option but to have complied.

Deliberately, therefore, he had chosen to keep her in the dark, a decision that had troubled him greatly ever since receiving the telephone notification. He had never told his wife lies, at any point throughout their marriage, so it sickened him to do so now. It was weighing heavily on his conscience.

However, Robert's subterfuge had had been successfully deployed, so far at least. The catalogue's arrival had been anticipated and to ensure his wife remained oblivious, he had taken to loitering by the front door each morning to intercept the post as it arrived. Odd behaviour he had realised, but fortunately for him, it had not triggered any awkward questions.

A smooth departure from the house was all that remained. Robert instinctively knew he had to be at the auction that morning, to safeguard their interests, come what may. So his plans must not falter at the last minute. Pinkney could still prove himself to be the rat Robert Erskine suspected he was, and if that should happen, he needed to be on hand to give the man a run for his money. If it came down to a contest on the day, then his wife would clearly learn of his deceptions afterwards and the consequences would need to be faced. Not a particularly welcoming prospect, he reflected, but at least he would have the chance to plea bargain before she passed sentence on him. Safeguarding of their futures was sure to be taken into account, he had reassuringly convinced himself. On the other hand, if Pinkney remained a man true to his word, then no harm would come of it and no-one need be any the wiser. The golf club would be gone forever and good riddance for sure. At least he would get to witness the event, which in turn would quell his own fears.

Standing at the front door with his car keys in hand, he had shouted his goodbyes to his Elizabeth before closing the door behind him. *'Damned if I do … damned if I don't',* had been in his mind as the door slammed shut. Hesitating briefly, he had felt strangely inspired as though a guiding hand was ushering him onwards. The moment had been brief, but it had been sufficient to spur him on. Jumping eagerly into his car, Robert had raced down the long drive towards the exit, more determined now than ever to be present at the auction.

His journey to Treddington Town Hall was taking Robert Erskine slowly past the Blue Bell Inn, the regular Rotary Club haunt. As he cruised past, he noticed the doors were shut firmly with no signs of activity at all, inside or out. A small notice had been fixed to the door and straining to read it at distance, he learnt the reason; *'Temporarily Closed for Decoration'*. Under normal circumstances, this would have caused no hardship to the resourceful Rotarians who, knowing plenty of other equally hospitable establishments close by, would simply have switched to somewhere comparable.

But these were no normal circumstances and no meeting had been planned requiring a change of location. Robert was shocked as he read the notice. It brought home how easily a small lie can quickly manifest itself into something quite unmanageable. He had been lucky this time, acutely aware of how that minor oversight on his part might well have led to his undoing that evening. Annoyingly his storyline would need to altered, becoming unduly elaborate now, just in case his wife was aware, or became aware, that the Blue Bell was closed for business. He could so easily have fallen headlong into a sticky situation by naively praising the hospitality of the establishment, only to find himself buried in the process. He cursed the owner of the Blue Bell Inn in passing. It only served to complicate matters even further.

Arriving at the Town Hall, somewhat flustered by now, Robert discovered there were no empty parking spaces available. Having expected to simply arrive and leave his car in the municipal car park around the corner, his misfortunes were now multiplying. The streets were thronged with vehicles of all descriptions and he realised, albeit belatedly, that he should have set off much earlier that morning. He was going to miss the start of the auction, a prospect that was making him frantic as he raced round the streets in search of that elusive parking slot. Robert was unsure how quickly the auctioneer would be getting through the catalogue, but if he delayed much longer he ran the risk of missing the main event altogether.

Up ahead, a car was indicating its departure, so Robert pulled up abruptly in the middle of the narrow street to let it out. Within seconds, a parade of cars and vans had begun falling into line behind him and it only took a few more seconds for one impatient wag at the rear to start sounding his horn, albeit from a safe distance. Meanwhile, the driver up ahead was making pitiful attempts to extract himself from the gap. To the casual observer, the reason was obvious; insufficient lock being applied to the steering wheel. Nevertheless, with the patience of a saint, the driver continued to replicate his mistakes, relentlessly it seemed. Forward then reverse, forward then reverse and so on and so forth, each time advancing his exit by only an inch or two.

All the while the queue behind was growing ever larger and the barrage of horns ever greater. Robert Erskine was losing precious time and those farcical manoeuvres ahead were not helping his composure in the slightest. Almost at the point of jumping out of his own vehicle to pilot the man through his difficulty, the car ahead finally broke free and was off down the road, leaving Robert with the now unenviable task of slotting into the gap whilst under close scrutiny himself. It took three attempts, all the while horns impatiently resounding. So when he finally pulled up the handbrake, his stress levels were off the scale.

But, he had no time to waste and a quick check of his watch confirmed the first twenty minutes, at least, had been missed. He crossed his fingers and prayed for a delayed start. Thankfully, his item was down the list a little, so perhaps his late arrival might not be that crucial, he convinced himself. Despite his thin optimism, Robert nonetheless needed to reassure himself with a bit of mental arithmetic as he rounded the corner. Racing up the Town Hall steps and following the directions towards the rear of the building, he calculated that at a rate of two minutes per 'lot', that would mean they would have got to 'Lot 10' or thereabouts. Plenty of time to spare.

Passing a group of people queuing at a make shift reception desk, Robert entered a cavernous room at a canter. A hammer was heard falling and a muffled something being shouted out from across the room, but at that moment he was more interested in finding a good place to sit or a free space to stand.

'Lot 37 ... an early twentieth century fish-tailed tennis racket with original mahogany press, both by Spalding. What can we say for this?' came forth the auctioneers request, 'So, who'll give me fifty?'

'Lot 37', Robert Erskine noted. It had been a closer call than he had imagined, but it still left plenty of time to get settled down before his golf club came up for grabs, so to speak. But the priority now was finding a vantage point that would provide the panoramic view he needed, somewhere to get a good look at all the bidders. His interest was not so much in the items for sale, more the people wanting to buy them. The auction was crowded and that surprised him, but it did at least explain his difficulty in parking. Robert was somewhat bemused at the level of interest in sporting memorabilia as there must have been over two hundred people in the room, he estimated. But *'each to his own'*, he silently conceded.

Very soon he found himself being squeezed from all directions as more and more people piled into the auction room. This prompted Robert to start skirting the outer perimeter to safeguard his hard earned view from being obscured completely. Edging sideways step by step, threading his way through the crowds, he scrutinised closely all those around him. Occasionally a small gap would appear ahead which prompted yet another dive forward, a further chance to scan yet more faces, some close hand, some from a distance. Those people seated, were easy to see, remaining in place as a regular feature. He was able to quickly reassure himself Charles Pinkney was not amongst the seated, at least. But the ones standing were a different proposition altogether. At best, only a quarter of the assembled crowd could be observed at any one time, which might not have been so bad had they remained static, with one circuit sufficient to account for them all. But they were in a state of fluid change, moving in and out of view in waves as the auction sale progressed. And this was hampering his task.

Constantly on the move, much to the annoyance of those around him, Robert took the opportunity to observe some auction protocol. He was a novice and had much to learn in a very short time. Bidding behaviour was the first thing he noticed, each person adopting a differing style. Most were staring down into their catalogues, presumably waiting on their items to come round. Or perhaps they were sellers, attending purely out of curiosity. Others occupied their time by marking down each and every sale results; a pointless exercise Robert thought. Those bidding, however, were the most attentive, raising heads and hoisting arms aloft to attract the auctioneer's attention. The whole process was fascinating him and for a short while he became distracted by waving arms, catalogues being fanned, heads nodding and eyebrows lifting. It seemed there were no hard and fast rules being applied, leaving it entirely up to the individual to choose a method that worked for them. Being noticed, regardless of how it was achieved, was the only thing that really counted. The auction had meanwhile moved swiftly on.

'Lot 57 next ... a box of six Dunlop tennis balls ... from around 1925 ... and in good condition these,' came a further announcement from the auctioneer's rostrum. 'I have fifteen, who'll give me twenty?' There was a brief pause before the auctioneer became animated once again.

'Twenty in the corner ...,' the auctioneer announced enthusiastically pointing over heads towards the far corner of the room.

Robert Erskine glanced down at his opened catalogue. The sale was rushing through the tennis items at a pace and he realised his golf club would be coming up quicker than expected. His heart picked up speed and the apprehension intensified within. Turning a single page was all that was needed to trace the start of the golf section. Scanning down the many entries caused him to suffer a moment of high anxiety. The Tom Morris putter was not listed. A frenzied thumb-through his catalogue, led to a folded piece of paper falling from the middle. Picking it up from the floor and almost gaining a wayward knee to his temple in the process, he remembered the club was listed on the addendum sheet and not in the catalogue itself. Unfolding the sheet, catalogue tucked under his armpit, he scanned down the list and found what he was looking for, *Lot 127a* with an estimate of fifteen to eighteen hundred pounds.

It was lost on him, he had to confess. How could a golf club possibly be worth anything like that amount of money, he wondered? But what did he know? Clearly it was, judging by the prices being paid that morning. But the Morris putter was no ordinary collectable. Not that anyone else would realise that, Robert thought to himself. Whilst he would happily pay considerably more than the estimate, should that prove necessary of course, he was bewildered why anyone else would be willing to pay hundreds of pounds for what, after all, was just an old golf club.

Thinking about the estimate reminded Robert that it had already crossed his mind a million times to bid for the golf club regardless of Charles Pinkney's presence there or not. He was still undecided, suspecting it may be regarded as unethical if he should. But something unquantifiable was causing him disquiet. It came down to a matter of trust, he supposed. So knowing little of the man was making an informed decision impossible. It would be left therefore until nearer the time, a time that was approaching all too fast for Robert's liking.

The auction had developed quite a momentum by now and Robert was beginning to feel somewhat intimidated by it all. A steady procession of new faces had spilled into the sale room and space was fast becoming a scarce commodity. He knew his desire to account for everyone was now a hopeless task from where he stood, he simply could not see well enough. So he set off on a slow traverse around the room once again, accidentally stepping on toes in the process and frequently having to apologise.

'Lot 68 is a Wimbledon Ladies Final programme from 1931, signed by one of the finalists ... a little indistinct ... so where can we start this?' the auctioneer asked out loud, 'Who's got thirty for me? ... twenty five then? ... a twenty pound note, surely?' There seemed a reluctance to bid on this item for some reason, the 'experts' suspicious about its authenticity, perhaps.

Eventually an arm was raised from the middle of the seated group, 'Twenty I have ... thank you Mr. Guthrie.'

The lot number did not slip Robert's notice as he poured himself strategically into position just to the right of the auctioneer. There was a bit more space where he now stood and he was grateful for some respite from the hurly burly, although he soon realised he was outside the auctioneers' field of vision. A few others had made a similar bee-line to enjoy the positions' relative tranquillity. A much better view across the room from here, he decided, although a touch more elevation would be just perfect. He surveyed his surroundings and noticed some steps directly behind him. The auctioneers' rostrum had been erected directly in front of a stage and these steps led up to the wings. Robert edged his way to the first tread then started his gradual backwards ascent. His view immediately improved although Robert was becoming ever more conspicuous the higher he rose. He felt the risk was well worth taking, however.

Robert's eyesight had never been perfect, a hereditary defect that rarely bothered him. He had always managed to get by. But looking out over the assembled throng, he soon realised its deficiency was now an impediment. Whereas the faces of those to the front half of the room where in adequate focus and he could easily account for them all, those to the rear were much less defined. Several could, quite possibly, be taken to be Charles Pinkney from this range. He was not feeling in the slightest bit assured that his positioning was ideal.

Without warning his mobile phone burst into life with a synthesised rendition Wagner's *'Ride of the Valkyries'*. Being so close to the auctioneer, the very obvious distraction caused a momentary pause in proceedings. Throwing himself down the steps to escape the limelight, whilst at the same time trying to silence the offending article, he noticed the call was from his wife. To his surprise, she was calling from her mobile, but his priority at that precise moment was to kill the call instead of answering it. In any event, he had reservations about speaking to her anyway, just in case he was placed on the spot and had to compound his lies even further. He would have plenty of time, later that day, to think of a plausible excuse for ignoring her call.

Recovering his composure and reclaiming his earlier place next to the rostrum, Robert was mindful of the new focus that was now bearing down upon him. When Peter Harrison lent over and asked him, in a voice designed to be overheard by all, if it was alright for the auction to continue, he was embarrassed beyond measure. Instead of doing the sensible thing and first observing, keeping a low profile and gaining that all important familiarity, he had chosen to spend his time lunging clumsily from pillar to post, drawing attention to himself and generally working himself up into an unnecessary state of alarm. He was in uncharted territory and was feeling over exposed and vulnerable. And time was slipping by much quicker than he realised.

Peter Harrison, centre stage and flanked by his assistant, was conducting proceedings with confidence and professionalism. He was being polite always, humorous on occasions and firm when required. The turnout was better than expected and those who were aware of the strenuous efforts made by the young auctioneer to ensure his first auction was a success, were in praise of his diligent preparations over the days leading up to the event. He was riding high on a crest of a wave and, judging by the smile on his face, the young auctioneer was clearly loving every minute of it. So far at least.

'So we come to Lot 87, ladies and gentlemen, a decorative early twentieth century ...,' he paused to read, then continued, '... biscuit tin depicting tennis players on a village green ... with elaborate artwork ... and I have sixty to start. Do I see sixty five?' he enquired.

'*A biscuit tin?*' Robert Erskine pondered, '*How can a biscuit tin be worth over sixty pounds? The world's gone mad,*' he decided. He was feeling a little irritable by this time which probably accounted much for his incredulity. It was also necessary to retreat back into the shadows, so he commenced his slow shuffle round the room once again, this time aiming for a central point towards the back, close to the entrance. The bidding continued whilst he painstakingly worked his way into position.

'Ladies and gentlemen, if you please?' Peter Harrison said, trying deliberately to attract everyone's attention. 'I have an apology to announce.'

All heads lifted.

'Regrettably, Lots 91 to 115 will have to be withdrawn

from the sale.'

The room erupted into a frenzy of murmurings with several people huddling together in consultation.

'I appreciate the annoyance this creates, ladies and gentlemen,' said the auctioneer calmly, 'but I have no choice in the matter. This is quite unprecedented I have to say, but we've just received a call from the seller.' His words were not pacifying a small group just off to his left who were now becoming more and more agitated and vocal in their objections.

'I can assure you we've made every effort to persuade the seller otherwise, but he was insistent. I apologise to those of you who have come today especially for those particular lots and it will be of small comfort to you, I'm sure, to learn we shall not be accepting any more entries from that particular gentleman in the future.'

Some heckling erupted and tempers became quite frayed but Peter Harrison continued, seemingly unperturbed.

'I can assure you that had we received prior notice then clearly we would have advised you much sooner, ladies and gentlemen. Again, I can only apologise for the inconvenience this may be causing you.' His tone reflected the annoyance he felt at being placed in such an invidious position

With growing impatience over the commotion which was now well established, the young auctioneer waited a few moments in the hope that things might settle down. But emotions were running a little too high for his liking, so he elected to call for a short recess.

'Could I have your attention again please?' Peter Harrison asked with authority beyond his years, 'That brings us coincidently to the end of the tennis items ladies and gentlemen and as we are now running a little ahead of time, we shall have a short intermission of about ten minutes or so ... before we progress onto the golfing items. Thank you.' And with that Peter Harrison detached himself from his microphone, got up and left the rostrum, accompanied by his assistant, leaving in his trail a barrage of taunts from an embittered small group off to his left.

The announcement triggered a wholesale movement within the room with tennis enthusiasts pouring themselves out and golf enthusiasts pushing their way in. With Robert being so close now to the entrance, he soon found himself caught up in the ebb and flow of bodies. His natural reluctance to assert himself meant he was ungraciously swept out of the auction room and back into the foyer, meaning he had to wait patiently for the ebb to subside before being capable of returning back into the main hall. Reassuringly for him however, the exodus now meant the room was much more peaceful and much less crowded. He let out a prolonged sigh to help control his ever-rising blood pressure. The brief respite was most welcome and he began to relax a little.

'Hello Robert,' came an unexpected voice from behind him, one that he instantly recognised and one that made him quake with trepidation. He turned around slowly to face the speaker, feeling the growing tension grip his body.

'Hello Elizabeth,' he spluttered ashen faced, 'But how?'

'How indeed?' she responded, 'Certainly not from *you* ... that's for sure.'

'But how?' he repeated, unable to formulate anything more constructive.

'A phone call my dear … this morning in fact … just after you'd left for your so called Rotary meeting,' Elizabeth said with the sarcasm laid on thick.

'From whom?' he asked ignorantly and more than a little stunned at his wife's unwelcome presence.

Breaking through the two word threshold was clearly proving a problem for him Elizabeth noted, before offering her husband an explanation.

'From the good people you have chosen to spend your time with this morning,' she pronounced, her arm sweeping round the room in an exaggerated gesture, 'Seems they have inadvertently dropped you in it … my darling.'

'But how?' he repeated once again. Robert felt his knees starting to buckle.

'They phoned this morning,' she explained with raised eyebrows, '… and asked for you … but I took a message instead.' Her eyes fixed on his. 'Well, it was actually more an enquiry than a message, I should say. They wanted to know if you would be coming to the auction or whether you'd prefer to leave something they called a commission bid?' Her head tilted to one side after she spoke.

Robert Erskine fidgeted on the spot and tried hard to avoid the eye contact his wife was beckoning, preferring instead to look around the room to buy some thinking time. Finally, he managed to muster a few pitiful words together.

'My dear, please forgive me. I never wanted you to find out like this,' he pleaded, 'but it was something I felt I just had to do. I can't explain why, but I've had a premonition of some sort, something that's compelling me to be here today. It sounds ridiculous, but it feels inherent somehow, something that's been dormant within, something that's now giving me direction of some sort.'

He paused for a few moments then added, 'I'm explaining this badly aren't I? You're not impressed ... I can tell.'

Elizabeth Erskine stood silent and motionless in front of her husband except for her darting eyes scanning his face. She was waiting for him to look at her, she needed to look into his eyes, she needed to interrogate the sincerity of his words, and there was only one way that could be achieved.

Robert quickly realised exactly what his wife was seeking and wasted no time in reciprocating, allowing her gaze to fix firmly on his. Her silent request had been granted and they held the pose briefly. Although it represented only a fleeting moment in time, it was long enough to serve its purpose. She reached out and took his hand in hers.

'Robert, I love you dearly and I trust you implicitly. I know exactly why you're here and I think I know why you felt compelled to keep it from me. You know better than most how stubborn I can be at times.' She squeezed his hand reassuringly, then carried on before her husband could speak, 'But we can talk about that later, my dear.'

Her husband's eyes began to moisten slightly as he mouthed a 'thank you'. It was a relieving of tensions for him, but before it turned into an overwhelming moment for the pair of them, Elizabeth Erskine took control.

'By the way Robert, you're explanation for being here

was bordering on ludicrous I have to say ... you should have heard yourself. ... but enough said, for now,' she declared resolutely, '... let's get down to business. Do you know if Pinkney's here Robert?'

'Not that I can tell. I'm pretty sure he's not, although there's more people coming in by the minute,' he said nodding towards the entrance. Having dwelt momentarily on his wife's words, he was feeling more than a little upset that the honest account for his attendance had been so casually dismissed.

'Chances are, he's received the same call we did this morning, so it's possible he might keep his profile low,' Elizabeth said as matter of fact, seemingly having now entered into the spirit, 'But I'm a little vague on how a commission bid works ... I think you have to leave a figure with the auctioneer and he bids on your behalf,' she added knowingly.

'Well if that's the case, my dear,' said Robert, 'then we'll just have to make sure we bid beyond Pinkney's limit.'

She looked at her husband closely.

'So you've decided you're going to bid have you?' she asked solemnly, a little taken aback it seemed, 'You've actually made that decision have you, Robert?'

'If I have to ... then of course I will,' he said with uncharacteristic assurance, 'I didn't come here just to be a spectator ... to watch Pinkney carry off the spoils.'

'But how will you know if it's Pinkney that's doing the bidding?' she asked with a wry smile beginning to emerge.

'Well, before you mentioned that whole commission

bidding thing, I was quite sure he'd be here … if that was his intention. If I saw him bidding, then I'd just simply follow suit of course.'

'And if he wasn't to be seen?' Elizabeth enquired.

'Well if that were the case … and I couldn't see him … well … then I'd probably have just let it pass,' Robert declared limply, before adding, '… I'm really not that sure to be honest,' he confessed, '… I was just going to go along with gut instinct at the time.'

'Good plan!' Elizabeth said sarcastically.

'But now I'm confused,' he said to his wife, 'It isn't quite as simple as that … is it?'

Elizabeth turned towards her husband.

'Robert, I have a small confession of my own.'

'What do you mean, my love?'

'I've been teasing you a little,' she said, 'just a little to get my own back you might say.'

'Teasing? …How?'

'Robert, I'm going to put you out of you misery. It's really much simpler than you think.' She playfully punched his shoulder, 'You're going to bid regardless and bid as much as it takes to secure that golf club of ours.'

This change of heart came as a complete surprise to Robert Erskine, but he still needed to know why his wife had decided to offer her encouragement. It was not what he had been expecting at all.

'But why are you so sure I should?' he asked keenly.

Elizabeth Erskine's face turned a little more serious at

this point.

'Because, Robert,' she said quite deliberately, 'because that scoundrel is not going to leave a mere commission bid … he's actually going to be on the other end of a telephone … the man from MacIntyre's told me this morning.' She clenched her fists before adding, 'He's trying to make a fool of me … sorry … make a fool of us my dear, and he's going to pay the price for crossing me.'

Robert Erskine's mouth dropped wide open. His suspicions about the man had been sound after all and his wife had just given him the green light to start a bidding contest. A smile crossed his face.

'But how did you find all this out?' he asked her, as the young auctioneer began to climb into his rostrum once again.

'Unlike you, Robert, I have a knack of extracting information out of people, even when they don't necessarily want to divulge it … I'm not quite as accepting as you are,' she said a little caustically, all the while glancing over her husband's shoulder and noting the preparations being made to recommence the auction.

'And by the way, looks like we're off again,' she added pointing in the direction behind him.

Robert turned around and watched as Peter Harrison, now comfortably seated in position, shuffled a few papers and cast an eye over the assembled throng.

'That's why I called you on your phone, Robert, to let you know exactly what was going down here today … to let you know that you must start bidding against that …,' she hesitated briefly whilst some inner turmoil resolved itself. Robert Erskine stepped back a little before she continued, '... against that bloody two faced cheat.' There was obvious venom in her uncharacteristic choice of words and her completion reddened in the process.

Not content, however, at having vented her spleen solely on Charles Pinkney, she continued without pausing, only this time taking aim at her husband.

'And as for you, Robert,' she said scolding her husband, '... you freaked me out completely when you switched your damn phone off. I was on my way here, struggling with traffic ... and you cut me right off ... I could have throttled you.'

'I'm so sorry, my dear,' he said trying to make his apology sound genuine. But it was met with a dead pan expression. In a submissive tone, he added, 'Is there any way I can make this up to you, Elizabeth?'

She thought about that for a little, deliberately stringing out her response time It was beginning to feel like an eternity for Robert, but finally his wife spoke.

'Well you can start by paying my parking fine. I'm parked right in the middle of the pavement ... just outside the front entrance here,' she said light-heartedly.

Peter Harrison made his broadcast to the fresh faces that now surrounded his rostrum.

'Ladies and gentlemen, we're ready to start once more, so your attention please. We'll be starting again at lot number 116 ... a pair of late nineteenth century scare necked woods ... both by Robert Forgan ... a driver and brassie ... good condition ... you've all seen them ...,' he said with authority. Glancing down at his notes, then raising his head again he shouted, 'Two hundred pounds with me on the books... so who's got the fifty, please?'

Elizabeth Erskine dug her husband in the ribs and they turned their attention in unison to events in the room. With arms rising from all quarters, the bidding had taken hold again. In no time at all, a price of four hundred pounds was reached and the hammer fell. And almost without pause, the next item was being called. The action was gathering pace quickly.

'Robert, get ready. Stand over there where you can be seen,' Elizabeth instructed, pointing towards a gap just in front, '... and make sure you don't miss it. It's coming up any minute now,' she added emphatically.

He duly obliged and positioned himself directly in front of the auctioneer, about twenty feet away. But, all the while his stomach tightened and he began to feel a little nauseous into the bargain. Being an auction virgin, Robert was much more nervous and apprehensive than he cared to admit. He looked furtively around, trying to pick up some last minute tips from those more experienced. Undecided whether the raising of an arm, the nod of a head or the exaggerated waving of a catalogue would be the best way of attracting the auctioneers' attention, he watched closely the others around him. It soon became quite obvious the auctioneer had no real preference, being quite content to accept any bids, no matter how they were conveyed. It was simply a matter of being seen at the right moment. So not wanting to run the risk of being overlooked, Robert finally elected to go for a flamboyant technique. Catalogue waving it would be.

The auctioneer was now racing through the lots and

Elizabeth Erskine manoeuvred herself adjacent to her husband to provide moral support and encouragement. On hearing the hammer fall on yet another sale, she leant over and asked a question.

'Can I take a quick look at the catalogue, Robert?'

'Only if you're quick,' he said sharply, 'I think our item is coming up in about three more lots,' he added to reinforce the urgency.

Robert handed his wife the catalogue and took the opportunity to take another good look around the room. Thankfully there was no sign of Charles Pinkney. But if the rogue was intending to use the telephone to place his bids, then there was no point in him looking anyway, he reminded himself. Glancing across, he watched as Elizabeth quizzically turned the pages back and forth with no obvious purpose.

'You'll not find it there … it's on the sheet at the back … I've put a big red circle round it,' he offered impatiently, hoping it might speed her up. He was definitely getting nervous. She turned to the back, removed the extra sheet and unfolded it.

'It's *Lot 127a*,' he added for expediency. She slowly read the description, placed the sheet of paper back inside the cover and then closed the catalogue.

'So how far are we prepared to go on this, Robert?' she asked quite seriously.

He thought about it long and hard then answered rather sombrely, 'We have no choice, my dear … we go as far as we need to I expect … wherever that might be.'

'And that brings us to the first of our additional items

ladies and gentlemen. You'll find it on the addendum sheet. *Lot 127a* which is a fine Tom Morris long-nosed putter ... in very good condition I might add ... we don't see too many of these nowadays, so please take this opportunity to acquire a piece of golfing history ... a quite stunning putter from one of the all-time great club-makers.'

Although a very informative announcement, Peter Harrison appeared to be stretching out his words and was observed looking frequently over to his right.

Robert Erskine followed the auctioneer's sight line and noticed three assistants, each standing and each holding telephones up to their ears. They were clearly talking to some anonymous persons on the other end. The auctioneer kept his eye on the telephone assistants whilst he continued talking.

'There has been considerable interest in this club ladies and gentlemen and I have to advise you that the estimate we placed on the item is expected to be well exceeded.'

Both Elizabeth and Robert Erskine were, by now, clinging onto each other for their dear lives.

'Are you ready, Robert?'

'Pass me the catalogue ... please,' he demanded rather brusquely.

'We have bids on the books and three telephone lines opened up for this item ladies and gentlemen ... and I'm looking over now to get a signal that they're all ready.' He raised a thumb hoping the gesture would be reciprocated by the assistants.

'Are we ready to go?' the auctioneer enquired. The three telephone assistants each raised a thumb in acknowledgement, whilst at the same time continuing their conversations with their respective clients.

'Pinkney must be one of them,' Elizabeth stated somewhat resentfully.

'I'm afraid you're probably right,' Robert responded, pointing to the central telephone assistant, a smart young women flanked by two older gentlemen more casually dressed, one being bald, the other one wearing a bright waistcoat. 'I reckon Pinkney will be on the woman's phone.'

'My bet's on the first man ... the one with the bald head,' Elizabeth added.

They looked at each other briefly and smiled in unison, realising how absurd they sounded. At such a crucial point in their lives, they were behaving like mere spectators, betting on the outcome of some trivial sideshow. It only just served to remind them how terrifying the situation had become.

Peter Harrison, having received his all-clear to proceed, then set about bringing the bidding alive.

'Ok, here we go then. I'll take the commission bids first and I have six ... six fifty ... seven ... seven fifty ... and eight hundred pounds ... so I'm now looking for eight fifty from the room,' he enquired. The auctioneer was not looking over to the telephones quite yet Elizabeth Erskine noticed.

Robert, standing on tip-toes for added elevation, waved his catalogue animatedly.

'I see you, sir,' Peter Harrison acknowledged with a touch of irony, 'But I'm taking that gentleman's bid first,' he added, pointing to somewhere far right. '... and eight fifty with the gentleman standing at the back of the hall,' he declared. Attention then returned his attention to his enthusiastic catalogue waver.

'Are you bidding nine hundred pounds, sir?' the auctioneer asked politely. Robert flicked his catalogue, a little more discretely this time.

'Thank you sir, now do I see one thousand?' An arm rose above heads from the far right once more.

'One thousand I have ... and eleven hundred I seek?'

Robert brandished his catalogue aloft once more. The auctioneer had anticipated the bid and acknowledged with a nod of his head before looking around the room again.

'Eleven I have with the gentleman in the middle ... twelve hundred therefore next ...'

This time no arm emerged above heads. Attention quickly switched across to the telephone bidders. Peter Harrison invited a bid and the women standing in the centre nodded her head first.

'Twelve hundred with *line two*,' Peter Harrison announced before looking again at Robert. On cue, the catalogue was flicked up and down. Robert was clearly growing in confidence having settled into a casual bidding style of his own. Elizabeth gave him an encouraging pat on the back.

'Thank you, sir.' Attention shifted once again with the telephones, 'Thirteen perhaps?'

The women spoke into the mouthpiece, then nodded. The 'bald man' and the 'startling waistcoat' both gave discreet signals to the auctioneer, indicating their respective clients were eager to enter the fray. But auction protocol required them to wait, at least until one of the two current bidders withdrew.

'Fourteen with the phone,' was the announcement. Robert flicked his catalogue once more and was acknowledged straight away by the rostrum. He looked across at his wife, who by now was totally engrossed with the telephone assistants.

But the bidding went on and on, ever higher, much to the fascination of all those in the know. The two thousand pound barrier was quickly exceeded with the *'line two'* bidder eventually backing down, only to be replaced by the waist-coated assistant who pushed the bidding to nearer the two thousand five hundred mark. This in itself generated a ripple of astonishment throughout the room. The putter was causing a bit of a stir, much more in fact than it deserved. The serious collectors amongst the ranks started consulting each other by way of reassurance, just in case they had inadvertently missed spotting something unusual. Frantic catalogue referrals were witnessed all around.

Robert Erskine bid the two thousand six hundred that was required, but if the pair had entertained thoughts that Charles Pinkney might be abstaining, they were quickly disillusioned. The bald assistant raised an arm and called out *'five thousand'*, causing a commotion to break out across the auction room. Peter Harrison turned to the telephones, a little astonished himself by the turn of events.

'Was that five thousand on line one?' he asked with mild incredulity. The bald assistant nodded an acknowledgement then continued his dialogue with his client. The auctioneer looked across, with raised eyebrows, at his catalogue bidder in the centre of the room.

'That being the case, my next bid will need to be five thousand five hundred ...,' and pausing to allow the message to be fully absorbed, went on to enquire, '...so are you bidding, sir?'.

Elizabeth and Robert Erskine were now very much centre stage, but they were oblivious to all the staring eyes that were now watching their every move. Strangely, the once over-crowded room had now respectfully granted them some space of their own and they stood now in splendid isolation, directly in front of the auctioneer. This withdrawal may have resulted from some peculiar reverence that was now being conferred on the pair, or simply a desire to stand back to get a better look at these high fliers.

For whatever the reason, Robert and Elizabeth were unaware it was happening. The couple stared solitarily at one another, in amazement, the realisation dawning that this was now going to be a bloody fight to the finish, a fight between two families with seemingly unlimited resources, albeit not particularly fluid for their own part, not at that precise moment, at least. The bidding was about to become incomprehensible to those watching and would bear no reflection to the clubs' true value. The contest would now centre entirely on what it represented and not on its worth. But no-one else in the room would be appreciating that. The bidding would appear simply ridiculous from here on in, and no doubt they would come to be regarded as foolhardy. Not that it would bother either of them in the slightest. All that mattered now was making sure that *'line one'* did not gain the upper hand.

'Are you bidding, sir?' came the all too sudden prompting.

For the second time, Elizabeth Erskine dug her husband in the ribs with her elbow. A small signal, but all the encouragement Robert needed. Without a moments hesitation, he raised his catalogue belligerently into the air and cried out loud, loud enough for 'line one' to hear his call.

'Ten thousand pounds!'

The offer that was greeted with gasps of astonishment, followed by some hurried words from bald man to his 'line one' client.

'Ten thousand with the gentleman standing in the centre,' called out the auctioneer, somewhat puzzled. 'Do we have eleven?' he continued nevertheless, his attention now having switched automatically to the telephones.

There was a brief delay as bald telephone assistant and 'line one' conferred. It appeared, to those watching, that the assistant was questioning the caller, seeking confirmation that the instructions were fully understood, without possible ambiguity. Finally, he shared his instructions with the auctioneer.

'Twenty five thousand pounds, sir,' he declared loudly and impressively. Peter Harrison was dumbfounded beyond belief, so quickly sought confirmation.

'I'm sure we all heard that, but just in case I misunderstood, I'd like to hear it once more, just to be certain that is,' the auctioneer said calmly, before asking, 'Do we have a bid of twenty five thousand pounds for the Tom Morris putter?'

The bald assistant nodded his confirmation immediately.

'Very well, this may be somewhat academic, but I'll ask the gentleman in front of me if he'd like to bid thirty?' His words prompted some laughter from the more established dealers.

All eyes were now upon Robert, and the speculation grew as to what his next move might be. After hesitating briefly and consulting Elizabeth once again, he calmly raised his catalogue, sparking off another round of murmurings. The young auctioneer lent back in his chair and tried to comprehend what was happening in his auction room, and by way of reassurance that all was genuine, he asked his current bidder to reaffirm his offer.

'Do I take it you're bidding thirty thousand pounds, sir?' he enquired politely, emphasising the amount.

Robert Erskine gave a categorical nod so there could be no misunderstanding of his intent, although his expression was starting to betray his growing concern over the direction in which the bidding was heading. The odds, Robert realised, were better than even that the price was about to go through the roof. Not that thirty thousand was a small sum in itself. Unless one of them was prepared to back down at some point soon, then the only recompense either would gain from losing this day would be some perverse notoriety from participating in the sale of the world's most expensive golf club. But losing was not an option. This was one battle he and Elizabeth simply could not afford to lose.

'Ladies and gentlemen ... please? ... Would you kindly keep quiet,' the auctioneer pleaded in an attempt to quell the growing disturbances breaking out across the sale room. 'We have some serious business going on here so please, be respectful and tolerant.' He waited until the noise subsided then reiterated his previous call,

'Thirty thousand pounds once again with the gentlemen standing in front of me.'

Peter Harrison switched his attention straight to his bald assistant who, by now, was actively and discreetly talking to his client, advising and seeking further instructions. He would, no doubt, be reminding his client that the next increment would need to be thirty five thousand pounds, a sum grossly disproportionate to the actual value of the club and would, no doubt also, be advising caution at this point.

If the bald assistant *had* been advising any of these things, then apparently little heed had been taken, as his next action was to turn to the auctioneer and call out *'fifty thousand pounds'*. The words were repeated one more time for absolute clarity, accompanied by a shrug of his shoulders.

The shock waves resounded around the auction room and all eyes shot instantly from the bald assistant to the Erskines. It was turning into something of a tennis match for the spectators. Some laughter began to emanate from a small group of dealers who, judging by the amusement they were animatedly displaying, were clearly finding the whole thing somewhat bizarre. One of the group was even heard to mockingly call out, 'Go on, make it a million!' This prompted more laughter from his immediate grouping, but he was quickly chastised by the auctioneer. Little did they know that Robert Erskine may well be prepared to ultimately do just that.

The Erskine's were oblivious to the antics going on around them and their only focus was now on each other.

Both were drained of all colour and had, by now, fallen silent. Despite this, Robert was in no doubt, knowing exactly what was required next. Just a small sign was all he required, something by way of endorsement from his wife. Elizabeth read the signs well, and provided her support with a robust directive.

'Go on Robert …do it to him!'

Before Peter Harrison had time to invite the next bid, Robert Erskine made his offer. There was no need to wave his catalogue this time to attract attention.

'Sixty thousand pounds,' he assertively called out.

The young auctioneer was way beyond the point of challenging the bidding by this time and simply accepted the call without question. He followed this up with the obligatory turn towards to his bald assistant who was fervently engaged in discussions with *'line one'*.

'Line one' was clearly being updated and everyone waited. The dialogue was more protracted than previously, which only served to heighten the tension. There was a definite feeling emerging that *'line one'* was turning hesitant, after all, the next bid would need to be sixty five thousand pounds and no-one believed any bidder would be that reckless. Two people in the room however, knew the delay was mere sensation, designed to simply 'up the anti', so to speak. And only they knew the bidding would undoubtedly continue, very soon, on its same course.

But the delay became marginally longer then the Erskine's were expecting. Keeping their eyes fixed on the bald assistant, they could tell from the body language that *'line one'* was doing something more than just prevaricating. For a brief moment they entertained the idea that they may have finally succeeded. But the moment was disappointingly short lived as the bald assistant with *'line one'* raised an arm and theatrically nodded his head one more time.

'Sixty five thousand pounds,' the auctioneer said in hushed tones, 'Do you wish to bid seventy, sir?' he enquired looking directly at Robert Erskine.

But the auctioneer's expression was a little different this time. He was displaying concern. Elizabeth Erskine was quick to notice this and wondered what lay behind. It occurred to her, it may be a subliminal signal from the young auctioneer, a request to halt this farcical nonsense from progressing further. It appeared he was trying to be benevolent, trying to avert some catastrophe which his bidders might live to regret for the rest of their lives. If only he knew, she thought.

Acknowledging the auctioneers gesture with one of her own, Elizabeth gave Peter Harrison an elegant nod followed by one of her most charming smiles. Understanding her response, he reciprocated with a modest smile of his own.

Robert Erskine, sensing their telephone adversary might well be wavering, wasted no time in driving home the small advantage he perceived had been gained. He made a swift follow up bid in the hope his decisiveness might overwhelm his faceless opponent.

'Seventy thousand,' he called out loud and clearly.

Collective heads turned once again to the telephone. The earlier amusement was no longer evident as people demonstrated a kind of empathy towards the odd couple in their midst. And speculation grew as to who they might actually be. Whispering and pointing was breaking out all around. Were they famous in some way, celebrities perhaps, or maybe just senselessly rich business people? No-one knew. But one thing everyone was undoubtedly agreed upon; this bidder knew absolutely nothing about golf collectibles.

'Line one' was clearly struggling with the prospect of bidding the necessary seventy five thousand pounds to stay in the game, as once more the conversation between telephone assistant and 'client' became stretched. With the auctioneer's commission on top, plus tax on the commission, the actual cost of a further bid would be close to eighty eight thousand pounds. And *'line one'* would know that precisely.

The Erskine's held hands and silently prayed. The telephone conversation continued unabated and everyone held their breath. Finally the bald assistant stopped talking and waited. A prompt from the auctioneer caused the assistant to hold up one finger, indicating he needed a further minute. The wait lengthened with the auctioneer keeping a close watch, until finally his assistant mouthed some words into the mouthpiece. Turning to the rostrum, the assistant slowly shook his head. His client had withdrawn from the bidding.

Elizabeth and Robert Erskine jumped into the air and let out cries of delight, much to the astonishment of all around. Elizabeth Erskine applauded herself whilst her husband wiped some tears from his eyes. After kissing publicly, they turned to the auctioneer, hardly able to contain their excitement despite the monumental price they had just been forced to pay. But they were quickly brought back to earth as Peter Harrison calmly spoke.

'Not over quite yet,' he reminded the couple, 'There's still one further question I need to ask before we get too carried away with success,' he added with a wry smile.

'Do I see seventy five thousand pounds in the room?' he asked playfully.

This question, quite predictably, caused some hilarity. One or two of the more seasoned professionals, pretended to place mock bids ensuring, at the same, there was absolutely no risk of the young auctioneer interpreting their offers as legitimate. Nevertheless, the wait itself was torturous for the Erskine's, the auctioneer content to bring down the hammer only when he was satisfied all other potential bidders had been accounted for.

'Anymore interest ladies and gentlemen?' he formally enquired. 'Seventy I have ... I'll take seventy five.' He waited and waited, hammer hovering over his desk. 'For the first time ...,' he paused, 'For the second time ...' he paused again.

For Robert Erskine the moment was unbearable and it reminded him of their wedding day; that infamous point in every ceremony where the minister asks '... if anyone here knows any good reason etc., etc.'

'And for the third time ...,' Peter Harrison called out, '... You've all had fair warning,' and with that, the hammer finally fell.

'Now you can celebrate,' he said looking across to the Erskine's. The sale room continued with the applause Elizabeth Erskine had earlier started. The auctioneer waited a second or two for the commotion to quieten down and then addressed them with a question.

'Your bidding number please, sir,' he asked graciously.

Robert Erskine looked across at him, a little uncertain of what he had been asked, a blank expression to the forefront.

'Your bidding number please, sir?' the auctioneer repeated, but a little less genially this time.

Robert shrugged his shoulders, 'I'm sorry, I don't think I have one,' was his sheepish response.

The room fell silent at this point. Everyone, except the Erskine's, appreciated the implication of those few innocently spoken words.

Peter Harrison looked perturbed as he spoke. 'Are you telling me, sir, you don't have a bidder's number?'

Robert Erskine looked to his wife for support and asked, 'What does he mean by bidder's number?' But all she could do was shrug her shoulders as well. The young auctioneer demanded a quick reply.

'Sir, are you telling me you do not have a bidder's number?' Without waiting for the reply, he turned to his assistant in charge of *'line one'* and beckoned him to hold onto the caller.

'No, I don't have a bidder's number,' came Robert Erskine's indignant reply, 'But if your telling me I need one, then how do I get it?' he asked in all innocence.

From the auctioneer's reaction, Elizabeth Erskine knew immediately there was a huge problem associated with this. A flurry of activity could be seen at the rostrum as Peter Harrison held up his hand placing a halt on proceedings. He spoke discreetly to another of his assistants seated to his left. For now, Robert Erskines' enquiry was being disregarded and the auctioneer's focus seemed more on seeking some procedural advice from others. After a brief delay, Peter Harrison invited the Erskine's over to his rostrum and whilst they made their way forward, he made a quick announcement.

'There will be a short break whilst we sort something out here. I'm sorry, ladies and gentlemen, but I ask for your patience in the meantime. This should only take a minute or two. Thank you.'

By now the couple had reached the base of the rostrum and the auctioneer came down his steps to talk to them privately, well out of range of his microphone. His expression gave them cause for immediate concern. Robert Erskine spoke first.

'Look, we're very sorry about this whole bidding number thing ... we simply had no idea we needed one.'

'I'm afraid you certainly do,' was the auctioneer's less than sympathetic reply.

'No bother then. Just let me know where I get one ... and I'll give it to you. Perhaps you could even give me one yourself,' Robert responded in a slightly patronising way. 'My name's Robert Erskine ... your office called us this morning,' he informed the young man, expecting that particular revelation to resolve the matter once and for all.

'I'm afraid it isn't quite as simple as you imagine, Mr. Erskine. We have a very awkward situation here and you'll appreciate I have to act in the best interests of my client as well as being seen to be even handed in the way we conduct business here in our auction house.'

Elizabeth Erskine cut straight to the chase. 'Are you

telling us this *awkward situation* you describe means our bid is not going to be accepted?' she desperately enquired.

'I'm afraid that's exactly the situation we find ourselves in here. Look, I have no reason to doubt who you are … and I recall our conversation from the other day, Mr. Erskine, but the fact remains you didn't register before bidding. You should have obtained a number and you didn't. It's as simple as that I'm afraid. Our rules are quite explicit and well publicised … I'm sorry but your bids are void,' he said quite apologetically.

The Erskine's looked aghast and waited for the other to speak first. As neither did, Peter Harrison spoke again.

'Look … there is absolutely nothing I can do about your lack of bidding number. We had a similar situation here recently and I'm afraid a precedent has now been set. If we accept your bids on this occasion, then we run the risk of complaints being raised by others who were similarly refused in the past. I'm afraid my hands are tied on this, I'm sorry. I have to play this by the book I'm afraid.'

Seeing his comments were causing obvious distress, the auctioneer nevertheless felt obliged to offer them a small crumb of hope.

'The way I see it, we only have two options here,' he said calmly and deliberately, making sure the Erskine's listened closely to what he was saying. 'First and foremost, my duty is to protect the interests of my client, in this particular case, the seller. Because of the quite extraordinary sum involved here and the very remote prospect he could ever attract a similar offer ever again, it's imperative I safeguard his current position. Do you understand what I'm saying?' he asked of them.

'Yes, I think we follow you so far,' said Elizabeth Erskine.

'Good. Well having said that, there are a couple of things which might now happen, but it all depends on the attitude of the under-bidder,' cautioned the auctioneer.

'What do you mean?' asked Robert, a little too shell shocked to fully appreciate what was actually taking place.

'It means Mr. Erskine, the under-bidder will be given a choice at this point. And that's where our two options come into play,' he informed the couple.

Elizabeth Erskine was becoming extremely frustrated by now and encouraged him to continue as quickly as possible. 'Please go on Mr... ?' She hesitated, before saying somewhat aloofly, 'I'm sorry, you didn't introduce yourself … what's your name?'

'Sorry, Harrison … Peter Harrison.' He turned to address her instead. 'Anyway, the circumstances will be explained to the under-bidder in a minute or two, and he will be asked if he wishes like to stand by his maximum bid … sixty five thousand pounds I believe was his last bid … and accept the club at that price. If not, he will also be given the option of a re-run, allowing you time to pre-register … and then we do the whole thing all over again.' He paused to let it all sink in, before adding, '… So, it all depends on your under-bidder and what *his* preference might now be.'

And with that, Peter Harrison walked over to the telephone, took hold of the receiver for *'line one'* and started talking to the person on the other end, leaving the Erskine's to contemplate their fate alone.

'He said '*he*' didn't he?' Robert pointed out, still a little too stunned to really comprehend the significance of his oversight.

'You're right he did … That's bad, isn't it?' his wife asked rhetorically.

For the Erskine's the call seemed to last for an eternity, but was only about thirty seconds in fact. Peter Harrison concluded into his call and climbed his rostrum once again, ominously avoiding eye contact with the Erskine's, who by now where clinging onto each other for their dear lives. The auctioneer lifted his hammer and looked down at the Erskine's apologetically. The hammer descended and struck the rostrum with a resounding crack.

'*Lot 127a*, sold to the gentleman on '*line one*' for sixty five thousand pounds,' he declared. Peter Harrison looked down at the distraught couple.

'I'm ever so sorry,' was the only consolation he could offer.

Chapter 13

After practically an entire day's clock watching, the allotted time of three thirty finally arrived and Tom Hudson was all-clear to make his call to MacIntyre McBride. A call any sooner would have been too early with mid afternoon ideal for everyone, buyers, sellers and auctioneers alike. Being both a buyer and a seller, Tom was keen to learn the outcome, so sneaking once again into the office foyer, he eagerly placed his call.

The phone rang and rang with no reply and whilst waiting the decision was taken to leave the better news until last. First he would enquire about the 'porter' bids he had left. Eventually a voice on the other end offered an apology for the delay in answering, and then asked how she may help. Tom introduced himself, outlined his purpose for calling, and quoted his bidding reference number when prompted to do so. After a short pause and a request to confirm his address, a young woman read from her computer screen.

'Mr. Hudson ... I can only see three purchases against your reference number ... Lots 115, 116 and Lot 143. Would that be about right?' she enquired.

Tom looked through his notes and realised that, of the six bids he had left, the three he had actually secured were his least preferred. A little disappointing but he had, at least, managed to buy roughly forty clubs in total, enough to partially satisfy his new found Belgian customer.

'That sounds about right,' he responded, 'Maybe you

could tell me what they went for?'

'I'll just take a look, Mr. Hudson … just bear with me a second,' she said very slowly whilst waiting for her screen to change. 'Here we are ... Lot 115 went for eighty five pounds ... Lot 116 went for two hundred and thirty five pounds and ... Lot 143 went for one hundred and forty five pounds.'

Writing the figures down as she spoke, he compared them to the commissions he had left. He soon realised there had been no bargains that day, having paid his top line on two out the three. Nevertheless, he thanked the young women for her assistance and assured her he would be coming round to the Town Hall before six that evening, to pay for his purchases and to collect his clubs.

'Thank you, Mr. Hudson. We'll be closing down here around seven, so six will be fine,' she informed him helpfully, 'Is there anything else we can do for you, Mr. Hudson?' she asked politely.

'Yes there is,' he replied, 'I did have one item up for sale today … *Lot 127a*. Perhaps you could tell me how it did?'

'Of course, just hold on a minute please and I'll find out for you.'

He was all-expectant and quite excited at the prospect, already knowing at least two people were pursuing the club quite eagerly. Whilst he waited for the news, he speculated as to what price his putter had achieved and decided he would be disappointed if it had fetched less than three thousand pounds, given all the effort put into making it available for a second time. The young women soon spoke once more.

'Could I just check that lot number again please?' she enquired, doubting perhaps she had heard correctly in the first instance. 'Did you say *Lot127a*, Mr. Hudson?'

'That's right ... *Lot 127a*. Is there a problem?' he asked with growing concern.

'No problem at all from what I have in front of me here on the screen. It looks more like a case of congratulations from where I'm sitting,' she said enviously. 'Are you sitting down as well, Mr. Hudson?'

'No, but please put me out of my misery, anyway,' he pleaded with her.

'Well according to my screen it went for sixty five thousand pounds,' she announced with astonishment. '... So, less the ten per cent commission and tax, the right hand column here says you'll be getting a cheque for exactly ... fifty seven thousand three hundred and sixty three pounds fifty pence, Mr Hudson ... What do you think about that?'

Tom Hudson was totally speechless.

At precisely that same moment, Charles Pinkney was once again welcoming '*Mr. Smith*' and his roguish friends into his home. He had hastily called the meeting and only the promise of significantly more business had persuaded the so called Mr. Smith to accept the invitation and alter his plans for that afternoon. As with the previous meeting, the older man was accompanied by a larger man and a smaller. After some courteous small talk, Mr. Smith sat down and spoke.

'You're fast becoming one my most regular customers, Mr. Pinkney,' he said with a slight grin on his face, 'so how can I help you this time?'

Charles Pinkney needed considerably more cash and he needed it quickly, that afternoon in fact. Only a few hours earlier he had come off the phone having committed himself to purchasing one *'Tom Morris long-nose putter, Lot 127a'* and it was going to cost him exactly seventy six thousand four hundred and fifty six pounds twenty five pence, including the buyers fifteen percent commission and tax. The auction house had explained they could not accept a cheque for that amount, so payment needed to be in the form of a bankers draft or an electronic transfer of funds into their business account by noon the next day. He needed cash immediately, to enable a deposit into his own account so that a transfer could take place. Without the cash and without the transfer, he would run the risk of losing the sale and the whole escapade would have counted for nothing. A deal had to be struck there and then, regardless of the ludicrous terms and terrifying guarantees Mr. Smith would no doubt be extracting. He was over a barrel and it would very soon become apparent to the well dressed gentlemen sat in front of him. No doubt he was about to be exploited to the hilt, but regrettably there were no other options for him to pursue.

The intended nature of Mr. Smith's terms mattered little to Charles Pinkney. He was feeling cocksure with his success earlier that day and was quite happy to write off a couple of hundred thousand pounds if, in doing so, he secured his stake over the Erskine estate. But time was of the essence and all he now wished was to get his hands on at least seventy five thousand in cash, sign whatever needed to be signed and get these three thugs out of his house before they took up permanent residence. If all went according to plan, he could have the cash securely deposited into his bank account by five o'clock that afternoon. Judging by the size of the briefcase the smaller man was holding, Charles Pinkney felt confident Mr. Smith had come along fully able to satisfy even the most outlandish request.

'Mr. Smith, thank you once again for coming to see me at such short notice,' Charles Pinkney said respectfully, 'so, I'll come straight to the point. I need a further fifty thousand pounds ... and I need it today.' He paused to gauge the reaction, but Mr. Smith maintained his deadpan expression. 'Can you help me once again, Mr. Smith?'

A moment or two of mutual sizing up first took place before finally the smartly dressed older man spoke.

'I appreciate your directness, Mr. Pinkney, and yes I could help you ... and yes, I may ... but this sudden need you have for large amounts of cash is a little disconcerting for me you will understand.' He leaned forward. 'It doesn't bother me if you're in some sort of trouble ... that's your business after all, I'm only interested in your enthusiasm to repay the loan at the end of the day, after all ...,' he hesitated and rubbed his chin thoughtfully, 'although if it's trouble I can help you with? ... you'd let me know wouldn't you?' he added somewhat menacingly.

Charles Pinkney responded swiftly, 'No trouble at all, I can assure you of that, Mr. Smith.'

'Pity...,' said the older man, still rubbing his chin, pausing briefly to scrutinise Charles Pinkney's sincerity. 'Never mind,' he conceded, 'back to the business in hand. Quite a large sum of money, Mr. Pinkney, is it not?'

Charles Pinkney got the man's drift immediately and set about reassuring his 'guest'. He briefly summarised the situation he faced, the prospect of imminent and substantial gain and the need to secure certain funds to unlock some equity. He was deliberately vague in his summary and attempted to avoid disclosing any specifics, despite some blatant probing on Mr. Smith's part. The recital seemed to satisfy his lender to a degree, but he could sense Mr. Smith was beginning to show an unhealthy interest in the detail. Drawing upon years of boardroom stage management, Charles Pinkney was nonetheless able to alter course successfully and bring the conversation back in-line to the only business he wanted to discuss, Mr. Smith's financial assistance.

'Very good Mr. Pinkney, just so long as we understand each other, and just so long as you understand I will be asking you to sign another piece of paper.' Mr. Smith clicked his fingers which prompted the smaller man to instantly produce from his briefcase yet another contract. 'This paper Mr. Pinkney, gives me preferred creditor status, if you know what I mean?' His outstretched arm swept full circle round the drawing room leaving Charles Pinkney in no doubt how the penalty clauses were to be applied should he default in some way.

Mr. Smith took charge of the papers, read them himself, made a few alterations and then handed the papers over to his now anxious customer. Charles Pinkney carefully read the words and began to perspire as a consequence. From what he could gather, he would need to write-off more than the many thousand of pounds he had earlier assumed. Additionally, Mr. Smith had just added some new freehand conditions, conditions which were clearly non-negotiable. He lamely queried the terms, but to no avail, Mr. Smith simply leaning back and folding his arms.

Clearly having no choice in the matter, he once again put pen to paper. A shake of the hand sealed the deal, the money was handed over and the three men were shown politely to the door. Only when they were out of the house, did Charles Pinkney permit himself a modest celebration, a large malt whisky accompanied by a drop of iced water to heighten the flavour.

Feeling a need to relieve the stress and having time before heading off to the bank, he returned to the drawing room and sat back in his favourite chair to reflect on the auction and the drama that had unfolded that day. 'So near and yet so far', that had been the probable outcome, but it had turned unexpectedly in his favour.

He had been in serious competition from someone within the auction room that day, competition he could only presume was coming from the Erskines, competition he had presumed had have been much earlier eliminated. Clearly that had not been the case and he wondered why they had undergone a change of heart. Perhaps they had seen through him from the start, or maybe just got wind of his intentions? He would never know and it mattered little. The club was now his, and that was all that counted.

It had been a close call, he reflected. His reserve of twenty five thousand had quickly been exhausted. But that had been the limit he had set himself, never expecting a need to go beyond that figure. So when the bidding went through his self imposed ceiling and continued upwards and out of sight, he was venturing then into no-mans land, with no prospect he could honour whatever commitment he might end up entering into.

It had turned into a real predicament for him as the bidding rose. And a fifty thousand pound throw of the dice had represented his last chance of success. But even that had been genuinely beyond his means. So when it came to the point of placing bid of seventy five thousand pounds, he had been forced to reassess his situation on the hoof. He had quickly calculated the real cost would have been nearer the eighty eight thousand mark, and that was simply impossible for him to contemplate, particularly knowing the prospect of raising such amount at short notice was a mere pipedream. He had requested a brief respite and the auction house had duly obliged, albeit for one minute only. During that time, he had attempted to contact Mr. Smith on the man's mobile phone, but the call had been, not unsurprisingly, diverted to an answer machine. Realising he had no probable access to funds, his predicament had worsened as the auction house lost patience and pressed him hard to make a final decision on the bid.

His inclination, quite naturally, had been to continue on regardless, pushing the price as high as possible, even if he ended up being unsuccessful. At least that would have caused the Erskine's to pay through the nose for the club, and consequently his estate. But a strange sensation had engulfed him, a sense of panic he had never experienced before. His financial worries must have surfaced from his sub conscience, suddenly coming to the fore in one giant accumulation of concern. That unexpected surge had been sufficient to scramble his powers of rational thinking and before he had time to place those worries into some sort of context, he had signalled his withdrawal when vigorously pressed for the final time. A sum of seventy five thousand pounds, or something equally high, was always going to be his nemesis, so his concession had perhaps been inevitable.

With no time to reconsider, the hammer was heard falling on the other end of the line. His only prayer, after that, would be a reliance on the Erskine's misplaced sense of honour and decency to resist following through with the threat of eviction. Better still, it may have been sold to some unsuspecting fool, someone oblivious to the '*Morris Men Agreement*'. A forlorn hope and well he knew it.

But lady luck had unexpectedly dealt him back in, at sixty five thousand. He had been asked to hold whilst an issue of some sort was resolved in the auction room and that extra time had granted him a chance to reconsider in the cold light of day, released from the urgency to think on his feet. The delay allowed a fresh risk assessment to be carried out with a clear head, and when the option to buy at sixty five thousand pounds was inexplicably presented to him, the choice had become a much clearer and simpler one. Such a golden opportunity must not be allowed to slip from his grasp and his acceptance had been practically immediate. Although it was still financially marginal, it was nevertheless possible.

Thank goodness for Mr. Smith's rolling bankroll, he now thought to himself, and thank goodness he had been able to contact the man. It had been a huge gamble for him, no certainty of funding prior to acceptance. But it had paid off and he was now able to breathe a huge sigh of relief. He took a further sip of his whisky before placing the glass down on the table. He had a pay a visit to the bank shortly, but first, a phone call to Bainbridge & Bainbridge. He would insist upon an immediate appointment and with any luck, he would have the Erskine's ejected within a few days.

Meanwhile, Robert and Elizabeth Erskine had spent the rest of the afternoon at MacIntyre's main office, having been referred there by the auction officials. They were trying desperately to get the decision reversed, but to no avail. A combination of court action threats coupled with undignified pleas for compassion had all proved fruitless, none able to effect a favourable reversal to the outcome.

Peter Harrison had not been able to see them initially, having to first conclude the remainder of the auction at the Town Hall, but once coming free, he had headed straight back to the office to lend a hand to his now exasperated staff. Faced with a concerted effort to influence his thinking, he had reiterated, more or less, what he had earlier advised, only more forcibly this time. When that proved still unsatisfactory as far as the Erskine's were concerned, he had reluctantly offered to call Stuart MacIntyre for some adjudication, despite the principal being on vacation.

The call had been made in the Erskine's presence and surprisingly Stuart MacIntyre had promptly answered. He had been anticipating a call of some sort, not because of any concerns about the abilities of his novice auctioneer or his staff, more a suspicion the young team would be naturally jubilant after their first auction without him and would wish to include their boss in the celebrations. As expected, he got all of that from the call and was delighted, instructing Peter Harrison to convey his praises onto everyone involved. But when the issue of bidder registration had been raised and the incident that morning summarised, Stuart MacIntyre was adamant Peter Harrison had conducted himself properly and that the right decisions had been taken. He reinforced that by adding he too would have acted in exactly the same way and again congratulated his young assistant on a job well done. Even when Elizabeth Erskine insisted on speaking to the principal herself, he had left her in no doubt the matter was now closed.

It had been a sad sight indeed, watching the pair of them leave the offices of MacIntyre McBride in such a distressed state and the young Peter Harrison did feel a degree of sympathy, despite being utterly bemused at their desire to buy a two thousand pound putter for something approaching ninety thousand.

The Erskine's headed straight home and bolted all the doors behind them.

Maurice Bainbridge was feeling a little upset. He had just concluded a telephone conversation five minutes earlier and was distressing himself thinking about the implications that would inevitably follow. He had been very accommodating and conceded to Charles Pinkney's impolite insistence they meet the next afternoon at 2pm, despite a half day's holiday having been long ago planned. From their brief discussion, he was left in no doubt about the significance of the meeting and was heavy hearted at the prospects that now faced Mr. and Mrs. Erskine.

'What a dreadful business,' he thought, *'I wish I had no part to play in all of this.'*

It was all very unpalatable for Maurice Bainbridge and ever since this whole business had raised its ugly head, he had wished to play no further part. But that decision was not his to take and he was bound by professional obligation to see his instructions through to a conclusion, no matter how unseemly they may well be.

But that obligation did not console him as a human

being. Tomorrow, it seemed, he would be taking his final instructions and setting in motion a legal process that would see an innocent couple stripped of their entire belongings and their dignity. And to make matters worse, the beneficiary was a gentlemen he found to be somewhat distasteful and roguish.

Ever since the issue first arose, just a few short weeks ago, Maurice Bainbridge had hoped the club would never emerge from its hiding place. It had remained concealed for nearly a century and everyone had been living their lives in blissful ignorance of its significance. An equilibrium had been established whilst the contract remained secret, but its recent revelation had changed all that. These *'Morris Men'*, as they had chosen to call themselves, had selfish intent when they made their pact, he thought, and it saddened him to think its resolution had not been affected at the time. Had it been, then the distress the Erskine's were now confronting, would have been long since avoided. To never have had owned in the first place was ever so much different from having everything snatched from you afterwards.

He felt a great deal of sympathy for the Erskines because he was sure they had no malicious intent in pursuing the club, just a desire to protect themselves from harm. Pinkney, on the other hand had made his intentions quite clear from the outset. His motivation, throughout, had clearly been one of gain, and that angered the solicitor. There appeared to be no common decency in the man, he reflected, and Pinkney's' attitude on the telephone had been unpleasantly jubilant. The man seemed to be relishing the prospect of benefiting from this affair and harming the Erskines into the bargain.

However, the meeting would take place the next afternoon regardless of his personal views, so Maurice Bainbridge allocated time to pull the 'Morris Men" documents out from the filing system. Having gathered them all together, he made the short walk into an adjacent office and made sure his junior partner was available to attend the meeting and act as witness. Whilst returning to his office, his receptionist called him over and he was handed a small package received just a few moments earlier by courier. He glanced at the label and recognised the name of the company. Immediately his spirits were lifted. The discs had arrived safe and sound which meant he would now have unfettered access to Edward Bainbridge's diaries, and all the little gems of wisdom and insights they might well contain.

Chapter 14

'There you go, sir, your club,' Peter Harrison had said whilst proudly handing over the putter to Charles Pinkney, '... and a fine example of a Tom Morris club it is ... if you don't mind me saying.' The young auctioneer was attempting to engage his visitor in polite conversation.

'I would have no idea about that ...' Charles Pinkney replied somewhat rudely, '... and quite frankly I care even less.'

'I see,' said the surprised auctioneer, 'then may I be so bold to ask why you paid such an extraordinary sum for it sir? ... We're all very curious I might add.'

'Absolutely none of your damn business,' came back the dismissive and ignorant reply.

Peter Harrison was mortified with the impoliteness of the remark, but let it pass without brewing up further aggravation. The money had been transferred into their bank account fifteen minutes earlier and a phone call had confirmed the transaction.

And that was all that really mattered, as far as the auctioneer was concerned. The gentleman now had legitimate title to the club. The man's attitude may have been unfortunate but having been expressed, then the sooner he was out the door, the better it would be for all.

'In that case, sir, I'll bid you farewell,' he said gesturing towards the exit.

Charles Pinkney, nodded his head in acknowledgement,

made sure the club was firmly in his grasp, then strode out into the car park were his Range Rover was parked over two spaces, much to the annoyance of an elderly couple you were waiting patiently for somewhere to park. He jumped into the front seat and just sat there, gazing down at the article in his hand. There was no packaging, no labels other than a sticker that had *'Lot 127a'* written on it, in fact nothing at all other than the club itself, apart of course from his purchase receipt. The receipt was immediately screwed up and thrown into the back of the car and after a cursory inspection of the golf club, it too was tossed into the rear with no regard for the monumental price it had just cost him. With a turn of the ignition he was away, shooting past the old couple and barely missing their car by inches. Driving at full pelt down the road, he was eager to get to his appointment with Bainbridge & Bainbridge.

The offices of Bainbridge & Bainbridge were quiet that afternoon. Maurice Bainbridge had expected to be on a half days' leave watching cricket at Edgbaston, a tasty match between Warwickshire and the touring Australians in a one-day contest, a spectacle he had been looking forward to for some considerable time. Over several weeks, no appointments had been scheduled for that afternoon and barring a crisis of some sort, nothing warranted a change of plan. Until, of course, Charles Pinkney had called the day before and had insisted, quite unreasonably, that he be seen without delay. The man had been uncompromising, showing a complete disregard for any personal disappointment and disruption his demands would cause. But Maurice Bainbridge, demonstrating a sense of professional duty, had nonetheless reluctantly conceded and undertook to see Pinkney at short notice. Had it been regarding any other matter or any other client, his heels would have dug firmly in. But this appointment, he realised, was no ordinary request and this was to be no ordinary meeting.

So he had agreed, but his disposition towards Charles Pinkney was now at low ebb. He rather ashamedly hoped some accident might befall the man en-route but at that very moment, his receptionist called through to say his appointment had arrived. He thanked the young girl, asked if she would advise Mr. Simmons, his junior associate, and then requested she should show Mr. Pinkney through to his office. He had toyed briefly with the idea of keeping Charles Pinkney waiting for five minutes or so, but decided not to antagonise the man any more than was absolutely necessary.

The two men shook hands and the solicitor introduced his colleague, Mr. Simmons, whom he had invited along as witness. He then beckoned Charles Pinkney to be seated. Mr. Simmons took up position unobtrusively in the corner of his senior partners' office. Coffee was brought through and business commenced. Charles Pinkney spoke first.

'Mr. Bainbridge,' he opened politely enough, 'you will see I have brought something with me.' He triumphantly placed the Tom Morris putter on the desk in front of the solicitor, leant back in his chair and folded his arms as if inviting a congratulatory comment of some sort. Maurice Bainbridge cast a brief eye over the club lying before him and after a second or two, moved it to one side and opened a document file instead.

'Very good,' he said dismissively, 'but before all that, there are one or two questions I need to ask you, Mr. Pinkney.'

'Fire away,' was the man's casual reply.

'Thank you, I shall,' the solicitor commented without raising his head.' He continued. 'Firstly, am I to take it you are here in the capacity of *'Claimant'* in the context of the *'Morris Men Agreement'*, Mr. Pinkney?' he asked, this time looking over his spectacles at his client.

'If that's what you want to call me, then I guess so,' Charles Pinkney replied rather flippantly.

Maurice Bainbridge referred again to the documents before looking up to examine the man sitting before him.

'It is not *I* that has chosen to call you that, Mr. Pinkney ... the expression is explicit in the *'Morris Men Agreement'* ... I have merely taken it from that ... sir!'

'Look here, Bainbridge, we can play games here if you like, but the fact remains, I'm now entitled to the Erskine estate and the sooner we get this wrapped up ... and I'm out of here ... then the better for all of us,' came back the irritable reply.

The solicitor removed his reading glasses and closed the document file. His junior associate sensed what was coming next and smirked in anticipation, a gesture which did not escape Charles Pinkney's notice.

'Mr. Pinkney, there are two ways we can approach this,' Maurice Bainbridge said slowly and deliberately. 'The first involves you and I conducting our business amicably ... I ask the questions ... you reply as co-operatively and as cordially as you are able ... after all, we are discussing contract here and any entitlement that you may presume, first has to be demonstrated to my complete satisfaction.'

Charles Pinkney, not yet feeling in the slightest bit

chastised, enquired arrogantly, 'And what might this second way of yours be … Mr. Bainbridge?' derision clearly being expressed in his tone.

'Well, the second way … and the one I most favour I might add …,' informed the solicitor, '… is to simply ask you to leave here and now … which would then permit me time to head off to the cricket match I'd been looking forward to for several weeks now.' He checked his watch and without looking at Pinkney, then added, 'So if you could make your mind up straight away, I might only miss the first few overs.' It was now the solicitors turn to lean back and fold his arms.

Charles Pinkney was being challenged and it had come as a surprise to him. His first inclination was to become demonstrative, to create a fuss, to voice an objection at the way this 'servant' was treating him. Because that was precisely how he had viewed Maurice Bainbridge up until that moment, just someone at his beck and call, to kick around as he pleased, in the manner he had been accustomed to with his business associates. He was no respecter of office. But this man Bainbridge was demanding it. He had no choice in the matter.

'Very well,' he said a little more reverently this time, '…yes, I suppose I am very much what you refer to as the *'Claimant'.'*

'In that case,' said the solicitor, 'perhaps we can finally get down to business.'

Maurice Bainbridge then took a few moments to open his file once again, replaced his glasses and proceeded to neatly organise several piece of paper and documents in front of him. After satisfying himself all was in order, he addressed Charles Pinkney once more.

'Mr. Pinkney, you have stated here that you wish to present yourself as the *'Claimant'* under the *'Morris Men Agreement'*,' he said deliberately, 'so, I acknowledge that fact. That being the case, then I refer to the agreement itself and some of the provisions contained within,' the solicitor added.

'But what about the club?' Charles Pinkney enquired, 'Aren't you intending to even take a look at it?'

'In due course, but there are a few procedural matters we need to discuss before we get down to the club itself.' The solicitor advised, now well in control.

'Procedure, procedure. You solicitors just can't help yourselves, can you?'

Having had his bubble burst from the outset, Charles Pinkney could not resist the chance to throw one back at Maurice Bainbridge when the opportunity presented itself.

'Without procedures, the world would be a chaotic place, would it not?' the solicitor commented rhetorically. And with that, his junior associate settled himself down for what promised to be a long session. The solicitor consulted his notes, took the larger of the documents, turned it around and presented it to Charles Pinkney.

'What I've given you there, Mr. Pinkney, is the actual agreement that was signed by ...' he referred to his notes once more, '... signed by Sir Randolph Erskine and Sir Giles Pinkney, the latter being one of your long since departed relatives, I understand.'

'Great grandfather,' Charles Pinkney stated as a matter of fact. Maurice Bainbridge avoided an acknowledgement, instead choosing to carry on with his counsel.

'You will see there are many provisos, some of which simply make reference to the basis of the agreement, some of which give guidance concerning the actual mechanics for settlement. But the clause I wish to highlight is *Clause Eight*, Mr. Pinkney.' He waited for Charles Pinkney to find the provision for himself before continuing.

'That particular clause is designed to establish the basis of fee calculation for this practice when acting as executors to the agreement.' He then stopped speaking to allow Charles Pinkney to catch up and read the wording. After a minute or two, he looked up and spoke.

'Never miss a trick you guys, do you?' Charles Pinkney said resentfully, before adding, 'So let me get this straight.' He lifted one sheet of paper closer to his face and started quoting. 'Clause eight says ...,' he looked over the top of the piece of paper in his hand to see Maurice Bainbridge watching attentively, '... it says, and I quote:

The Claimant hereby agrees that in pursuant of a claim under the provisions of this Agreement and prior to the execution of clause five being the Authentication shall commit to the payment of fees to the Executors of this Agreement Messer's. Bainbridge and Bainbridge of Stratford upon Avon a sum equivalent to nought point five percent of the combined market value of the freehold properties known as Kerrington Manor and Grange Manor both of Gloucestershire which at the time of signing said value equated to five hundred and fifty five thousand pounds known as the base figure and that on the date of claim the market value shall be re-assessed and calculated on the basis of

*compounded five percent increase of the base
figure year on year and that fee together with any
statutory taxations applicable at the time of claim
shall be a debt due by the Claimant and payable to
the Executors within fourteen days regardless of the
outcome of clause five.*

'All a bit of a mouthful if you ask me,' Charles Pinkney
remarked, 'and I suppose the only bit you're only really
interested in, Mr. Bainbridge. But just for my sake, what
does all that mean in English, if you please?' he asked
wryly, before adding, 'And by the way, don't you people
ever use punctuation?'

'Never,' replied Maurice Bainbridge solemnly, 'we
people find it just serves to confuse matters.' Referring
back to his notes once more, and withdrawing a formal
looking document from his drawer, the solicitor placed the
document in front of Charles Pinkney for his edification.

'In plain English, as you requested Mr. Pinkney, it
means you sign this contract before we go any further,' he
said pushing the document closer. 'And by signing you
agree to pay this practice the sum of thirty nine thousand
two hundred and eighty pounds ... plus value added tax of
course.'

Charles Pinkney stared across at the solicitor and
without even looking at the contract, asked the obvious
question.

'And if I refuse to sign, what then?'

Maurice Bainbridge just smiled, selected a sealed
envelope from the documents laid out before him and held
it aloft.

'Well if that's the case, then I suppose we'll never know what's in this, will we?' he said with no small display of satisfaction,

'And what exactly is that?' Charles Pinkney enquired impertinently.

'This, here, is your one and only passport into the Erskine estate,' the solicitor said somewhat bitterly, 'It is, quite simply, the only thing that should really concern you, Mr. Pinkney. It's what we shall be using to *authenticate* your claim.'

A brief exchange then followed.

'In which case I have no choice, do I?'

'On the contrary, from where I'm sitting I perceive there are at least *two* choices open to you.'

'But only *one* if we wish to progress with this deal?'

'Correct.'

'And you get paid even if it all falls apart from here on in?'

'Again correct. That's the commitment you enter into if you wish to be regarded as the *'Claimant'*.'

'Sounds to me like it's a whole lot of money for nothing.'

'Precisely what I was thinking concerning your circumstances, Mr. Pinkney.'

There was an obvious lack of camaraderie between the two men and the sparring continued for some time, much to the amusement of Mr. Simmons who was sitting quietly in the corner. It proceeded at a pace, becoming more and more acrimonious. Maurice Bainbridge was missing his cricket and was therefore quite content to sit back and trade insults all day.

But it finally dawned on Charles Pinkney he was gaining nothing from the exchanges. He changed tack and brought the focus back to something he hoped would be much more beneficial to him.

'Enough of this, okay,' he conceded, 'I'll sign your blasted contract. Give it here.' And with that, he snatched the document from the desk and placed his signature on the bottom without even reading the terms. 'Maybe now can we talk about the club for a change?' he asked sarcastically.

'By all means,' said the solicitor, 'but are you happy with all the other terms contained in the *'Morris Men Agreement'*, Mr. Pinkney?'

'I have to confess I'm not really all that interested, Mr. Bainbridge, I just want to get through this meeting and take possession of the house in the next week or so,' he replied.

Maurice Bainbridge held up his hand to halt Charles Pinkney in mid flow, then quickly scanned the agreement.

'Here we are … found it,' the solicitor proudly announced.

'Found what?'

'The clause in the agreement that makes provision for an eventual transfer of ownership, Mr. Pinkney. I'm afraid your timeframe might be a touch too optimistic.'

'What do you mean?'

'Well,' said the solicitor, 'a complete inventory will be necessary from the outset undertaken by an independent body. You might not be fully aware of this, Mr. Pinkney, but the entire contents of the claimed estate are also included in the settlement.'

Charles Pinkney was now beaming and metaphorically rubbing his hands. 'But surely that need only take a day or two,' he suggested.

'Quite so, but I was going on to say, the transfer of ownership needs to be handled in the normal fashion, as if the house were being sold. There are deeds to acquire and to be transferred, local searches to be completed, registration of titles to be lodged, perhaps even boundary issues that may require settlement beforehand. All in all Mr. Pinkney, I think you're looking at three to six months as an absolute minimum,' the solicitor advised.

'I simply can't accept that,' Charles Pinkney declared irritably, the small matter of Mr. Smith's non-negotiable repayment deadline praying on his mind, 'but can we discuss all that later. Can we now get back to talking about the golf club, Mr. Bainbridge?'

'Certainly, as long as you're content you've been properly advised about the composition of the *Agreement*,' enquired the solicitor.

'Yes, yes ... and yes again man!' Charles Pinkney had clearly been pushed beyond his tolerance threshold with the solicitor's correctness.

Pointing to the club, which by now had been relegated to the edge of his desk, Maurice Bainbridge switched his attention.

'Is this what you're offering?'

'Of course it is ... do you see any others around here?'

said Charles Pinkney sardonically, lifting the club aloft for a final inspection of his own, '…the key to the door you might say.'

The club was handed to Maurice Bainbridge, who being a golfer himself, proceeded to grip the club correctly. He was momentarily lost in thought.

'Begging your pardon, Mr. Bainbridge,' Charles Pinkney impatiently interrupted, 'but is that the club … the one you said I needed to bring along … the one that's going to finally end this contest once and for all?

Acknowledging the importance of the question, the solicitor turned sombre once more as he placed the club back down on his desk. He shuffled through his papers and documents and found what he sought. Replacing his reading glasses, he read the words it contained to himself, before summarising for the benefit of all.

'According to this document, Mr. Pinkney, the very same document I read to you only a few weeks ago, we are looking for what is described here … and I'm quoting the words you understand … as *a late nineteenth century Tom Morris long-nosed putter, bearing the makers impression T Morris in capital letters on the upper surface of the stained beech head, with corresponding name, again in capital letters to the upper portion of what is described as a greenheart shaft, just below the sheepskin hide grip, the whole club being just under three feet long.'*

He looked up, 'All quite explicit, would you not agree Mr. Pinkney?'

'So let's stop talking and take a look then.'

The two men moved in closer for inspection, each

taking turns to scrutinise the club in great detail and to make the appropriate comparisons with the wording of the document. They seemed to be satisfying themselves that all was in order with both club and wording corresponding. But the solicitor's junior associate, Mr. Simmons, had now shuffled closer and he looked a little more concerned than the other two men. After a moment or two of peering over shoulders to get a better look at the club, he cleared his throat to attract attention to himself. The solicitor looked up to see his associate grimacing slightly, and indicating discreetly that he and Maurice Bainbridge should leave the office for a private discussion of some sort. The solicitor took the hint and offered his apologies to Charles Pinkney.

'If you don't mind, Mr. Simmons and I will leave you alone for a minute or two. Please feel free to continue your examination. We'll just be outside, but I'll leave the door open so we can remain watchful.'

Charles Pinkney appeared either oblivious to the solicitor's words or had chosen to ignore the comment entirely. The two associates stepped outside. Immediately, Mr. Simmons voiced his concerns.

'Just thought I'd better mention this, sir,' Mr. Simmons said apologetically, 'I'm no expert, I must add, but you stated greenheart shaft didn't you?'

'I can't really remember, but I'll take your word on that,' said Maurice Bainbridge, 'Please, go on.'

'Well, I'm no expert like I said, but I'm pretty sure greenheart darkens with age. My father had a collection of walking sticks and I remember him describing the different woods to me once,' informed the junior associate, offering an explanation for his doubts.

Maurice Bainbridge digested the words then asked, 'Are you suggesting that club in there might not indeed match the written description?'

'I think that's precisely what I'm saying, sir. The shaft is much lighter than you'd expect from greenheart. I'm pretty sure it's just ordinary hickory, but like I said, I'm no expert.' Maurice Bainbridge mulled this revelation over in his mind, before going on to compliment his junior associate.

'Well done young man. I'm no expert either, but I'm happy to go along with your opinion for now,' he said, with some amusement, 'Let's get back in there and see if you're right.' He beckoned Mr. Simmons to enter the office first, giving the young man an encouraging pat on the back into the bargain.

Charles Pinkney was leaning back contentedly in his chair when the two men re-entered the office.

'Looks genuine to me!' he announced before the two solicitors had even seated.

Maurice Bainbridge wondered whether now would be the best time to deflate the gentleman, but decided first to build his hopes a little higher. The fall would then be so much more painful, he devilishly thought.

'Very good, Mr. Pinkney,' said the solicitor, trying hard to contain his amusement, 'I think we've both concluded the club you've brought along, more or less corresponds to the description I've just read out, so I think it's appropriate we move onto the next stage … the actual *Authentication*.'

'And about time too,' said Charles Pinkney impolitely. The debate outside the office had irritated him considerably and his impatience was shining through.

Maurice Bainbridge again rifled through the documents on his desk and pulled out the sealed envelope that would be used for the purpose. Although showing signs of age, the waxed seal remained intact and the two faded signatures across the envelope could still be clearly identified. Both Sir Giles Pinkney and Sir Randolph Erskine had signed and dated in black ink, leaving no doubt as to the importance of the contents. He held it aloft and invited Charles Pinkney to inspect it ahead of announcing the next step in the process. Both men agreed it had not been tampered with.

'As far as I am led to understand, by the terms of the *'Morris Men Agreement'* Mr. Pinkney, the contents of this envelope are designed to verify the authenticity of any club presented and purported to be *'The Trophy'* as described in *clause two* and also referenced on the reverse of the two prints the gentlemen had chosen by way of token.' The announcement all seemed a little over dramatic for Charles Pinkney, but he nodded his understanding nonetheless. The solicitor continued.

'The contents of this envelope, whatever they might be, are final and binding. There will be no opportunity for you to object, query, question or otherwise seek adjudication of any sort. Do you understand that, Mr. Pinkney?' the solicitor enquired, making sure the ground rules were clearly spelt out and acknowledged in advance.

'Get on with it, man!' came Pinkney's' exasperated reply.

'I'll take that as a *'yes'*, therefore …Mr. Simmons, if you please … could you open this envelope in front of us both?' the solicitor formally invited.

And with that, the junior associate took the envelope, broke the seal, withdrew a small folded piece of paper that was contained within, unfolded the paper, offered it up to view, then handed it to Maurice Bainbridge. The solicitor read the short passage to himself, making sure Charles Pinkney's efforts to lean across the desk and catch a glimpse proved unfruitful. The solicitor finally made his declaration.

'Mr. Pinkney, if you please,' he asked politely, 'Would you please pick up your golf club and pay attention to what I am about to say.'

Charles Pinkney duly obliged, his eyes lighting up with the excitement of the moment.

'Mr. Simmons, if you would move a little closer and watch carefully please, I shall now quote from the *'Authentication'*.' And with the preamble concluded Maurice Bainbridge read aloud the wording taken from the paper in his hand.

'We, the undersigned, being Randolph Erskine and Giles Pinkney, together described as 'The Morris Men', hereby disclose the two distinguishing features 'The Trophy', referenced in 'The Morris Men Agreement', must possess for 'Authentication' when presented by 'The Claimant' as settlement of the said agreement, under the terms contained therein.

(a) An inspection mark, that of the maker, made by his own hand, in the form of a tiny spider on the nose of the putter.

(b) The signature of both the 'Morris Men', as identified in the 'Morris Men Agreement', placed on

the shaft, in ink, underneath the grip, to be verified by comparison to those contained on the agreement itself.

'Not very trusting of each other were they, judging by the lengths they went to in all of this?' the solicitor casually commented. He noticed Charles Pinkney, who just prior had been rotating the club quite fervently during the reading, had become somewhat agitated by this time.

'Is there something amiss, Mr. Pinkney?' the solicitor innocently enquired. The club was being frantically twirled and inspected at very close quarters.

'Does it say how big that spider mark might be?' Charles Pinkney asked desperately.

'I imagine big enough to be seen,' the solicitor offered somewhat unhelpfully. He waited for the anxiety levels to rise even higher before innocently enquiring further.

'Is there a problem, Mr. Pinkney?'

Charles Pinkney was in turmoil, being unable to find anything that resembled a mark of any description. In desperation he offered a small worm hole to Mr. Simmons by way of proof, but that was instantly dismissed. His next action was to start stripping away the old sheepskin hide grip, but all that achieved was the creation of an untidy pile of discarded leather strips and hessian wraps on the edge of the solicitors desk.

There was a complete absence of signatures. None to be seen, whatsoever.

'Oh dear!' was the solicitors only comment, as he and his associate exchanged smiles with one another.

'This can't be,' cried Pinkney in desperation, seemingly

on the brink of retching. 'This can't be. It came from my great grandfathers collection ... it has to be the one ... there weren't any others,' he cried out again. He was, by now, clutching forlornly at straws.

'Are you absolutely sure that note is genuine?' Charles Pinkney bellowed at the solicitor.

'Absolutely, Mr. Pinkney,' said the solicitor confidently as he basked in the satisfaction of the moment, watching the man break down before his very eyes. Maurice Bainbridge was far from sympathetic of the man's plight. As far as he was concerned, the outcome was more than equitable given the man's character. So he moved to conclude matters swiftly.

'Mr. Pinkney, it is evident to me and my colleague that as *'Claimant'*, you have not presented *'The Trophy'* and as such, we need take this no further.'

The solicitor's words were being disregarded as Charles Pinkney consulted the piece of paper once more.

'So if you don't mind, Mr. Pinkney, I would be most grateful if you could leave right now as we all have other business to attend to. By all means, please make a fresh appointment if you ever should acquire something that provides a closer match to the description ... but for now, we can help you no further.'

And with that the solicitor started to tidy up his desk. Despite this, Charles Pinkney remained motionless, looking every inch a broken man.

'Mr. Simmons, will you be kind enough to see Mr. Pinkney out?'

Duly prompted, Mr. Simmons rose to his feet and

placed a hand under Charles Pinkney's arm and managed to ease him out of the seat. Taking the hint, Charles Pinkney moved towards the exit unaided.

'You mark my words, Bainbridge, I'll be back,' he announced defiantly, brushing the helping hand away before turning on his heels and heading for the reception area, a solitary gripless club in hand.

The solicitor smiled and rubbing further salt into the man's wounds, called out whilst he still remained within earshot.

'And please don't forget my fee requires full settlement within fourteen days, Mr. Pinkney ...!'

Chapter 15

Tom Hudson received a letter one morning, postmarked Stratford upon Avon. It had been expected and he knew exactly from whom it had come. Disregarding all the other post that had arrived with the same delivery, he opened it eagerly, calling out to his wife as he tore into the envelope.

'It's here … it's arrived,' he shouted enthusiastically up the stairs.

The contents were pulled out; a receipt, a compliments slip and a cheque made out in his name. Anne Hudson had, by now, joined her husband in their small living room. They simply danced around and around, waving a cheque for £57,363 triumphantly in the air.

Mail was falling through someone else's letter box. It was also postmarked Stratford upon Avon, but this one had not been expected. Robert Erskine, dishevelled and unshaven, standing there in his dressing gown, placed all others to one side and examined this letter in particular. It was intriguingly addressed to both he and his wife in elegant handwriting, so his curiosity grew as he opened the envelope with a small penknife. Inside were two sheets of paper, the first letter headed, and the second a continuation sheet. Both were written in the same hand as the envelope, the second page having been signed by Maurice Bainbridge.

His heart missed a beat as he assumed the worse. Why else would Maurice Bainbridge be writing other than to formally announce the bad news he and his wife had been dreading?

Since the auction, they had cut themselves off from the world, not daring to venture out of doors unless absolutely necessary, becoming very protective of what they had, at least for what little time remained. All telephone calls were now being screened. He knew Bainbridge & Bainbridge had tried on several occasions to contact them by phone with requests to call their offices having been left on the answering machine.

But why should they aid the process? If Pinkney wanted in, then he would have to do it the hard way, without their co-operation. Plucking up the courage, he sat down and began to tentatively read the words.

Dear Mr. & Mrs. Erskine

I am writing following unsuccessful attempts to contact you directly over the telephone. I have news and guidance I would like to impart personally. My preference would have been a discussion, privately of course, but that has not been possible. So I write, and in doing so, you must accept I do this without prejudice, which simply means you cannot subsequently rely on my statements as a matter of record. Nevertheless, I expect you will be encouraged by what I am about to say.

Robert Erskines' worst held fears evaporated in an instant with those few words of implied encouragement from the solicitor, and he called out to his wife to join him quickly. He read on:

I have one piece of good news and one piece of advice. The good news, you will be delighted to learn, is you remain the rightful owners of Grange Manor, both for now and in the foreseeable future. Mr. Charles Pinkney has recently and unsuccessfully attempted to conclude what has become known as the 'Morris Men Agreement'. A club he presented, which he claimed to be the legitimate 'Trophy' under that agreement, failed to satisfy the 'Authentication' and there is little immediate prospect he can satisfactorily do so with any another in his possession. Forgive me for using an Americanism, but it appears you have 'dodged a bullet' on this occasion.

'Elizabeth, quick … come here my darling,' he shouted out at the top of his voice, 'We're in the clear … we're in the clear.' He eagerly carried on reading:

That is the good news and I now offer my advice. There is a way you might be able to avoid a repeat of your recent circumstances. Having completed further research into the matter, research prompted by an archive diary entry made around the time the Agreement was initiated, the conclusion being drawn is that one or more party to the agreement may be able to retrospectively protect themselves. This may be achieved by placing in Trust to their unborn children, their entire estate, thus passing title, theoretically, to someone who does not exist and, therefore, from whom title could not be acquired by a third party. It sounds implausible, but my preliminary examination of the law has led me to conclude this principle has merit in practice and I encourage you to make an appointment to visit my office, as soon as possible, so we may progress this possibility further.

Robert Erskine read the remainder of the letter, which was simply an expression of best wishes, good fortune and an offer to be of further assistance. By this time, Elizabeth had joined her husband and without comment, he simply handed the letter over for her to read it herself. He watched with delight as she too experienced the same emotional roller-coaster he had just ridden.

In a small village just outside Monte Carlo in the south of France, the Frenchman called Bertoise was cataloguing his collection of scarce golf clubs. Mostly sourced from the United Kingdom, some from the United States and the odd one or two from his homeland, he was proud of the ensemble that was laid out before him. He cherished each and every one, frequently rotating his displays, generally substituting his older acquisitions for the more recent.

Unsurprisingly, he was now holding one of the clubs he had recently purchased from Tom Hudson and was trying to decide how best to present it. Should he hang it horizontally on his study wall, or perhaps it would look more appealing hung vertically? It mattered little to him knowing it was a replica, an exact copy of a club that, had it been original, would have been twice its age. But he had paid only a fraction of the price a genuine article would have commanded, yet despite that, it looked genuine enough. Only an expert, like he, would be able to tell the difference, so in his mind it was money well spent.

He held the club under a lamp for closer inspection. Whoever had made this copy had been a gifted a craftsman, as gifted, in fact, as the original club-maker he had attempted to imitate, even down to the personal touch, a small inspection mark he knew some of the master club-makers had occasionally employed. With his free hand he searched for his magnifier in his pocket, pulled it out, flipped it open and placed the lens to his eye, drawing a small area of the club head into sharp focus. The mark was one he did not recognise, but that was not surprising as they were rarely used and scarcely seen. Only a small percentage of clubs ever made were blessed with these special endorsements, individual clubs picked from a batch of thousands, chosen especially for their perfection. He looked once again and decided it was in the form of a beetle, but a second count of the legs confirmed something different. It had eight legs and it was definitely a tiny spider.

Charles Pinkneys' exact whereabouts remained a mystery after his disappearance. It was known he had abandoned his Gloucestershire home shortly after the auction, leaving his financial affairs entirely in the hands of a trusted provincial solicitor with whom he corresponded only by post office box number. He had become practically untraceable otherwise, not even turning up for work in the City, a situation that was tolerated for only a short while before the inevitable termination was posted. The few fair weather friends he had acquired over time, abandoned him quickly thereafter, whilst several suspicious characters were understood to have been making intimidating enquiries about him recently, fuelling the rumour mill even further.

What is known for certain, however, was a hastily arranged sale of Kerrington Manor shortly after his departure, a consequence of mounting debt according to local gossip at the time. The sale had been handled discreetly, no advertisements boards on display, just some well placed canvassing by one of London's more reputable property agents. The asking price had been pitched low to generate maximum interest, sensible enough to entice a cash purchase, it was again rumoured. After only six weeks, a single removal van was observed entering the grounds and within forty five minutes, it had departed once more, passing a procession of incoming vans half way down the driveway. Whatever Charles Pinkney had managed to retain at the end of it all, it had amounted to very little indeed.

The new owners, a young Scottish couple named Cuthbertson, together with their small family, soon established themselves in the local community, a community delighted to witness their early commitment to reverse the years of neglect which had befallen such a beautiful estate. Tradesmen became regular visitors and local employment was generated, especially amongst the young who found opportunities at Kerrington Manor to work in the grounds, to work in service and to work with newly introduced animals, particularly horses and deer. Within a short while, the estate became vibrant once more, commercially and communally, hosting regular fetes, garden open days, horse riding school and leisure breaks for the hunting fraternity. Ironically, they also became close friends with their neighbours the Erskines who, quite naturally, avoided any mention of *The Morris Men*. During occasional visits to Kerrington Manor, they had noticed virtually all of Pinkney's former furnishings and possessions had remained in-situ after his departure and it always occupied their thoughts that the *Pipeshank* print, the one which had sparked off the whole affair in the first place, may well be hanging still on a wall somewhere within the house. But of course they were too cautious and apprehensive to ever have mentioned it.

Maurice Bainbridge promoted his junior associate, Mr. Simmons, to full associate within a short space of time. Although fresh to the profession, entering as a graduate and a little wet behind the ears at the outset, he had nevertheless shown outstanding promise, demonstrating a confidence and commitment that had encouraged the senior partner to invest more heavily in him. Mindful of the cut throat competition that existed in the legal circles and the emergence in recent years of dedicated head-hunters, he was keen to protect his interests by offering the young man an enhanced status within the practice, more responsibility, more reward and some specialist training. These had all been gratefully accepted and in return, the young associate had given a pledge to commit to the practice in the longer term.

But there was also an ulterior motive. Maurice Bainbridge was no fool and possessed, amongst other skills, a practical head on his shoulders. With delegation of responsibility, he could invest more time in promoting his practice, something that Bainbridge & Bainbridge had traditionally neglected. Historically, the practice had relied almost entirely on the repeat business from existing clients, but times were changing and clients were becoming fickle. The status quo was no longer an option and commercial survival was dependant on generating new business through marketing and networking.

Maurice Bainbridge saw his principal responsibilities moving more in that direction and he was encouraged by early successes, mostly as a consequence of his well received after-dinner speeches and recitals. Talking to mixed audiences, and in a style that amused as well as informed, he noticed a modest celebrity status was now following him, which meant his diary remained active and full, ever in demand as his reputation spread. But he now had a rich vein of anecdotes to tap into and he never forgot to give credit to his illustrious scriptwriter, the late and great Edward Bainbridge. And of course acknowledgement of *'The Bainbridge Diaries'* as they had now become fondly named by the practice.

Epilogue

The architect was completing her survey, gathering precise dimensions of the drawing room's interior, floor to ceiling, wall to wall, opening sizes and the like, each time carefully converting the ultrasonic measurements onto layout sketches she had prepared earlier. Kerrington Manor was to be sympathetically extended, another wing added to accommodate the growing number of landed gentry and wealthy business people who now made regular visits to enjoy the hospitality, the fishing and shooting rights and some simple indulgences that a great English country estate had to offer. But internal access needed creating between the existing building and the new. And the optimum route was directly into the drawing room, an area to be designated for guest's relaxation and general conversation during the evenings.

Panelling surrounded the room and the architect was determined to retain this impressive feature with minimum disturbance. But some demolitions were unavoidable, so it was just a question of limitation. Tapping the panelling at the chosen point, there seemed to be an unexplained void behind and this troubled the architect. Having concerns that some additional structural provisions may be necessary, she called for the assistance of a joiner who was working elsewhere in the building. Within no time at all, several secured panels had been delicately removed and placed to one side, revealing plasterwork, as expected. But a final panel, approximately three feet across and three feet high, fell unexpectedly before the joiner had raised a hand. The pair of them moved swiftly to prevent it crashing to the floor. But it had revealed an obvious void; purpose built it appeared. Unbeknown to the architect and joiner beforehand, the panel had been secured in position with a simple hinged mechanism, a mechanism that had been loosened from the plasterwork when the adjacent panels had been removed. Amazingly, they had discovered a secret compartment, and a secret compartment that clearly housed something inside into the bargain.

Not wishing to be accused of tampering, the architect thanked the joiner for his assistance and dismissed him. He was clearly reluctant to leave, curiosity now grabbing hold. But her insistence eventually proved effective. She called Mrs. Cuthbertson's mobile phone using her own, and being close by at the stables, the owner was able to join her architect in a matter of just a few minutes.

The discovery, a single article it seemed, was first prodded by way of examination, and then tentatively removed for closer inspection once the pair had fully satisfied themselves it harboured no spiders or insects of any description.

Placed on a side table, about three feet long, it sat there for a few moments whilst the speculation grew. Whatever it was, it was neatly wrapped in newspaper, and an old newspaper at that, given its fading. Mrs. Cuthbertson was intrigued and invited her architect to open it up. Her architect was equally intrigued, but felt it more fitting that her client perform the honours. The selection was eventually made with a toss of a coin and the architect hesitantly started the unwrapping, with sheet after sheet being painstakingly removed and handed to her client. The object inside was long and slender for the most part, but thickened at one end. The thicker end, they soon realised, accounted for most of its weight and it looked, for all the world, very much like a baton or cane at that particular moment.

Soon, Mrs. Cuthbertson held an entire edition of *'The Gloucestershire Times'* in her hand, the pages randomly sorted, but each bearing the date, *21st September 1922,* in the top right hand corner. The mystery object finally revealed itself to be an old golf club, unusual by modern standards, made entirely out of wood it seemed, but a golf club nonetheless. Mrs. Cuthbertson looked the more disappointed out of the two, but turns were taken to examine their discovery. It was definitely old; they were both agreed on that. And it appeared to be in reasonable condition, except for what they both called the 'handle end' which had loose and tattered leather bindings, consumed in part by insects it appeared. A few firm taps on the edge of the table confirmed 'nothing nasty' was still in residence, which paved the way for some preliminary dissection after part of a word was seen to be hidden underneath the leathers. The architect took the lead on this, whilst Mrs. Cuthbertson, whose interest in the club was now fading rapidly, diverted her attention once more to the void in her wall, hoping to find something a little more exciting.

She peered inside and was rewarded with the sight of a small envelope. Withdrawing it eagerly, giving it a quick shake to remove some plaster dust, she followed up with a final blow to clear away the residue. She read the hand written inscription on the outside. It simply said;

'To be opened in the event of my incapacitation' followed by *'Sir Giles Pinkney, September 1922'*

By now, her architect had delicately exposed the wording beneath the impoverished grip, and there, on the wooded shaft, were two fairly indistinct signatures. She called her client over, whilst at the same time, made her own attempt to decipher the names. The only one for certain was *'Giles'* in the middle of one signature, and *'Erskine'* at the end of the other, together with a quite clear date of *'1 Aug 1921'* tagged on at the end. Mrs. Cuthbertson headed back across, still clutching the unopened envelope, and after taking her own look, was intrigued to decipher *'Pinkney'* and *'Erskine'* amongst the words. She was convinced those were the names, names which held no significance for her architect, but names with whom Mrs. Cuthbertson was entirely familiar, one having been her vendor and former family in residence at Kerrington Manor, the other being that of her friends and neighbours. She was intrigued, momentarily forgetting the envelope in her hand, until, that was, her architect enquired.

The gummed seal had perished and it opened quite easily. Inside, there were two pieces of folded paper, each the same size but one was clearly of better quality than the other. Mrs. Cuthbertson unfolded the inferior first and discovered, somewhat disappointingly, it was merely a bill of sale from someone called *'Samuel T Turner, Master Craftsman'*, whose address was local. It was signed and dated *'Sam Turner, 18 September 1922'*, stamped *'Paid'* along with a description which simply read;

' 1 off replication: T Morris: 15 shillings '

The second piece of paper was folded tightly and after unfolding, was found to be written on both sides. Pressing it flat down on the table, Mrs. Cuthbertson read it out loud;

'The mere fact you are reading this note indicates you have found the instructions I retain constantly

within my wallet, leading you here to my private vault and this declaration. It also means my incapacitation is sufficiently serious to warrant your involvement, in fact, I may even be deceased. The details of this declaration must remain guarded and undisclosed to others, but the exploitation of its disclosure will remain entirely discretionary.

Accompanying this declaration is the original and actual Tom Morris putter referenced in the 'Morris Men Agreement' as 'The Trophy' and is the only club that will satisfy authentication under that agreement. All others will fail that test, including the very putter which Randolph Erskine and I shall contest each year, that particular article being an exact and convincing replication of 'The Trophy', complete with spider indentation, except insofar as it shall not display the 'Morris Men' signatures beneath the grip, nor shall it be dated 1 Aug 1921. Messrs. Samuel T Turner can vouch for this, their receipt being appended for reference purposes.

The purpose of this deception is twofold:

(a) If, at the time of my incapacitation, I hold the title of 'Challenger' under 'The Morris Men Agreement', then the 'Victor' under that same agreement will be unable to legitimately elevate his own status to that of 'Claimant' and benefit from all that the title will confer. (fundamental)

(b) Should I, at the time of my incapacitation, hold the title of either 'Victor' or 'Challenger' then any of my successors, under that same agreement will be able to legitimately elevate their own status to that of 'Claimant', regardless of objection, and

benefit from all that the   title will confer.
(discretionary)

Randolph Erskine is oblivious to this deception and has no knowledge of the substitution, a substitution made possible with the attainment of my first victory last month and presentation of the very club you now possess. I effected a substitution, but his ignorance must continue undisturbed as disclosure will undoubtedly compromise your own position. Leave him content in the challenge of a futile chase. He can never legitimately win our contest, but he need never realise this until the very end.

In reading my words, you may regard me as a cheat, but I care not. Your own security has been indirectly assured by my actions and you may later thank me for that. I cannot be sure which of my descendants may be reading this, it may be any of my three sons or one of my many grandchildren perhaps, but whoever you are, I pray that you have not inherited any of my less enviable traits.

Sir Giles Pinkney

September 1922

Mrs. Cuthbertson folded the sheet once more and thanked her architect for bringing the find to her attention. Of all the treasures it might perhaps have been, to discover it was a mere golf club, along with some unspectacular confession, was a touch disappointing, she had decided. The reference to an individual called *'Randolph Erskine'* was the only real interest, but even that was insufficient to raise her excitement. As for the author of the confession, *'Sir Giles Pinkney'*, well apart from the vendor having had been called *'Pinkney'* the curiosity ended there. That particular gentleman was long gone, and now an irrelevance as far as she was concerned.

The *'confession'* seemed a touch overly dramatic Judith Cuthbertson and her husband Douglas that evening decided. They had spent several hours discussing the find, speculating over the references to a *'Morris Men Agreement'*, *'The Trophy'*, *'The Victor'*, *'The Challenger'* and *'The Claimant'*. Clearly, there was a connection to golf and the golf club must have been a prize of some sort. Suspecting the two men may simply have been painfully formal over the outcome of a particular golf match, even to the extent of involving a solicitor, with the prize seemingly the tattered old golf club that now rested on their coffee table, they jointly dismissed the find as totally insignificant.

But what to do with the articles, they wondered? The first inclination was to cast them out with the rubbish, the club showing worrying signs of woodworm with what appeared to be a small bore hole on the end of the wooden head. With so many valuable antiques in the house, they could ill afford an infestation breaking out. Alternatively, they could sell the club, but the prospect of actually having to invite interest seemed all too troublesome, especially over something that might only be worth a few pounds.

Their third option was much more appealing, so Judith Cuthbertson made the phone call, there and then.

A couple of days later, Elizabeth and Robert Erskine arrived at the Cuthbertson's home, having accepted their invitation to come round for *'a couple of drinks and to see something that might interest you'*. Robert Erskine, was particularly excited, believing it must be the new Alfa Romeo his friend, Douglas, had been promising to buy; the same model Robert had set his own sights on. Elizabeth, on the other hand, had needed a little more persuasion particularly as she would be missing the final episode of her favourite TV drama.

Nevertheless, they were now entering Kerrington Manor and being welcomed most enthusiastically. Judith Cuthbertson was wearing a peculiar smile, Elizabeth Erskine had noticed, as they were politely led through to the drawing room.

Drinks were served, the conversation was amiable and Elizabeth soon forgot the disappointment she had earlier expressed to her husband. The two couples had become quite fond of each other since the Cuthbertson's arrival at Kerrington Manor and frequently met for light social occasions such as these. The talk was mainly of country pursuits, but Robert, being impatient to see the new acquisition he had convinced himself was going to be proudly displayed that evening, very soon decided to hurry things along in that particular direction.

'Douglas,' he said casually, by way of a preamble, 'so what's this 'something' you hinted might be of interest to us?'

The Cuthbertson's winked at each other and Douglas left the room briefly, before returning with one arm tucked behind his back. It was clear to all he was hiding something from view. Judith Cuthbertson spoke first.

'Elizabeth and Robert, we're going to ask you a question,' she announced.

The Erskine's curiosity was now heightened.

'Have you ... by any chance ... ever heard of something called the *'Morris Men Agreement'*?' she went on to ask innocently, 'I can't imagine you have,' she added helpfully, 'because it's over 80 years old now.'

Robert Erskine's mouth dropped wide open, whilst Elizabeth Erskine quickly covered hers. They were stunned by the question and unable to respond. Taking their silence as confirmation they were oblivious to its existence, Judith Cuthbertson kept the excitement simmering.

'Well, it just so happens we've come across a little discovery in the house ... something that Douglas and I have no interest in ... but something you might find a use for.'

As if on cue, Douglas Cuthbertson revealed the object he had kept from view, a sad looking old golf club, but one the Erskine's recognised immediately for what it was. They clutched each other tightly and a silence ensued, neither being sure quite what to say.

Douglas Cuthbertson, not in the least surprised by the Erskine's apparent lack of enthusiasm, decided to lighten the moment.

'Look, I'm with you on this one ... It's not much of a gift I know ... but here, take it ... it's yours.'

'You're actually *giving* this to us?' Elizabeth asked incredulously.

'I'm sorry, Elizabeth,' cut in Judith Cuthbertson apologetically, 'I know it's not very exciting looking ... but there is a particular reason why we're gifting it to you.'

'Which is?' Elizabeth asked cautiously, and rather

impolitely, she realised straight afterwards.

'There's a reference to your family name, you see … here on this piece of paper that came with it,' she said, handing the sheet of paper across.

Elizabeth snatched it, and hastily read the words silently to herself. Robert took charge of the golf club without acknowledgement. The pair then exchanged club and paper, after a moment or two, Robert taking his turn to read the words, whilst his wife painstakingly inspected the club.

The Cuthbertson's were left to stand ignored, a little embarrassed, thinking their friends might be feeling awkward, not knowing quite what to say, perhaps. It was ever so apparent their guests had not yet thanked them for the gifts. No comment at all, in fact. They began to believe their goodwill gesture may well have back fired, causing insult rather than the amusement they had intended.

The Erskine's exchanged knowing looks, simultaneously drawing the same conclusions. This was the club they thought they had been chasing all along, a chase that clearly now had a fruitless inevitability about it. The club they had fought so hard to acquire at auction, was so obviously now the wrong club entirely. It was such a blessing they had not wasted a fortune in buying it.

So the real thing had actually been hidden all along in this house, Kerrington Manor, under the very nose of that despicable Charles Pinkney fellow. There was poignancy in that thought. The rogue had set out to cheat them and in return, had received his just deserts.

But it appeared Charles Pinkney was just the latest in a long line of Pinkney cheats, with Sir Giles seemingly the pick of the crop. Not for the first time a member of the Erskine family had been duped, it would seem, with Sir Randolph tricked into thinking he was actually playing for 'The Trophy', when all along it was just a worthless replica.

Elizabeth and Robert continued their dumbfounded silence, standing face to face, their thoughts merged into one.

Believing the Erskine's were perhaps too affronted to speak and attempting to switch the collective mood to one more affable, Douglas Cuthbertson made a rallying call.

'Elizabeth ... Robert ... just forget it okay. Instead come with us and take a good look around the house,' he invited, 'we've made lots of changes ... and we're sure you'll be impressed ... so much so, we're convinced you'll simply want to take it off our hands and move right in ...' Douglas added jokingly.

'Now there's an interesting thought!' the Erskine's said with one accord ... somewhat creepily; their eyes eagerly scanning their surroundings with what appeared to be extraordinary relish.

And in that instance, the Cuthbertson's felt jointly and inexplicably uncomfortable in their neighbour's presence.

The End?